THE SHADOW MISSION

THE SHADOW MISSION

SHAMIM SARIF

An Imprint of HarperCollinsPublishers

HarperTeen is an imprint of HarperCollins Publishers.

The Shadow Mission
Copyright © 2020 by Shamim Sarif
All rights reserved. Manufactured in Germany. No part of this
book may be used or reproduced in any manner whatsoever
without written permission except in the case of brief quotations
embodied in critical articles and reviews. For information address
HarperCollins Children's Books, a division of HarperCollins
Publishers, 195 Broadway, New York, NY 10007.
www.epicreads.com

ISBN 978-0-06-284963-2

Typography by Torborg Davern
20 21 22 23 24   CPIG   10 9 8 7 6 5 4 3 2 1
❖
First Edition

For Hanan, Ethan, and Luca, always

»»»

1

I'M FINDING IT HARD TO breathe.

Sweat drips down onto my hands, which cling so tightly to the handlebars in front of me that my knuckles pop out, bone white beneath my skin. Trickles of perspiration trail along the muscles of my arms and onto my thighs; muscles that are screaming at me to stop pedaling. But I won't.

I'm winning this race: edging, bit by tiny bit, ahead of Caitlin and Hala. Each of us stares up at the screen illuminated on the wall before us. Our avatars, linked to the exercise bikes we are on, creep slowly around the glowing outline of a virtual track. The three of us are getting toward the end of two hours of early-morning training here at Athena's headquarters.

"Is that the best you can do, Cait?" I say. "I've seen grandmothers pushing shopping carts faster around grocery stores."

I'm gulping for breath but just the fact that I eked out a sentence that long is my way of taunting Caitlin.

"Yeah, Jessie?" she pants. "Well, not mine. She just chases down chickens for dinner."

I grin. It's a funny image and just possibly true since Caitlin grew up in a tiny Kentucky town.

Hala doesn't ever participate in much banter so I just steal a glance at her, a sideways look she won't catch. Her face is tight with the pressure of riding at this resistance and intensity, her dark hair damp with sweat. She'll never boast or taunt, and she's a gracious loser (I should know, I beat her a lot) but she has a competitive streak as wide as a river.

"Slow down," says Amber, from behind us, her tone officious. "You're beating your all-time records for speed, but you're creeping into the danger zone for heart rate."

Well, that's a momentum killer.

"Amber!" Caitlin and I exclaim at the same time. Feeling the competition drain out of the room, Hala lets out a mild curse in Arabic. My foot slips off the pedal and the spinning rubber catches on my calf, shearing off a thin layer of skin. I gasp and pause for a moment.

"Sorry," Amber replies, in a tone that makes it clear how *not* sorry she is. "But this is training, not an ego contest."

Amber is head of Athena's technology department and also oversees our training, which she controls mainly by compulsively tapping data into an iPad. I love statistics and numbers, but Amber is off the charts when it comes to tables and graphs, and she might be just a tad obsessive about logging and tracking everything, from our lung capacity to her collection of old vinyl music records. But that obsessive attention to detail also makes her incredibly good at other things, like finding connections between shell companies and offshore bank accounts. Those are the kinds of connections that help Athena to bring down traffickers, terrorists, and a host of others who target mainly women and children. The kind of people that governments rarely have the time or budget to pursue. The kind of people our bosses, Li, Peggy, and Kit, built this rogue agency to fight against.

I get my feet back onto the pedals, ignoring the scrape on my leg that's just beginning to ooze a thin film of blood, and Caitlin gets her pace up again too, till we are both matching Hala. But the thrill of the chase has passed. We finish the track without the same intensity, leaving Amber stressing about our mediocre speeds.

"Li's not going to be thrilled with these results," Amber says, trailing us all toward the door that leads to the showers. She's probably right about that. It usually takes an effort of superhuman proportions for Li to offer anyone a word of appreciation.

"Then it's a good thing it's only ever you that I want to impress." I smile.

"Sorry to break it to you, Jessie, but you're failing miserably—" Amber's retort is cut short by a message flashing up on her phone. She glances at it and then at us.

"What's up?" asks Caitlin.

"Clean up and report back to the situation room in ten minutes," she says.

I'd rather spend the short time we have in the locker room soothing my tired muscles under a scalding shower than wielding a hair dryer, so I leave my washed hair damp and tied back and meet my teammates by the elevator. Hala steps in first and lets a small beam of blue light from the unmarked control panel sweep over her iris. Once it recognizes her, the lift starts to move up.

None of us speak, and Caitlin leans tiredly against the sidewall. So tiredly that her eyes actually close for a long moment. I'm just about to throw her a sarcastic comment about being out of shape, but a concerned look from Hala stops me. We both sneak glances at Caitlin again. Shadows form gaunt dips beneath her eyes and there are fine frown lines on her forehead. Caitlin has decided she wants to slowly come off the anxiety meds that she's been on since her military tours in Iraq. Maybe that's not helping, or maybe she's reducing them too fast. Either way, she feels us staring.

"What?" she asks, opening her eyes.

Always reluctant to get too personal, Hala just shrugs and looks away.

"You look rough, that's all," I say.

A tiny sigh escapes Caitlin's lips, a sound that's almost apologetic. I wait for her to elaborate, but the elevator door opens and she chooses not to answer but to stride out ahead of us into the corridor that leads to the situation room. Coming down to meet us, as he always does, is Thomas. Like Amber, Thomas has been integral to Li's team since he was out of college. He runs Li's many agendas, anticipates her requests, arranges her meetings and travel—and yet to call him an assistant feels like it misses the point. It's more like he's an extension of Li's brain; at least the part that organizes the insane schedule she keeps.

"Good workout?" Thomas asks by way of greeting.

"Workout?" I sniff. "It was a bit tougher than your usual jog around the park."

Thomas smiles, unfazed by my sarcasm. His hair is swept back and perfectly styled; his three-piece suit and shirt are crisp and wrinkle-free. He sports a pink tie and delicate silver cuff links. I'm quite sure that when Thomas slipped out of the womb, his parents asked, "Boy or girl?" and the midwife said, "Neither. You have a beautiful, healthy men's fashion ad."

The door of the situation room clicks open at the touch of Thomas's pass card and he holds it for us to enter, reserving a special smile for Hala as she passes him. Thomas has a crush on her. It's become apparent to all of us over the past months, from the longing looks he throws her, not to mention the way he always manages to stock the situation room with Hala's favorite bran muffins, green apples, and mint tea. It's crossed my mind that maybe it's more than an unrequited attraction, that maybe they're seeing each other—but since Thomas is the soul of discretion, and Hala would rather eat dirt than reveal much in the way of feelings, I haven't been sure.

Thomas sits beside Amber, who has staked out her usual spot at the long table, surrounding herself with multiple laptops and tablets. Across from us are all three of the Athena founders. Li Chen taps on her phone, which sports a very cool red leather case that matches her crimson tailored suit. As the head of one of the world's largest privately owned technology companies, Li projects the kind of self-assurance that gives everyone the impression that she is definitely *in charge*. And not just of Chen Technologies, but of the entire universe.

Kit Love, another cofounder, also happens to be my mother. In stark contrast to Li, she wears faded blue jeans, a printed silk shirt, and cowboy boots. My mother is a music star—or used to be—and wherever she goes, she always just feels like someone you need to pay attention to.

Between Kit and Li sits Peggy Delaney. One of the first African American women to be a US ambassador to the UK, Peggy is also a trained lawyer, and a woman whose global connections always manage to surprise us. Nobody wears a Chanel suit or a string of pearls better than Peggy, and on top of that, she's just one of the kindest people I've ever met. Of everyone in this room, it's usually Peggy who will get up to greet us all with hugs. But today, even she makes do with brief smiles of welcome. There's a nervous tension hanging in the air and we all settle in quickly.

"Let's begin," says Li. "Time is of the essence."

Briskly, Amber flicks a picture onto the screen. A sixty-year-old man with a thick beard flecked with gray, heavy eyebrows, and small, sharp eyes. It's a face we have become familiar with. Imran is from Pakistan. He is the tribal leader in the village where Peggy, Li, and Kit opened a school for girls two years ago under the auspices of the United Nations. And he took it upon himself to burn down that school, while the girls and their teachers were still in it, because he believed that girls should be married off by the age of fourteen. Li, Kit, and Peggy lobbied and fought for justice and got absolutely nowhere. It was a dark few months, but something *did* change in the end. When no government would help and the UN seemed tied up in political knots, all three women took a stand—a deeply secret stand—and our agency, Athena, was born.

"As you know, Imran escaped any consequences for . . . what he did," Li says. Unusually, she seems emotional, and tries to cover it by talking more quickly. "And as you also know, we've done our best to track his movements ever since. It hasn't always been easy, but we've had help from this man, Asif. His twin daughters died in Imran's attack."

A new photo pops onto the screen: a young man with high cheekbones, a light growth of beard, and eyes that look older than the rest of his face. Kit's eyes flicker away from the photo, a tiny muscle in her jaw clenched. It was Kit who convinced Asif to put his daughters back in school when he was afraid of what Imran and his Taliban backers might do. To say it still haunts her would be an understatement. But at least now she deals with it through her work with Athena rather than by staring at the bottom of an empty vodka bottle.

"Asif gets information from Imran's housekeeper and passes it to us. The housekeeper is a man who's worked with Imran for years. He's been very helpful."

"How?" Hala asks.

Amber chips in: "He's helped us keep tabs on which phones Imran uses so we can always monitor him. He switches handsets and SIM cards like he's changing underwear—rather frequently. And now, something's come up through the phones." She pulls at the ends of her spiky, purple-highlighted hair, tense.

"Imran is planning a terror attack in India," says Li.

"What kind of attack?" I ask, sitting up.

"We don't know."

"What's the target?" I try.

"We don't know that either." Li looks pained at the admission.

"What *do* we know?" asks Hala, biting into a muffin.

"We know it's happening tomorrow at four thirty a.m. Indian time."

The three of us start to look at our watches and phones, but Amber spares us the math. "That's in just over thirteen hours from now," she announces, her voice serious.

"Where?" Caitlin asks.

"Somewhere in Mumbai, we think."

"*Somewhere* in Mumbai? A city of, what, twenty million people?" I ask, stressed. "How are we supposed to protect the target?"

"You're not," Kit says. "You're going to track Imran on the ground and find out what the target is. He's gone completely dark in the past few hours—burner phones included. It's standard practice for terrorists ahead of an attack, to reduce the chances of being caught or foiled."

Peggy chimes in. "You have to keep it clean and simple. No

fighting, and minimal danger to the three of you. Amber will out-line possible strategies as you fly out. And once you know the target, I have a direct line to the Indian ambassador here and we can get the Indian police involved to stop the attack." Peggy's long and illustrious diplomatic career has left her with a wealth of contacts all over the world. I don't doubt she can arrange an intervention in another country, but the whole mission sounds pretty vague.

I stand, suddenly too keyed up to even stay in my seat. Pacing around sometimes helps.

"And what do we do with Imran?" I ask.

"Hand him over to Asif and his neighbors. They've been planning to take back their village for some time. The extremists supporting Imran have moved much farther north and his funding is drying up."

That's all fine and dandy, but another question is bugging me. "Why is Imran targeting somewhere in India? When he's over the border in Pakistan?"

"He's working with a relatively new group called Family First," Peggy explains. "They are so new we don't have anything much on them, but he's referenced them in connection with this upcoming attack, and there is intelligence out of India about them. They are against gender equality, anti-LGBTQI+, and their biggest focus is to stop women and girls being educated or working, because it erodes traditional family values."

Hala makes a face that communicates her disgust with that manifesto.

"Have they committed attacks before?" Caitlin asks.

"No," says Peggy.

There's a brief lull, but it seems like these scraps are all the information there is. Li nods to Amber to deliver the practicalities.

"You'll be on a private flight to Lahore two and a half hours from now," says Amber, reading from one of her tablet screens.

"Can't we leave sooner?" I ask.

"It's not a walk in the park arranging private planes to places like northern Pakistan," replies Amber crisply. "I've done my best and the plane you'll take is faster than a commercial flight. You'll be in the air for just over seven hours. When you land, a stealth helicopter will be waiting for you. Caitlin will pilot. Estimated time to get to Imran's village is around thirty minutes. Giving you over an hour to get the target details out of him."

Well, there's not much margin for error there. The room falls silent, probably because we're all wondering at the immensity of the task. Only the sound of Li's manicured nails tapping compulsively on the table fills the air. It's not a sound I've ever heard before from her—the sound of nervous tension. And it doesn't make me feel great.

"I'm not happy about this," Li admits, at last. "It's rushed. But if we do nothing and people die . . ."

There's a moment's pause, broken finally by Caitlin. The oldest of us agents, she's our team leader and often our unofficial cheerleader too. "I think I speak for all of us in this room when I say we never met a challenge we said no to," she says seriously. "Let's get our asses in gear."

"How poetic," Amber comments. "I think Shakespeare may have said that first." She packs up her workstation.

"Possibly Maya Angelou?" says Thomas. I snort and even Kit and Peggy stifle smiles.

"Gimme a break, all of you," grumbles Caitlin, getting up. We all follow her and rise to clear the room.

2

KIT MEETS ME AT HOME, where I've rushed back to grab some things before I head to the airfield to board the flight to Pakistan. We live together in an expansive house in Notting Hill, a part of London that Kit moved to fifteen years ago. It's not as manic as the middle of the city but there are still a ton of great places to hang out, good restaurants, and lots of vintage clothing shops where Kit can satisfy her occasional shopping cravings.

It takes me about ten minutes to pack. Everything I need is within reach, and though the inside of my closet might look like the aftermath of a burglary, I know where everything is. When I'm done, I haul my backpack into Kit's bedroom, an oasis of distressed wood floors, crisp white linens, and subdued modern art. My mother has lit a couple of citrus candles, sending warm flickers of light onto the pure white walls. The sounds of whale song and ocean waves issue softly through the ceiling speakers. These weird soundscapes are apparently designed to enhance our well-being, but I find it a bit disorienting to hear crashing breakers on some Hawaiian beach when there's only a little green English lawn outside the window.

Kit is busy rummaging around in the vast expanse of her walk-in closet.

"I have to go," I call.

My mother hurries out with a pile of shirts hanging over her arm.

"What about these?" she asks.

I sigh. My backpack is stuffed full of plain T-shirts, which vary only in that some of them are white and some of them are black. Unsurprisingly, most of Kit's clothing just *looks* like it belongs to a music star, and none of it is really my style.

"Seriously, Mum?" I ask. "If you want to help, why don't you—"

The doorbell interrupts me. I'm closest to the video monitor panel mounted next to Kit's bed. The image is in color, high definition, crisp and clear. I feel like I've seen the man standing there before, also on a screen . . . then I realize where. I've seen him on the TV news. Not to mention in person, just once.

"That's Jake Graham," I say.

"The journalist?" Kit asks.

"How many Jake Grahams do you know?"

"Bloody hell," Kit sniffs.

"He trashed you!" I remind her—as if she wouldn't remember.

During our last mission in Belgrade, Kit went undercover and gave a performance for the human trafficker Gregory Pavlic. It was purely as a distraction so that Caitlin could break into Gregory's office and find the evidence we needed to bring him down. Despite our best efforts to keep the concert quiet, the story hit the press, and it was written by Jake Graham, the crusading social justice reporter. And so it looked like my mother was a money-grabbing has-been singer who'd played a gig for a scummy criminal. It turned public opinion against Kit, but she shook it off, deciding it was a good thing. Nobody would suspect a sell-out singer of running a secret agency to help women.

The bell rings again. Long and hard. I stay quiet and wait, watching the wheels turn in Kit's mind.

"Stop worrying," I tell her. "Jake has no idea that Athena exists."

"I know. But it's just better that he doesn't connect you to me," she says. "Just in case."

"Then don't answer it," I suggest.

But she takes a step toward the stairs, toward the door.

"I need to find out why he's here." She flicks on the recording app on her phone and pockets it. "Listen from up here, Jess, and stay quiet, okay?"

I nod. Kit disappears down the stairs while I stay out of sight at the top of the landing, sitting comfortably so that I won't have to move a muscle.

Kit opens the door and there's a wary exchange of pleasantries. Like the pushy reporter that he is, Jake asks if he can come in, but Kit doesn't let him past the threshold.

"What do you want, Jake?" she asks.

"Look, Kit, I know my piece about you and Pavlic must have hurt, but people have a right to know the truth," he says.

"Do you make a point of apologizing in person to everyone you expose? Or is there something else you want from me?"

I smile. I can just imagine Kit's steely stare.

"I want to talk about Cameroon," Jake says.

That wipes the smile off my face. I lean forward, straining to catch every word, to sense Kit's response.

"The country in Africa, you mean? Isn't that where Cameroon is? Or is it the Caribbean . . . ?" wonders Kit.

Jake makes a slight noise—maybe a laugh, maybe a snort of disbelief.

"What do you know about those schoolgirls who were saved by an unknown private army a couple of months ago?" he demands.

"Unknown private army." That would be us. For a moment I'm a little bit flattered that just the three of us agents on the ground in West Africa gave someone the impression of a whole platoon.

"Jake, I'm busy and you're talking in riddles. If you have something to ask me, contact my manager or my PR firm. Their email addresses are on my website."

"You're friends with Peggy Delaney, right?"

Another left-field question. And I'm sure Jake has noticed that it's keeping the front door open and Kit planted on the step. She makes a sound of acknowledgment. There are pictures of Kit and

Peggy everywhere, from the White House to Pakistan, so there's no point in denying it.

"Peggy was helping the Cameroon government take care of those girls. I bumped into her at the embassy."

That freaks me out even more, because I was *with* Peggy when Jake spoke to her at the embassy. I am 100 percent sure he wouldn't remember me, though. I bite tensely on a nail. Okay, 95 percent sure. Jake's still talking:

"That was right after the operation in Cameroon. The attack on Ahmed."

Boy, he's really smart. Planting a name that we know well, just to see if it sticks. But my mom is smarter.

"Who is Ahmed, for Christ's sake?" Kit sounds exasperated.

No explanation from Jake. A bit of shuffling. Then:

"Here. This is a female soldier. Do you know who it is?" Jake asks.

There's a short pause, during which I imagine Kit is looking at whatever image he's showing her.

"Are you serious? It's grainy and—well, it's not even in focus. Jake, I'm sorry. Even though you made sure I can't walk down the street without someone spitting at me, I kind of respect your reporting. But you're really pissing me off right about now, and if you don't take a hike, I'll call the police."

"I can't tell if you're for real," says Jake.

"Trust me, I just need to push this panic button and the cops will be here in three minutes."

"Not about that," Jake continues, perfectly cool. I really want to run downstairs and punch him. But I sit on my hands and make myself breathe (quietly).

"About Gregory Pavlic," continues Jake, and his voice has dropped now, like he's trying to genuinely connect with Kit. "Your whole women's rights campaigning thing, all these years? It always struck me as, well, honest. And then you go and sing for a notorious trafficker. It doesn't feel right, Kit." There's a long pause. I lean forward, straining to listen.

"With Pavlic—I'm not proud of it, but I needed the cash," Kit lies, managing to sound broken by the admission. "That's what you wanted to hear, isn't it? Now go to hell," she says, her voice quavering.

The door slams, cutting off Jake's reply. I wait where I am. Kit stands silently by the front door for a moment then trudges up the stairs and jerks her head for me to follow her into her bedroom. It overlooks the back garden, not the street, but we both stay far from the windows in case Jake is still hanging around, sniffing for scraps.

Kit paces up and down the pale wooden floor by the side of her bed, staring at the planks beneath her feet. She's literally wringing her hands together. I can understand why. Nobody sanctions what we do at Athena. If we're found out, it would mean jail time for all of us; not to mention an end to our work. Something has clearly spooked my mother. I can guess what it is too:

"That picture he showed you? The female soldier? Where was it from?"

"From the mission we ran in Cameroon."

My stomach drops. "Was it me?"

There's a brief moment of relief when Kit shakes her head. But then my mother looks up, her face pinched with worry. She brings a hand up to rub her forehead and the hand is trembling, just a bit, as her gray eyes meet mine.

"It was Caitlin," she says.

3

THE AIR UP HERE IN the northern hills of Pakistan is fresh and touched with scents of pine and herbs. It's also pretty damned cold, especially when you're at the open door of an airborne helicopter. I scan over the landscape below, green and vague through the night-vision contact lenses that are irritating my eyes. There's certainly not much down there at 3 a.m. in the way of lights, or vehicles, or factories— but there could be people, hidden, watching. This particular region isn't under the control of religious extremists anymore, but there's no reason why insurgents and fighters might not still be living in the tiny hamlets and caves that dot the barren countryside. The cold grasps at me, eating into my bones, as Hala and I crouch at the door of our stealth copter. Caitlin lowers the aircraft, carefully, painstakingly, close enough to the rocky ground that we can both jump down and start running.

Our chopper is so quiet that we can barely hear the soft whirr of the blades whipping the air as Caitlin flies up and away from us. We've landed about a mile from Imran's village so that we don't attract attention, and we race over the rough landscape on foot, our pace steady, our feet hitting the ground together. We are late. Not by much, but we still have very little time left to mine Imran for information.

"Hey," I say to Hala. "Shall we go a bit faster?"

All three of us are connected to each other for sound, so a whisper is all it takes to communicate.

She just nods but picks up speed.

"I didn't think it would be this cold," I add.

"Hmm."

I decide not to bother with any more attempts at conversation. The fact is that even on a good day, Hala isn't the world's chattiest person—in her native Arabic, or in English. I've seen professional mime artists that have better small talk. Anyway, we're nearly there. The village begins with a long straggle of homes built along the dirt track that passes for a main road.

"I'm a hundred yards due north of where I dropped you. Let me know when you're five minutes out for pickup."

Caitlin's Kentucky drawl is so full and warm in my ear that it's like she's standing right next to me. The sound of her instruction, the knowledge that she's back there, waiting, with her hand on the helicopter controls, ready to spirit us out of here, calms the rising tension I feel as we move toward our target.

As we run through the village, we circle past the main cluster of houses and huts—and then I see it. Hala follows my gaze to a patch of empty land that holds rows and rows of small clay pots. Each one is filled with oil and each one burns with a small, persistent flame. Flames of remembrance. We both slow down for just a moment, out of respect, watching those oil lamps cast their tiny sprays of light into the black night.

This is the place where the village school used to stand before the twenty-three young girls and two teachers inside it were killed. These gentle lights are a memorial, one for each death—but the flickering fires only remind me of the brutal arson attack that took those lives. I try not to, but I can't help but imagine what it must have been like to be inside when the doors were nailed shut. Maybe those kids and teachers heard some hammering, but thought it was the last bits of building work, and just carried on with a math lesson. Maybe they ignored the soft slosh of kerosene on the outside walls and didn't even hear the fizzing strikes of the matches that followed. Beside me, I feel Hala shudder.

A noise attracts our attention. Someone's approaching through the solid black of the night, emerging from among the main cluster of homes. Hala and I step behind a wall and pull up the scarves that are swathed around our necks, masking our faces. We watch as a man pauses, looking around. Through my night lenses, his outline is clear, despite the black clothes he wears. He carries a long, thin knife in his hand and, by the stretched skin of his knuckles, I can tell that he's grasping it hard. The darkness is too thick for him to see us, though he seems to sense us as we circle closer. But by the time he turns, my hand is on his knife, my foot has kicked up behind his knees, and he drops to the ground while I press his own blade hard against his throat. Hala is right behind me, ready to help, but I've got this.

"State your name," I whisper.

"Mary Poppins," he whispers back.

Really, I don't know where Amber comes up with these code words. Maybe it livens up her desk job at Athena. I lower the knife away from the man's throat and Hala shines a tiny LED flashlight into his face. It is the face we were expecting. His eyes widen as he takes us in. My guess is that he wasn't expecting two young women to be the ones dropping in to help him take back his village. He rises to his feet, then shakes hands with both of us. It's a polite gesture and somewhat rare in this part of the world where, sometimes, men don't think it proper to touch a woman who isn't their wife.

"Asif," he whispers, giving us his real name.

We just nod mutely in return. Turning away, Asif leads us off into a tight alleyway between small wooden pens where goats and donkeys are tethered up for the night. As we approach the end of the narrow lane, he points to a stone building with barred windows.

"This is the village jail," he explains. "When you are finished with Imran, we will keep him here and put him on trial."

Imran was arrested at the time of the arson attack—the international uproar meant that the police could hardly leave him untouched. But news cycles move on fast and forget even faster. With extremists' money and weapons backing him, the police didn't have the courage or inclination to press charges against Imran, and he was released within weeks. He returned to his big house here in the village and nothing changed. The villagers who lost their daughters swallowed their rage, fearing their sons might be next. But now, the fundamentalists have retreated north and Imran's power base has crumbled. And so, Asif and the others are willing to take back their village and rebuild what was burned. Some justice for the loss of those young girls with big dreams of going to school; the girls whose hopes, and bodies, turned so quickly into dust and ash.

"We'll deliver him as soon as we are done," I assure Asif. "Thank you for your help so far."

"There are three guards outside his house," Asif tells us. "Once you get past them, the housekeeper will let you in the kitchen door." Using his phone, he shows us a picture of the housekeeper so we don't trust the wrong guy.

"Got it," I confirm.

Asif points us on our way but Imran's home is not hard to find—a sprawling, whitewashed house that squats heavily on a plot considerably larger than any of the others in the village. A forbidding wall at least twelve feet high and two feet thick forms a protective square around the dwelling.

I extract a small dart gun from the holster that clings to my body armor. We pace with light steps along the outside wall of the house. As we reach the front, I take over the lead position from Hala and sneak a look around the corner. Two men in white robes lean against the wall, smoking, looking more than a little bored of guarding the place. Concerned, I turn back to Hala and indicate that there are two guards there, not three, as Asif said—when the third man materializes like a specter, out of the darkness behind her. He advances on us, a crowbar raised high over his head. In a flash Hala ducks, giving me a clear shot. My dart fires into his neck and he falls like a stone before he can bring the weapon down. But the sound of his body and the crowbar crashing to the ground has alerted the other two. Their steps pound toward us, and I move out quickly from my cover behind the wall, and shoot again, twice. They both drop, drugged into unconsciousness that will last for a couple of hours at least.

Within moments, Hala is high above me, scaling the smooth surface of the wall as easily as if it were a staircase. Only once does she slip, but she rights herself, and makes the summit in seconds. She carefully slices away the curls of barbed wire that festoon the top, then drops a climbing line down to me. Quickly, silently, we use the line to make our way down the other side, into the heart of Imran's home.

We find ourselves in a wide, open-air courtyard that clearly forms the entrance into the house, which lies ahead of us, looming darkly in the night. The word "courtyard" always feels kind of romantic to me—it makes me think of cool shadows, high pillars, maybe candles. That's definitely not happening here. For a start, a stench of raw sewage wafts up from a blubbering drain to our left. And the only light source is a lurid fluorescent bulb dangling by a wire inside a wooden outhouse across from us. The scent of jasmine wafts past for a second, but it's soon lost under the odor from the drain. Light glimmers in a room at the far end of the courtyard, sending a splash of white onto the rough concrete floor before us. Through those lit windows we can see the outline of cooking pots hanging from the ceiling and, against the wall, a wood-burning stove. Harsh bulbs give the white walls a greenish glow, and inside, a tiny old man moves about—the housekeeper. Through Asif, we've learned that there's not much in the way of nine-to-five hours in Imran's house—if you work for him you can rely on being on call twenty-four/seven, and he has a habit of staying up most of the night, plotting and planning with his cronies, and then sleeping through much of the day. What we're expecting tonight is that Imran will indeed be awake, anticipating the attack that's due to happen in less than forty minutes from now. And what we really want is for him to talk to one of his buddies about it, preferably in exquisite detail, giving the London team the details they need to alert the Indian police.

Hala taps lightly on the back entrance to the kitchen. The housekeeper startles, then scampers over to open the door with quick, neat movements. For a moment, he stares, stunned by the fact that we are women; then he gets over it. He looks at us questioningly, like he's awaiting instructions. Hala turns to a platter of crisp pastry samosas sitting ready on the table and she sticks a clear, wafer-thin microphone dot onto the base of the plate. She shows the housekeeper, who nods, impressed that it's invisible. Then he pulls us into a dark corridor and indicates that we should wait there. The passageway that we stand in leads directly into the living room, where we can now hear Imran and his comrades chatting. It's good to be out of the coarse, bright light of the kitchen—I feel less *visible* out here, even though we are closer to Imran. But now, I use sign language to urge the housekeeper to get going. It's driving me nuts that Imran is jabbering away and we're not picking up the conversation.

The old man hurries down the long, dark corridor to deliver the plate. Within seconds, in our left ears, Amber's super-cool tech feed gives us a constant translation of the Urdu conversation that the mic is now picking up between Imran and his friends. There's a delay of about three seconds, no more. I glance at Hala, relieved. But if we were hoping for high-level terrorist discussion, we're out of luck. Right now, they're taking turns complaining about their families and how the first wives are so jealous of the second and third wives. Everyone has their cross to bear, I suppose, but somehow, I can't get there with the sympathy. I check my watch, which has a handy countdown timer that only makes me more stressed. Only thirty-five minutes to go. We have to get the information soon for Peggy's contact to have any chance of mobilizing the police and evacuating the potential victims. In our ears, the chatter from the living room pauses. Then, finally, Imran speaks:

"Not long now," he says. He sounds pleased with himself, his tone arrogant. I glance at Hala. She looks hopeful. *Please*, I pray, let this be it.

"Four thirty in the morning, everyone will be sleeping," says one of his guys, like he's congratulating Imran on his genius.

"Maximum casualties," confirms another.

My heart is pounding, with stress, with willing them to say more. *Where* are these casualties meant to be?

"I never thought us Pakistanis would be working with Indians," laughs Imran. "Muslims and Hindus—sworn enemies. But Family First is a bigger cause that unites us all."

Murmurs of appreciation rise up for Imran's comment.

"What made you choose this target, brother?" asks a different man, with a high voice.

Imran gives a low chuckle. "This target? This met all the requirements for Family First—but for me, it was also personal, my friend."

Next to me, I feel Hala tensing, leaning forward just a bit. We're getting close. Keep talking, Imran, I think. Just a little more detail and we can hand you over to the villagers and hightail it back home.

And then something blurs past us, right through the corridor, and then it stops, just as suddenly. I stare, my eyes wide open, my ears filled with the sudden hammering of my heart.

It's a little boy, maybe six or seven years old, tousle-headed, sleepy. One of Imran's kids, probably. The boy turns in surprise and stares openmouthed at the dark outlines of me and Hala standing there like statues in the corridor. Time slows to a crawl. I feel the blood pulse in my ears, as I watch, dull-headed, unable to think. Hala makes the tiniest move forward, then stops. Because I can't think of what else to do, I put my finger to my lips. Wide-eyed, the boy watches us in fright for a moment more, then turns and runs, screaming, into the room where Imran sits.

4

WE ARE ALREADY RACING THE other way, back up the corridor. In our ears, there's an echo of voices—a translation of the child's frantic warnings, and then the questions, the surprise from the men in the room as they rise and hurry out to investigate. A shot blasts into the corridor behind us, lodging into the wall just as we hurtle into the kitchen. The housekeeper is at the sink. Before he can even turn at the commotion, Hala has pushed him to the ground, using the table to cover him as best she can. Hala and I throw ourselves out into the courtyard, but more shots come, splintering the door moments after we run outside.

"The outhouse," I call to her. Desperate for cover, we both dive into the wooden building across from the kitchen door and pull out weapons—she has a real gun, I have my dart pistol. The team in London is hooked up to the feed from tiny body cameras sewn into our clothing. Amber's voice comes in:

"Just intercepted a text. Imran's requested backup."

Now, Li's voice sends an order into our ears. "Extract now, from the house."

"On my way," Caitlin replies.

I peer around the outhouse doorway and shoot—first one, then another of Imran's friends. Both fall, drugged. Then I get the third. Suddenly alone, Imran drops to the ground for cover and lies there, waiting, a pistol in his hand. I don't want to shoot him with a dart, because if he's tranquilized, he can't talk. In my ear, Caitlin comes in:

"I'm approaching the south wall."

But we can't move—we are in a standoff with Imran. He's not stupid; he knows where we are. He's seen three of his men drop from shots fired from our direction. Through a crack in the wooden wall, Hala and I watch his head lift off the ground, looking our way. Without getting up, he raises his gun at the outhouse. His bullets will blast through the rotting wood like a fist through a paper bag. So quickly that I hardly feel her, Hala pushes me aside and rolls herself out of the door. Imran's hand sweeps across to track her, but she shoots first, getting him in the elbow. He screams and drops his gun.

I'm out in a flash, running toward Imran. He flails his other arm out, looking for the gun, but my boot moves it out of his reach. I scoop it up and press it to Imran's head, holstering my dart pistol. At the kitchen door, women and children cower, drawn downstairs by the sound of gunfire. Hala fires into the air and barks at them to stay back. The kitchen door slams shut, leaving us alone with Imran in the courtyard.

"We have him," I say on my comms.

"Get out of there," Li says. "This is not the plan."

But if we leave, Imran gets what he wants—the attack in India will happen. I ignore Li and push Imran's head down closer to the ground.

"What's the target?" I bark.

He turns to me. Fleshy lips protruding from a dry beard. His mouth opens, as if to speak. I lean down close to hear him. But he only spits at me. Gross. I push the gun harder into his scalp.

"Incoming car carrying two guys, ETA three minutes," says Caitlin, from the copter. "This is a mess, get over to me now. . . ."

"I'm bringing Imran with us," I tell Caitlin.

"Li?" Caitlin asks.

There's hesitation from London, which is all the permission I need. I yank Imran upright as the copter lowers down just outside the wall. Holding our captive between us, Hala and I hustle him outside and through the downwash from the helicopter blades, pushing us back like a small hurricane. But we get him to the door. With one arm useless, bleeding from his gunshot wound, Imran is not able to fight us off.

"Can you control him?" Li asks.

"Taking Jessie's lead on this," replies Caitlin.

Hala clambers into the chopper and hauls Imran up by the shoulders while I push him in from behind, with the gun thrust into his back. I follow him into the open door as the chopper starts to rise from the ground. Below us, a car screams to a stop outside the house, and two men jump out. They appear smaller and smaller to me as we take off and climb higher, but I get a glimpse of them opening up the trunk of the car and pulling out something large.

But I leave Caitlin to keep tabs on them—I have Imran to deal with. He watches us, focused, alert; not complaining at all about the injury to his arm. It's bleeding everywhere and must be painful as anything.

"Put your good hand behind you," Hala instructs.

Still facing my gun, Imran obeys. Hala pulls out plastic ties to attach Imran's uninjured hand to the frame of the copter. But even as she tries to secure him, we both see something streak past the window and explode into the air just behind us.

"What was that?" I ask.

"They have a SAM," Caitlin says grimly. A surface-to-air missile. I feel tension—even more tension—flood my veins.

"They'll get a lock on us, those things are accurate . . . ," I reply, stressed.

"I'm using ECMs," she says. Electronic countermeasures can help confuse things, and there is another explosion, but also another miss. Hala glances at me in relief but now Caitlin makes a steep turn and banks upward—and in the back, we all tumble over each other. I'm on the floor of the helicopter, with Imran flung on top of me. Hala staggers up, looming above us, and grasps Imran by the collar to pull him off me.

"We're out of missile range," reports Caitlin from the pilot seat. "Okay back there?"

I don't reply because even as Imran turns and gets up onto his knees, with Hala's fingers grasping his tunic, I realize he's pulled the dart gun out of my body holster. I kick my leg up at his hand, at the gun, but he turns and shoots it at Hala. Her eyes widen in shock before she collapses onto the floor, drugged.

Caitlin glances back at us, cursing under her breath. As Imran tries to turn the dart gun on me, she twists the chopper from side to side, throwing him off his feet. I'm tossed around too, but at least he can't hit me with a dart. On the floor, Hala rolls around with the movement, out cold. I'm dizzy, but I aim a kick at Imran's wounded elbow. That puts him in enough agony for me to find my footing, struggle upright, and hit him again, in the face. The dart gun drops, and Imran is on the floor between the tiny bucket seats. I'm on top of him in a flash, my knee on his chest, my hand squeezing his windpipe.

"What's the target?" My face is right up against his. We're both sweating, stressed. His blood is everywhere, making it tough to keep my grip on his throat. Time is passing, every second dragging us closer to some unknown attack, unknown lives ruined, untold fear spread. All of it is pain that I have to believe we could still avoid.

"You CIA pigs," he hisses. "You think you will stop me?"

So, he's assumed that we're black-ops Americans. He literally snarls and then bites at my fingers, so I snatch my hand away from his bared teeth and use it to punch his eye. I cast a look toward the front of the chopper, checking on Hala. She's still lying there, drugged.

"Torture is what you know," he says, accusingly. "Nobody will torture me."

"What do you want?" I ask, desperate to make him talk. "Freedom? Citizenship somewhere? I can arrange it." Maybe he'll believe me if he thinks I'm CIA. "But you have to tell me what Family First is targeting."

Frustrated, I yank at his collar. I don't want to hit him again. He's already lost blood from the gunshot wound; I don't need him passing out on me.

Imran stares at me for a long moment, then he breaks into a smile.

"I will tell you," he says.

I wait, getting my breathing under control. Caitlin flies smoothly now, and my earpiece is silent as everyone in London waits. Only the soft chop-chop-chop of the blades of the helicopter and the dull throb of white noise in the cabin fill the space. Grasping Imran's neck, I glance at the watch on my wrist. Twelve minutes to go.

"Two years ago, imperialists—women imperialists—came here to *my* village, to interfere in *my* culture. Sending girls to a school. Girls who should marry, look after families. Women have a sacred place in the family. . . ."

For crying out loud, will this guy just get to the point, already?

"That's a great story," I interrupt through gritted teeth. "Now, what's the target?"

"Those imperialist women still educate girls," he says, managing to smirk through the pain of his arm.

I hesitate. I'm assuming the "imperialist women" he's talking about are Athena's founders. As for education, all three of them run foundations involved with schools, universities, and career training for women, dotted all around the world, including some in India.

They own some of them, fund others, or are on boards of governors.

"Let's get specific, shall we?" I press my knee harder, lower, into Imran's solar plexus, and it makes him gasp.

"I will tell you," he says. "Because you are too late to stop it."

I clench my jaw as I watch the countdown dip toward nine minutes.

"The most disgusting of these women is a whore," he spits. "A singer, entertaining men on a stage."

He means my mother.

"What's her name?" I say, just to be sure.

"Kit Love," he says. "She has two schools in Mumbai. In a few minutes, she will only have one."

Even having to look at him makes my stomach turn.

"Did you get that?" I yell at my team, but my question is drowned in a sudden cacophony of voices and instructions in London. They got it, all right. The audio drops out suddenly, but there's nothing wrong. It's just that the London team won't want us distracted with whatever they are doing.

I scramble up, grasping Hala's handgun, and turn it onto Imran. I'd rather control him without having to be on top of him. For one thing, I can't stand to be near him, and for another, it gives me a chance to check on Hala. She's unconscious but breathing fine. With my free hand I slip her own kit bag under her head and arrange her limbs more comfortably. At the back of the chopper, Imran pulls himself to his feet.

"You can't stop this," Imran says. "This is bigger than one attack. It is bigger than me. It is a movement, and it will only end when family values are restored to the whole world."

With a sudden movement from his good hand, Imran flips open a control panel attached to the rear door right beside him.

"Don't touch that," I command, moving closer, threatening him with my gun.

But his hand is out, feeling for the red lever that opens the rear hatch of the helicopter.

"Or what?" he sneers. "You won't shoot me. You want me alive, so you can torture me for more information. . . ."

"No," I begin. But he slams down the lever. Behind him, the rear door cranks open, letting in a windstorm of icy air.

"What the hell is he doing?" says Caitlin from the pilot's seat, her voice rising with stress.

The sheer volume of air rushing in at this altitude makes it hard to see. Water fills my eyes suddenly, a reaction to the cold, the wind . . . I grasp hold of the seat behind me and cling on, because my first thought is that Imran wants to throw me out of the speeding chopper. But that's not what he has in mind. As my eyes blink and clear, I watch Imran watching me. His gaze does not leave mine, and it carries an air of triumph as, cradling his wounded arm, he takes three steps back and falls out of the helicopter and into thin air.

5

THE CHOPPER FEELS STRANGELY SILENT as we fly south toward the airfield where we picked it up, not even two hours ago. I'm in the copilot seat, next to Caitlin. Behind us, I've settled Hala as best I can to sleep off the drugged dart that Imran hit her with. And now, on my wrist, I watch the timer count down the last few seconds toward 4:30 a.m. in India—the scheduled time of the attacks.

Our communications devices, phones, earpieces, everything, are eerily quiet. The rest of our team will be frantically trying to evacuate the schools in Mumbai that Imran referred to. There are two boarding schools funded from the charity that Kit set up back when she made a ton of money as a recording artist. Both are focused on educating girls aged eleven to eighteen, and between them they give places to around a hundred and twenty students— girls from small villages where they would usually be married off as they hit puberty, if not before. The schools are not only places to live and study, a safe haven where the students learn reading, math, and science skills; they also keep girls out of arranged marriages while they're still children. Instead, the curriculum sets them up to go to university or get a job and, either way, get equipped for some independence.

I reach into my backpack for wipes and use them to clean my face and hands. I can feel sweat, and congealed fluid, probably Imran's blood, seeping into my clothes, pooling under my nails. It also gives me something to do while we wait—and the waiting is painful as we stand by to find out what has happened. At the moment that Imran finally spoke up, there were only eight minutes to go; it's hard to imagine that any kind of attack could have been averted. And that's assuming that Imran even bothered to tell us the truth. Leaning my head tiredly against the back of my seat, I watch Caitlin fly. Her calm demeanor, her methodical movements, are soothing. Her kind blue eyes glancing encouragingly at me remind me of all the good things in the world. But then, Peggy's voice crackles into our ears. I sit bolt upright. We both do.

"How's Hala?" Peggy asks. Her voice is heavy.

"Vitals are fine. It'll take another hour till she's conscious," I say. "Peggy? Tell us."

"There was a bombing at one of Kit's schools." She sighs. There's a crack in her voice when she continues and the sound of it makes me feel ill. "There just wasn't enough time. By the time the message reached them, they had only started to evacuate. . . ."

Caitlin looks at me, her eyes full. She swallows down tears.

"How many casualties?" Caitlin asks.

"Still waiting to find out. I'm afraid the number will be high," Peggy says.

I put my head in my hands. "Peggy, I'm sorry," I say.

"You did everything you could, you all did. We got so close."

"How's Kit?" I ask.

Peggy hesitates. "She's taking it hard. She's off comms right now, getting ready to head to Mumbai on the next flight out, to meet the families of the victims, attend funerals. . . . I'll travel out too. Separately."

There's a moment of quiet, of respect and reflection, before Caitlin gently breaks the silence with a question.

"So, what's our plan now?"

Li chimes in, focusing us all with a set of efficient orders:

"Amber will get you to Mumbai this morning," she says. "You have three things to do. Find the bombers. Investigate this Family First outfit. And protect the remaining girls."

We are all tired, but in the early-morning traffic of Mumbai, the possibility of sleep fades pretty fast. I've never tried drugs but negotiating the city's dense traffic from the back seat of a taxi, with windows open to the damp, surging heat outside, feels like some kind of bizarre rush. Even Hala, who claims that roads in the Middle East provide the true test of driving ability, hangs on to the passenger strap as we career past acres of land covered in tented slums and into town.

"Feeling okay?" Caitlin asks Hala.

"No. We failed in our mission," Hala replies, ignoring the fact that she was clearly being asked about her recovery from the sleep dart. But her churlish reply is only self-blame, directed outward. Caitlin looks at me, pained, but says nothing more to Hala, who turns away, sullen, and goes back to watching the road beside us.

The truth is that we've all spent the past few hours replaying the whole Pakistan mission in our heads, trying to think of ways we could have done better, ways we might have coaxed Imran to speak earlier. Our only consolation is that since Imran's cronies were drugged, Asif was able to mobilize the village to drag them into jail. There were more than enough angry fathers and mothers to take on the extra men who turned up with missiles too. Now that the power balance has shifted, and especially in light of Imran's death, it looks as if the village will at last be back under the control of the farmers who live there.

Ahead of us, a truck crammed with chickens bursting out of wooden crates wavers as it turns a sharp corner. To our right, three goats are driven along by a young boy. To our left, a family of four cruise by, all of them riding on one moped and with one helmet between them. I pay attention to how our driver negotiates the whole mess. He's certainly skilled in a way they don't teach you at any driving school. He spots gaps where the rest of us would see only bumper-to-bumper gridlock and wheedles the taxi in and out of different traffic lanes with minimal fuss but plenty of horn tooting.

Our first stop is a monolithic, faceless apartment building in

Andheri. We approach it along side roads where people linger at tea and food stalls built in ramshackle lines along the sidewalks. It's here that Caitlin and Hala will stay. The building is popular with tourists who can book its apartments through an online app, so it's a place where newcomers are always coming and going. This way, they should attract as little notice as possible. They exit the cab and collect their backpacks from the trunk. Before I continue on in the taxi, Caitlin looks in at me through the window, while Hala waits behind her.

"We'll go get some food and clothes. Then we'll explore how to secure the girls at the other school," says Caitlin.

"Keep me updated," I say.

"Yeah. Enjoy your swanky hotel." She smiles briefly, trying to lighten the heaviness we all feel.

"I will," I say, giving the taxi driver the address of the hotel where Kit will be staying when she lands later today. The plan is for me to stay at the same place, posing as an investigator working for her foundation, the person she wants the police to keep apprised of their findings. I check my watch. Kit will be on the plane, mid-flight by now. She's on a commercial flight, but she will be greeted off the plane by the airline's special services crew, who cater to celebrities and make sure they don't have to negotiate the queues at immigration with people who might gawk at them or try to snap a selfie.

In the absence of any air-conditioning, a fine mist of sweat gradually coats my arms and forehead as we drive. We pass a temple, tall and white and gleaming; then a shopping mall; then a line of shanty homes. They form incongruous neighbors on this one stretch of street. Soon, we veer back onto the main road and the sea comes into focus on one side. The shoreline curves around, lined with high-end clubs, restaurants, and hotels; places that can afford to buy or rent a coveted view of the ocean. Along the way, I ask the driver to stop at a drugstore. He swerves to the curb in front of a row of tiny shops, their merchandise piled up on all sides, protected from rain only by tarpaulins stretched across to form an insubstantial roof. But one of the vendors has all the paraphernalia of a drugstore, including the hair dye I need. Quickly, I make my purchase and get back into the taxi. As we go to turn into the driveway of the hotel, private armed guards stop the car.

"What's going on?" I ask the driver.

"They check for explosives," he says. "Since Mumbai suffered the hotel terror attacks years ago."

I watch as the guards look beneath the vehicle with mirrors on poles, check inside the seating area and trunk, and finally wave us through.

The lobby is enormous; an air-conditioned, high-ceilinged, marble-paved oasis. A fountain trickles peacefully. A smiling bellman spirits my luggage up to my room. The receptionist offers me a complimentary beverage. I glance at the windows. But smoked glass now protects me from a view of the messy, busy street outside, and the soft tones of Billie Holiday singing "Stormy Weather" drown out any external noise that might penetrate the soundproofed windows. It's a weird contrast to the crush of life on the streets beyond.

I grab a hot drink and pastry from the hotel's high-end espresso bar then go up to my room.

I unpack by opening up my bag and upending the contents onto the bed. Then I go straight into the bathroom and apply the hair color to my head. While I wait for it to work, I call Amber.

"Where's my package?" I ask.

"Good morning to you too," she says tiredly. "My tracking shows it was delivered to the hotel ten minutes ago. . . ."

"Thanks—I'll check with the front desk."

But even as I'm heading for the phone next to the bed, there's a knock at the door of my room. I open up and a square box, tightly wrapped in layer after layer of plastic, is handed over to me. Still on the line with Amber, I take it, lock my door, and cut it open using my penknife. I smile.

"Got it," I tell her, stuffing the contents into my backpack.

"Good to know," she says dryly. "Send pictures of yourself. I'd like something to throw darts at."

I smile and hang up. It's time to rinse off my hair and get over to the school where the attack happened.

Sitting in the cab, watching my driver edge forward about ten inches every five minutes, I have plenty of time to assess how the traffic works here. Most trucks have a sign on their backs asking for "Horn Please." Far from blaring horns to indicate annoyance, the driver explains, horns are used all the time to ask slower vehicles to move to one side, so that the car behind can pass.

"It's a wonderful mode of communication," he explains ecstatically, in lilting English. "It means everything runs smoothly."

Well, that's a rather optimistic take on the traffic carnage outside our window, but I let it pass. After a few more frustrating minutes, I bail out on the bumper-to-bumper gridlock and walk the remaining mile to the school. On the way, I pass an electronics store where televisions line the windows—on each one of them the attack on Kit's school is the major news story of the morning. In all, eleven girls have lost their lives. I pause to watch. Old photos and concert clips of my mother are interspersed with live footage of the crime scene, sealed off by police guards and reams of police tape. Family First has taken responsibility for the bomb, releasing a brazen statement that demands that foreigners stop coming to India to corrupt young women and enslave them with Western values. I feel my temples throb with anger as I watch the news feed, but I turn away newly energized by my mission to track down the monsters who find it acceptable to kill young girls to make their point.

As I approach the school itself, I slow down so I can scope it out from a distance. Mournful threads of smoke still curl up from a damaged roof. Blown-out windows gape emptily. And police guards are everywhere. The school sits on its own large plot at the corner of a busy city block, much of which is sealed off right now. But two streets along is a row of shops and restaurants thronged with people; probably locals hanging around to see what's happening in the aftermath of the attack. I choose a bustling burger place crammed with customers, and hurry inside, making straight for the bathroom.

As I empty my bag, I look at myself in the chipped mirror that sits over the sink. My hair is much darker now, almost black. It looks natural but my skin still feels too pale for this ruse to work, surrounded as I am by Indians with a richer skin tone. But there's not much I can do about that now, other than inserting dark brown contact lenses to cover the green color of my eyes. I pull on the items that Amber had delivered to my room—khaki pants and standard lace-up shoes that pinch at my toes. Next, I button on a khaki shirt with chest pockets and epaulets. It fits snugly on top of my skinny T-shirt. Lastly, I try on a navy cap carrying an embroidered logo on the front, and the words "Mumbai Police" on the side. I tug the cap down, trying to hide as much of my face as I can. Thrusting my jeans and boots into my backpack, I head out into the street, trying to look as if I know where I'm going.

Walking with an air of confidence, I circle around toward the school, looking for an entry point. There are police on all the corners of the building, while at the front gates, TV news vans, photographers, and reporters jostle for position. There's certainly plenty of confusion there, and because of that, a possible way to slip in, unnoticed, but it also feels very exposed. Then, from the corner of my eye I see a police van pull up to a side street. A group of twelve officers, a couple of them women, jump down and wait to be deployed. I sidle closer as someone senior in plain clothes comes over to them and barks some instructions in Hindi. They all start moving, briskly, toward the school, and as they duck under the police tape, I step in alongside them and move inside too. There's a sense of urgency to everyone's movements, which means no one stops to talk or look much at each other, thank goodness. I don't wear out my luck though. As soon as I can, I drop back, a little behind the others, and duck into the first doorway that I find.

I've been briefed that there are eight classrooms in the three-story whitewashed structure, as well as a computer room, music room, and, upstairs, several dorms for the girls, who are all boarders, since they often come from smaller towns and villages some distance from Mumbai. The place is empty, now, of course. I'm in a corridor that leads away from the classrooms. Much farther ahead, I can see more police tape hanging in limp ribbons around the section of the building where the explosion must have happened. There's a pit in my stomach as I think about the devastation that so recently occurred there. I make myself turn away and focus. Putting my head into each doorway, I find a large kitchen, mostly intact, and next door to the kitchen are the rooms I'm looking for—administrative offices.

It's not my job to crash the heart of the crime scene and potentially mess up forensic evidence. That needs the police, coroners, and a whole host of pathologists—and, presumably, they are all hard at work this morning. What I'm looking for is any information about the running of the school. Who works here, who might have been a recent hire, who might have been a temp worker. Anyone who could have been in on this plan; anyone who may intentionally, or even inadvertently, have given the bombers access.

It's also important that I don't get caught impersonating a police officer. Most jurisdictions find that unpalatable, to say the least. In any event, my disguise has already done its job, allowing me to get into the crime scene. Swiftly, I pull off the police uniform, revealing just my T-shirt. Then I pull my jeans back on. I step back into the kitchen and hide the uniform by stuffing it deep inside the back of a washing machine that's under the sink. Lastly, I remove the brown contact lenses. Then I turn my attention to the offices.

I hack open the desktop computer and start uploads of the data to a secure cloud server; a server that is monitored directly by Amber in London. Then I start working through the sheets of paper on the desk and in the drawers. There's even a filing cabinet—how irritatingly retro in a cloud storage world. Like I have time to filter through the paper crammed inside. And it's going to be hard enough getting out of here under the radar without dragging stacks of files along with me.

Sitting at the desk, I quickly become absorbed in recent paperwork tossed in a tray, perhaps waiting to be filed. It details annual maintenance work completed just two days earlier by a local plumbing company. I snap some photos of the documents, then slip my phone back into my pocket and lean down to check inside the desk. And it's while I'm down there, my head deep in a drawer, that I hear the click of a gun safety being removed. I freeze.

"Put your hands where I can see them," a voice says softly.

6

I OBEY, RAISING MY HANDS high and moving my head extremely slowly back up above the desk. A young woman stands there, aiming a gun at my chest. But she's not in a police uniform. She wears a navy pantsuit over a crisp white shirt. Under her jacket a badge of some kind gleams.

"Look, I'm terribly sorry," I say, dusting off my own British accent but dialing it up a bit, to help me sound like a fish out of water. I throw in a gulp and stutter too, like I've never seen a real gun before. "I work for Kit Love. She sent me here, and I couldn't find anyone to ask permission from, so I just came in. . . ."

"Hands on your head. Interlace your fingers," the woman commands.

I do as she asks. "Can I show you my ID?" I try again. My hand slips down from my head to reach for it, but a jerk of her weapon persuades me not to.

"Get up and stand facing the wall," she says. Once I'm there, she approaches, still holding me at gunpoint.

"Where's your ID?" she asks.

"Back pocket of my jeans."

She pats down my pockets and extracts the fake ID that Amber gave me. On it is a fictional name—Jessica Flynn—instead of my real name, Jennifer Archer. It means I still get to be called Jessie, though, which makes my life easier; at least I don't have to train myself to respond to a name that's completely new to me. The ID also has a different date of birth, one that puts me a little older than I really am. The woman gives a sound of acknowledgment.

"We were told by Kit's office to expect you, Jessica. You can turn around," she says, holstering her weapon.

I turn and offer her my hand. "Kit has asked me to oversee the investigation."

"Detective Riya Kapoor," she says, ignoring my hand. I drop it, taken aback. She is probably mid- to late twenties, my height, slim with wide, brown eyes and improbably long lashes. Her dark hair is pulled back into a loose ponytail and she wears no makeup, making her look even more youthful.

"You seem very young for a detective," I say, taking a gamble that charm might be my best strategy.

"You seem very young—and not very bright—for an investigator," she returns.

So much for the introductions. I cross my arms, a bit riled.

"Tell me, Detective, did you flunk out of etiquette school, or is it just your job that's made you cynical?"

She raises an eyebrow at me. "Why don't I ask the questions?" she says. "And the obvious one is—why are you prowling around my crime scene, disturbing evidence?"

"*Your* crime scene?"

She bristles. "I'm one of the detectives assigned to this case. And you are not allowed in here until the police investigation is over."

"I'm appointed by the owner of this school. Maybe you should start thinking about it as *our* crime scene."

"I don't think so," she says simply. She takes off her jacket and drapes it over her arm, revealing a shoulder holster containing the gun she threatened me with. It is sweltering in here.

"I'm happy to share information once we have it," she concedes finally. "But just to be clear—I don't have to." She casts a suspicious glance at the desk, then at my hands. "Did you take anything?" she demands.

"Of course not," I exclaim, as if I'm insulted at the mere idea. The detective seems to relax a bit more at my assurance. Meanwhile a tiny blue light flashes at the base of the screen of the desk computer, reminding me that its contents are uploading to Athena's servers as we speak. At the doorway, a policeman appears and asks something in Hindi. Detective Kapoor rattles off a reply that sends him packing. Then she looks at me.

"Come with me," she says.

I resist the urge to look at the computer again. When the

upload's complete, it should switch off and leave the desktop looking completely normal.

"You can't stay here unsupervised," the detective continues. "Everything is potential evidence."

"Yes, but how long will it take the police to go through all of it?"

She starts walking, leading me away from the body of the building.

"You're from England?" she asks.

"Wow, you really *are* a detective," I say. The snark makes me feel better, but it doesn't earn me much love from my companion. She narrows her eyes at me.

"What are the police like there?" she asks, ignoring my sarcasm.

"Bureaucratic. Overworked."

"Well, it's no better here, and possibly much worse," she says. "They'll get us what they can as soon as they can." She turns to me. "Believe it or not, we do our best, ma'am."

"Call me Jessie," I offer, trying to cut through the formality and mend some fences. "Can I call you Riya?"

"No," she says curtly. "Anyway, here in Mumbai, it's the same as in most cities. A lot of crime, and not enough manpower."

"And I get that," I answer. "That's why I'm here to help however I can."

With my gaze, I try to convey how earnest I am, how much I want to cooperate. She watches me for a moment and then smiles suddenly. It's a great smile and it lights up her whole face. Finally, some glimmer of a real person under the officious exterior.

"You really want to help—Jessie?"

I nod, eager to get her on my side.

"Then stay the hell out of my way," she says abruptly. "There, that's the exit," she continues, pointing to the street. Just for good measure, she pauses to call over a uniformed cop. "Anil here will escort you out."

Since Detective Kapoor threw me out, my scope for snooping around the crime scene is much more limited, but at least Amber has the computer uploads and the pictures I took of the recent plumbing maintenance that happened at the school. While she goes through everything, I hail a taxi and head over to the next district, Bandra, where the second school is located, to check in with Caitlin and Hala.

Bandra is a busy area of the city, but one that also fronts the sea. It has plenty of leafy streets too, shaded from the brutal sear of the sun. Back lanes filled with old heritage buildings, arts and crafts stores, and cool cafés create a gentle contrast to the blaring traffic on the main roads. Driving along the seafront road, I take in an old fort that rises at the edge of the foaming waves. Beyond the worn stone of the fort, the bright, clean, ultramodern Bandra-Worli Sea Link bridge stretches out effortlessly across the bay, its enormous girth laden with cars moving from one side of the city to the other.

I have the driver take me past the other school, which is currently empty, just to have a look at it. The pupils and staff have been evacuated, and police guards are set up here as well. The building is on a residential street, which is otherwise a mix of small houses and low apartment blocks. Taller blocks rise up in rings all around the school, in the immediate vicinity and then radiating out from there. Mumbai is a city where land is so much at a premium that even billionaires build their dream homes upward, in towers that reach toward the sky. Driving on from the school, we turn into a side street where Caitlin has messaged me the name of a café where we can meet.

Inside, the atmosphere is cool, freshened with air-conditioning. Both my teammates are sitting at a wide table made of polished wood. Handcrafted cushions liven up the bench seating, and art by local painters covers most of the wall space. I order a coffee before Caitlin presses me for an update.

"You get anything?" she asks.

"I got interrupted by an obnoxious police detective," I sigh. "But Amber's working on the hard drives from the school, and there's this. . . ." I show her the plumber contract on my phone. She zooms in on it, looking for the date.

"They waltzed in there two days before the attack?" Caitlin frowns. "That looks more than suspicious."

"Yeah. I want to talk to the headmistress about it."

"Her name is Jaya," says Caitlin. "You'll find her at the hotel where they evacuated the girls. It's like, five minutes from here."

"How long are the girls going to stay there?"

"Just till tomorrow. Then they're coming back to the school," Caitlin says.

Hala catches my skeptical look. "Peggy's hired private security," she says.

"The Indian ambassador recommended them, and she trusts him," Caitlin adds. "But she's also got a couple of former Navy SEALs that she knows personally coming out to India from the States tomorrow."

I smile to myself. Of course Peggy has the most highly trained military men in existence on speed dial. Why wouldn't she?

"But still," I wonder. "Wouldn't a safe house be better?"

"It's been tough to find something secure enough so far," Caitlin replies. "Plus, even if lessons were stopped, *some* adults would need to be trusted to supervise them. Food and water would still have to be brought in. There would be some supply chain that could still leave Family First a way to find the girls, *if* they're looking."

"As far as we know, this attack was a one-off," Hala reminds me.

I nod. I also know Kit is not keen to bow to terrorists by abandoning her existing school buildings. With the extra security, plus some kind of uniformed police presence, I suppose terrorists would be deterred from trying to strike the same type of target twice. I gulp down my macchiato. It's time for me to go and interview the headmistress.

I'm reassured by the fact that it takes several minutes for me to get past the police that are guarding the hotel where the girls are currently staying. Only by cross-checking my ID with a list of trusted names that Kit has sent through will they eventually let me in to speak to the headmistress.

A uniformed officer walks me into the hotel lobby, a cozy space that is now deserted. Down one hallway, I catch a glimpse of hotel meeting rooms. The doors are ajar, and I can hear the sounds of lessons going on. The policeman leads me farther back, into the dining room, where the furniture has clearly been rearranged. Instead of intimate tables of two and four, there are now two very long tables stretching down the length of the room, transforming a hotel restaurant into a dining area that feels more like a school lunch hall. These tables are empty except for two women sitting at one end, talking. The officer points them out and leaves me to make my approach alone.

I can tell immediately which of the two is Jaya, the headmistress, because the other woman is none other than Riya Kapoor, the detective who so recently put me in my place. Great. I take a breath and stride over, holding out my hand and introducing myself to Jaya. In my mind, I'd painted the headmistress as stern and ancient, but the reality is that she is probably late thirties, no more than five feet tall, somewhat round, and carrying so much nervous energy that even while she just sits here, it feels as if the edges of her are slightly blurred. Her eyes are rimmed with red, probably from exhaustion and crying.

"So marvelous to meet you, Jessie-ma'am," Jaya says. She grasps my hand firmly and has a ready smile. "And I am so deeply, deeply sorry that this tragedy has occurred, and on my watch."

"It's not your fault," I assure her. "And I'm sorry for your loss. The girls . . ."

As tears spring to her eyes, Jaya looks for distraction and turns to her companion.

"This is Detective Kapoor," she says, introducing us.

"We've met," the detective says to her before turning to me. "And, you can call me Riya."

"Are you sure?" I ask, deadpan. "I don't want to rush our relationship, you know, if you're not ready. . . ."

Riya tosses out a tight smile before fixing me with a focused stare. "What are you doing here?" she demands.

"I have some questions for Jaya," I reply.

"Great. I'd love to hear them," Riya says, pulling a notebook from the inside of her suit jacket.

Suppressing a sigh, I sit down beside her, so that we are both opposite the headmistress, who's keen to offer me a beverage. I decline, politely. Nevertheless, small glasses of milky tea appear before us within minutes. Riya picks hers up and knocks it back quickly, while I focus on Jaya.

"Can you tell me if there was any maintenance done at either school recently? Like, annual checks or any equipment that needed servicing . . ."

Jaya nearly bounces out of her chair. "Yes, yes, there was. The detective just asked me the same. There was a plumbing company that came to the school just a few days ago."

I don't feel I ought to whip out my purloined photos of the contract right in front of Riya, so I ask Jaya for the company name. No surprise, it's the same one that I found the paperwork for.

"Is this a company you used before?"

She nods. Not that using an established firm means anything at all. It would be the easiest thing in the world to pay off the contracted workers to go and have lunch while someone else dressed in their overalls got access to the schools. Or for any company to hire in a temp worker.

Jaya looks stricken. "It didn't connect for me as a problem. Till now."

"It still might mean nothing," Riya reassures her.

"Did your staff take any copy of an ID for the maintenance men?" I continue.

"It was only one man, and yes. Our practice is to take an ID copy and a cell phone number for anyone who enters the building where the girls are. It's routine but we always do it."

Riya looks at me, as if she's just ever so slightly impressed that my opening questions were not completely idiotic. I take a sip of my tea, which is a troubling combination of scalding hot and tooth-achingly sweet.

"They scan the ID and store it digitally on the desktop computer in the office," Riya says. Clearly, she's decided she may as well save me the same line of questioning she's just gone through. "I sent our tech guys in there just now to find it but the folder it should be in doesn't have anything new from the past few weeks."

Jaya wrings her hands. "I hope the administrator didn't fail to follow procedure," she says.

"I'll talk to your admin person next," Riya tells her. "Unless you want to?" she adds dryly, looking at me.

"Nice of you to ask," I comment. "Does this mean you're start-ing to trust me?"

"Not in the least. I was being sarcastic," she returns.

I feel like she's always got me on the defensive. She's still watch-ing me, and somehow her gaze makes me self-conscious. I pull out my phone and ask Riya to let me know what she finds out. Whether she will bother to keep me updated or not, I can't be sure yet, but I give her my temporary Indian cell number, one that no one else contacts me on. To my surprise, she gives me hers in exchange.

"In case you turn something up," Riya tells me. She glances down at the table for a long moment and when she looks back up at me, her eyes are dark and serious. "Those girls have had their futures taken from them, brutally," she continues. "Their families will never recover from the loss. I want to do everything I can to find the people who did this and to make sure they don't do it again."

Across from us, an audible sob escapes from Jaya. I pass her a tis-sue and she blots away the tears in her eyes. I watch Riya, who looks younger now, even vulnerable. Her earnestness feels honest and it makes me like her more.

"Please know that I feel the same way," I assure her. "I'll be in touch as soon as I have anything."

7

IT'S NOT GREAT THAT THE maintenance man's ID scan appears to be missing, but I'm hopeful that Amber might have found it somewhere, maybe misfiled on the hard drive. Or it could be that she's tracked down the plumbing contractor and we can trace the guy from that. While I'm stuck in traffic on the way back to my hotel, I check in with Amber. She sounds animated, the way she does when she's got something up her sleeve.

"Good timing," she says. "I was getting ready to call you."

"The police say the plumber guy's ID is missing," I tell her.

"Utter nonsense. I found it within ten minutes, sitting in a folder on the computer's desktop, which has a hundred other pieces of crap in it," Amber replies. "Someone was just too lazy to file it."

"Why didn't you call me earlier?"

"Because the ID is all but useless. The name on it is fake."

That's hardly surprising, but still, it's a letdown and I sigh, looking out of the window. In the distance, row upon row of slums whip past as we drive by. Closer to me, blurs of color strobe, attracting my attention: clusters of women in technicolor saris walking along the road; massive billboards advertising the latest Bollywood blockbuster movie.

"However," Amber continues, "the cell number the plumber gave the school, though no longer in use, was once connected to a social media account. And that account belongs to the man in the ID photo; so the same guy. I imagine he couldn't resist checking his feed even while doing something dodgy. His real name is Hassan Shah."

"Great! Did you find him?"

"Well, there's good and bad news. The bad news is, Hassan Shah there is like the name John Smith here. There are hundreds of them in Mumbai alone."

I get the impression, just from her tone, that she's already cracked this problem, but the thing with Amber is, she delights in giving you every little detail of how she did it. I try my best to be patient.

"And the good news?" I ask.

"*Our* Hassan's social media account shows that he has two kids. A fourteen-year-old son and a younger daughter. Now, the son's got a social profile that geo-tracks him, you know, so his friends can find him when they go out. . . ."

"Yeah, thanks, I get how that works, Amber."

"Well, within the past week, he's also geo-linked to three places that he's been with his family, including his father. So, I'm hopeful that the next time Hassan hangs out with his son, we'll get an alert on the son's social media."

I smile. "You're a genius."

"Yes, it does feel that way, doesn't it?" Amber says.

"And modest too," I add.

"I'll let you know when I have anything more," she says, and hangs up.

I make it to the hotel just after Kit and Peggy have checked in. On the street outside the driveway, reporters and TV cameras jostle for position. I hope they are here waiting for some Bollywood superstar to emerge and not hoping to get pictures of my mother on her way to see the deceased girls' families or the schools.

I stop in at Kit's room. She greets me with a long, hard hug. It's clear from her bloodshot eyes, shadowed with dark circles, that she's hardly slept, and when she pulls back to look at me, her face holds a manic, strained energy that I haven't seen in her since the days when she was drinking. When alcohol was the only way she felt some relief from the sharp edges of pain. It makes me very uneasy.

"Mum, are you okay?"

"Fine."

"Are those paparazzi outside waiting for you?" I ask.

"Like vultures circling their prey," she remarks, disconsolate.

"I'm sorry."

She waves off my concern. "Here, give me a hand, Jess."

She turns away and starts dragging a sofa across the polished wood floor. The hotel room that she has is miles bigger than mine, a suite really, with enough space to hold a small soccer match and possibly a stand for the audience too.

"Mum, not this again . . . ," I plead. But I go over to help her.

Once Kit is happy with the placement of the sofa, she makes me help turn the desk around. She does this often when she travels—rearranges hotel rooms to facilitate the flow of *chi*, or positive energy. It's a *feng shui* thing, and I'm not convinced it makes any kind of difference, but Kit looks so stressed out at the moment that I just keep quiet and help out.

Next, she starts unpacking. I help her hang up floaty shirts and printed jackets. Along with them are a couple of white *shalwar kameez* outfits—long tunics that go over fitted trousers.

"These are nice," I say, trying to cheer her up, but it seems like I fail epically because Kit sits heavily on the end of the bed and just starts to cry.

"They're for the condolence visits and the funerals," she says, her voice breaking. Sitting beside her, I put my arm around her, but it feels pretty meaningless and not much help compared to the grief, or guilt, she's going through. Finally, the weeping subsides, and I take her hand.

"When did you last eat anything?" I ask.

She shrugs.

"Mum?"

"I can't remember."

"Then let's get Peggy and find some food."

An hour later Kit's taken us all out to a small restaurant with a patio that's open to the baking late-afternoon sun. A long line of commuters and local residents stands waiting for their turn to be served for takeout, but Peggy has managed to grab us a table, and within minutes, a waiter deposits our food in front of us. We are each given a large thali platter. Arranged upon it are lots of small bowls filled with different vegetarian curries—smoky lentils, chopped eggplant, paneer cheese, and spiced cauliflower. On the side are dishes of rice, pale green coconut chutney, and paratha bread, hot out of the oven and oozing with butter.

"This looks divine," Peggy says, surveying her plate.

"I've been coming to this place since the nineties," Kit says. She's been to India tons of times, for the schools that she founded, but also from years ago, when she was searching for enlightenment but mainly found dodgy gurus. I'm super hungry. Peggy watches with a small smile as I tuck into my meal. I glance up at her, questioningly.

"How does this fit with your diet sheet, Jessie?"

Li's nutritionist provides Caitlin, Hala, and me with an individual eating plan that gives us perfectly measured amounts of each food group, tailored to our specific body shape, blood types, metabolism, and general food tolerances. It's all wrapped up in a sexy app that Li has had coded in-house that combines data on our sleep, movement, heart rate, and body temperature, all of which is taken from a regular tracking ring. It's all very impressive and we're all super fit, but sometimes you just need that burrito, or a bag of fish and chips. Or rice and curry.

"I don't think there's anything here that's off-limits," I say.

My brazen lie makes Kit smile at least, and even though she only nibbles at her plate, the food seems to help restore my mother a little too. Meanwhile, I ask Peggy if there's any news on Jake Graham.

"On the face of it, he still doesn't have enough for us to panic about. But he's persistent," Peggy sighs. "He called me and left a message, just yesterday."

"Did he say what he wants?" I ask.

"No."

"But it was right after he came to see me," says Kit. She falls silent, brooding.

"Amber's still working on it," Peggy says, trying to be upbeat. "There's no point tying ourselves in knots. We all have enough on our plates right now."

I nod. Just as I contemplate starting in on Kit's leftovers, a new message from Amber comes into my earpiece. I've been wearing the comms unit since after our last conversation, to make sure I don't miss anything.

"Is it Hassan?" I ask.

"Yes, I've found him," she replies. "His son just checked in on social to say he's helping his father by working after school. It appears that Hassan owns a small car repair place over in the Santa-cruz area of the city."

"So, he's there now?"

"Right now. I've sent details to all of you. Caitlin's going to stay and keep an eye on the girls at the hotel, but Hala will meet you there."

I arrive at the car repair shop by auto-rickshaw. Rickshaws are just that bit narrower and more nimble than a taxi, and I don't want to risk losing our target by being snared in traffic jams. On the way over, I imagine how it would go if I shared the information we just gained on Hassan and his whereabouts with the police, with Riya. The problem is, even if the police manage to get to him, whatever they learn would never be passed back to us. And Hassan is most likely a cog in a big Family First wheel. And it is Family First that we really want to cripple. Delivering the man who may have planted the bomb and giving him a big, splashy trial would be a huge win for the police in Mumbai—but the truth is that people like Hassan are the hired hands who execute the strategy. We need to find out who's pulling the strings.

The garage is wide and deep, with two cars cranked up so that mechanics can work beneath them. Several other cars are scattered around, with their hoods open. Hala joins me outside the place. She and Caitlin hired motorbikes and she's managed to arrive ten minutes ahead of me, giving her time to spot and watch Hassan.

"He's the one in the banana shirt and shades," she says. Indeed, Hassan is in oversized sunglasses and a short-sleeved yellow shirt with green bananas printed all over it. It's a depressingly memorable style choice. Currently, Hassan seems like he's on a break. He lounges against the back wall of the garage, chugging back a bottle of orange soda, and talking to a young boy in overalls, possibly his son. After a minute, the boy slides beneath one of the cars to work on it, and Hassan leans down to give him some advice. Then he finishes his soda and saunters out toward the front, toward us, where he stretches and takes in the street, which is jam-packed with cars inching slowly along.

Hala and I step back behind a stall selling kulfi ice cream, keeping out of Hassan's eyeline. Behind us, a group of men play cards for thin stacks of rupee notes. Meanwhile, our mark pockets his sunglasses and lights up a cigarette, leaning against the wall to enjoy his smoke.

"Where are we going to talk to him?" Hala asks.

"Right there. He won't want a drama in front of his kid. Anyway, what else are we going to do? Ask him to dinner?"

"What if he runs?" she asks.

"Two of us, one of him," I reply.

"Weapon?" she asks.

"Not seeing anything on him, are you?"

She peers at Hassan one more time and agrees.

"I'll go talk to him, you run backup," I tell her.

Hala stays where she is while I start walking toward Hassan. He has a strong face, all jawbone and angles, with a broad forehead that juts out like a cliff face, leaving his eyes in shadow.

"Hassan Shah?" I say.

He throws down his cigarette and a tendril of acrid smoke curls up from where it lies, still burning, on the ground. I raise the heel of my boot and grind down the butt with my foot.

"I need to talk to you about the school attack that happened this morning."

"What attack?" he says, his eyes holding mine, aggressive. Well, either I just found the only man in Mumbai who hasn't heard about the bombing, or he's already lying.

"Your photo ID is on record, visiting the school. If you don't want to end up taking the blame for this, we need to talk."

He hesitates, probably trying to figure out who on earth I am.

"Who are you? British police? What are you doing here?"

His upper lip starts to sweat. He glances back into the garage, at his son's legs, sticking out from under the car.

"Your son doesn't need to know."

He nods, his breathing shallow.

"Just relax. Why don't we step around the back and talk . . . ?"

He nods again. And then he takes off. He just runs, propelling himself across the road, between idling traffic and into a tiny side street. He moves faster than I would have imagined. Pounding after him, I calculate that he has a hundred feet on me already. Out of the corner of my eye, I see Hala running like mad, coming up on my right side.

"I told you he'd run," she complains.

I pick up speed, intent on catching him quickly, but Hassan turns fast and is smart enough to go straight for the heart of a looming slum area ahead. It looks like a warren of tiny lanes and ramshackle tin houses. He probably knows it inside out too, making it the worst possible place for us to keep track of him.

I glance at Hala. She gestures upward, and as we veer to the right to follow Hassan's trail, she clambers up a single-story home and gets onto the roof. From there, she stays high, running across the roofs of dwellings that are built tightly together, bounding across gaps like a mountain goat, following him from above. But I've lost Hassan completely.

"Turn left," Hala directs me in my ear, from her bird's-eye view. "Then first right."

Following her directions, I slide into another tiny street, my feet skidding into something wet that I think it's better I ignore—and now I glimpse his banana-print shirt up ahead. He hurtles along, veering left suddenly. I follow him directly into someone's house— he's upturned a cooking pot, people are gasping, and then yelling at us. Up ahead of me, my target runs out of the back door, ripping his way through a bright blue sari that's hanging out to dry. The soft, winding cloth billows up, settling gently right in my path, entangling me for a moment.

"Where are you?" Hala pants in my ear. "Turn left, he's in the tunnel."

Pushing aside the sari, I sprint to try to make up time, and find myself hurtling into a dark concrete tunnel that runs under a bridge. Pounding through, I can see the dark silhouette of the guy as he exits the other side of it.

"Can't you jump him?" I ask Hala.

As I run, the walls echo my pounding steps off all sides, drowning Hala's reply. I emerge back into the beating sunshine and turn right, tearing after a glimpse of Hassan's shirt and into a road that stretches around between tightly packed street vendors. Chaos descends on me like fog. There are so many people, suddenly, jostling between stalls that sprawl out all over the narrow lanes. I keep running with smells, sounds, images blurring around me. Pots and pans hanging off hooks clatter as I pass, long ropes of chilies dry in the sun, some kind of street food sizzles in hot oil, hawkers shout, piles of vegetables loom up before me, a cart pulled by a cow crosses my path. Surprised shouts from people in the street follow me as they watch me barrel through. Up ahead, a painfully thin dog is snapping at the heels of someone who's just disappeared. I follow, avoiding the dog, who is standing still now, barking like mad, but I can't see Hassan. This side street is quieter and it winds uphill, long and thin; there's no way he could have gotten to the end of it already.

"Where is he?" I pant to Hala.

A noise of frustration in my earpiece tells me that she has no idea either. Glancing up, I see Hala appear on a roof opposite, still moving, still scanning around for any sight of him. Then I see it, crumpled in the gutter ahead of me. The banana-print shirt.

"He's taken off his shirt," I tell her. Smart move, considering how conspicuous it is.

Looking for a bare chest helps her. "Got him!" she mutters.

She leaps across to another roof, then bounces like a strip of lightning along a thin wall, a hundred feet ahead of me. In a busy jumble of people up ahead, I catch sight of our shirtless man moving quickly, but now he's trying not to run and draw attention to himself. I scramble to follow. He slides into a tiny street barbershop and plucks something from the counter, then whips back out and runs left. Hala is far ahead of him, so I veer left to try to head him off. My feet pound through a narrow lane where a naked toddler chases a chicken. A mechanical sound and a waft of oily fumes drift over to me, but I hardly notice as I hurdle over the flapping bird and the kid and keep going, skittering out of the alleyway in the hope that our target will run right into me.

But that sound and those fumes belong to a train. Thick iron tracks rear up right before me, right next to the densely packed buildings we've been running through. A freight train has just rumbled through. Car after car of containers move inexorably, slowly, up a route that winds off into the distance, where the sun is just beginning to lower into the late-afternoon sky. And our shirtless target is far ahead of me, running alongside the final car. With a magnificent leap, he grabs hold of the metal railing on the end of it and hauls himself up. He's too distant for me to catch now; I can see him panting as he turns and gives me a long look. From back here I can't really tell if he's smiling, but it feels like he might be.

8

I WATCH HASSAN AS HE moves away from me, clinging to the side of the train—but now it's my turn to smile. Because I can see something that he can't. Hala is on the roof of that train, walking toward the very carriage that he's hanging off. Her gait is careful but relaxed. Now that I've caught my breath, I start running again. I can't catch up, but I can keep the train and our target, not to mention Hala, within range.

"I think he has scissors or a razor—from the barbershop," I tell her over the comms. I watch him struggle to open the freight car door. He can't manage it, so he starts climbing the metal rungs that lead up onto the train roof.

"He's right below you, climbing up now," I say.

I watch him climb, estimating the moment that his head will pop into Hala's view.

"Four, three, two, ONE," I call.

On my count, Hala thrusts out a leg that jabs him in the face before he can even register what's happened. She follows it with another sharp kick, and I watch her in awe. She never comes close to losing her balance. Hassan tumbles off the train and rolls away down a gentle slope that ends in a trash heap. I veer off and run toward him. Hala clambers lightly down the side of the train and hops off, jogging up to join me.

He's up and eager to escape again, but he's hobbling on an ankle that seems to be twisted. I draw close enough to fling myself at his legs, bringing him down with a tackle that hammers the wind out of both of us. But I surface fast, going for his arms, his hands. I grab his wrist just as I feel the whoosh of a straight razor slicing past my face, missing me by millimeters. Hala arrives and helps me to twist the blade out of his hand. I press it lightly against Hassan's abdomen as we hoist him up.

"Walk with us, no sudden moves."

Keeping close on either side of him, we guide him into a small shack that sits near the tracks, tired and lopsided. The walls are corrugated iron and inside are a couple of kids, playing. I pull out a few hundred rupees and hand them to the children, indicating they should get lost. They leave fast, slamming the door behind them. It's dank and dark inside, but with enough light to make out a layer of putrefying sediment on the floor, as well as a street cat with ginger, matted fur. The cat turns and regards us coolly over its shoulder while we push Hassan down into a chair. I remove the razor from his side and place it gently against his windpipe while Hala finds his wallet and snaps pictures of the contents, sending them straight through to Amber.

"What do you want?" he asks. Thin trails of sweat wind down from his temples onto his neck.

"Who do you work for?" I ask him.

There's a tense silence. I press the razor a little harder against his throat.

"I don't know names," he says. "I just do the job."

"The *job*? Killing children is a job?" I hiss.

"I knew nothing about that," he pleads. "I was told to go to the school and open up the drains. For access."

"Access to plant explosives?"

He squeezes his eyes shut, fearful.

"Who told you to do this? Who hired you?"

His eyes stay shut and his mouth stays closed.

Angrily, Hala thrusts a hand into Hassan's trouser pocket. On instinct, he grabs her fingers and is rewarded with a sprained wrist. Hala ignores his moan of pain and pulls out his phone. It's a nice model. She turns it over in her hands.

"How's the camera on this?" she asks, conversationally.

He swallows. "Good," he croaks.

"Don't make me use it to send footage of you to your wife. And your son. And your daughter."

Hassan whimpers and clamps his eyes shut, fearful. Hala moves closer to him.

"Look at me," she says. He opens his eyes and finds her gaze drilling into him as her voice drops, close to a whisper: "Kids have a really hard time recovering from seeing their parents die violently."

I look down, uncomfortable. What she just described is pretty much what she went through in Syria, when her village, mostly full of Palestinian refugees like Hala's family, was attacked by ISIS. The horror of it is right there on her face and in the weight of her quiet words—just for a moment. But it's long enough for Hassan to sense the deep truth that underlies her tone. It terrifies him, and tears spill out of the corners of his eyes, mingling with the sweat to form a rivulet of stress that drips onto the floor right by our feet.

Hala still stares him down. Hassan squeezes his eyes shut again as if not wanting to watch himself betray anyone.

"The company is called AAB Enterprises," he says.

Of course it is. Why do criminals always pick such boring names for their shell companies?

"We need more," I say.

"AAB Enterprises," he repeats, desperate. "Check the wire transfer app on my phone. . . ."

We do, and sure enough, that is the name of the company that just sent him a hefty chunk of change. There are a few texts that look related too, but they are from unknown numbers, most likely disposable burner phones. Hala pulls out Hassan's SIM card and drops it into her pocket, just in case. Then Amber comes in over our comms. She dictates Hassan's home address here in Mumbai and we let him know that we have discovered where his children live.

And that our associates are on their way to visit his family. His face crumples in fear. Impatient with his whimpering, I bang the side of the tin wall, making him jump.

"Please," he pleads. "I speak to one guy, only by phone. And I don't have his name."

"Is his number in here?" Hala brandishes the phone. Hassan shakes his head.

"We only got handsets we could throw away."

Annoyed with the lack of progress, Hala fishes in the pockets of her combat pants and produces a bunch of plastic cable ties. Efficiently, coldly, without looking at him any further, she binds Hassan's hands together. Then she does the same to his feet. Once that's done, she takes out a knife and makes a big show of testing the sharpness of the blade. Sweating, Hassan starts to pant and beg, fearing that he's about to be executed.

"I have an address," he bleats at last. "That's all. They sent me there to collect my uniform and ID, and the location of the school."

"So, give me that address," Hala commands.

Hassan dictates it to Hala. She looks it up on her satellite map, and only when she's cross-referenced streets nearby with Hassan's description and recollection does she accept it as correct.

"Who did you meet there?" I ask. "Who gave you the ID and uniform and stuff?"

"Nobody. The place was empty. Everything was ready and waiting, in a plain bag, right outside the entrance. I picked it up and left."

Hala steps away, frowning, and I nod. We both feel like we've gotten all we can from Hassan. He relaxes slightly.

"Can I go home?" he asks.

"Sure, but you must be exhausted," I tell him. "We'll send someone to collect you."

Tapping quickly, I send Riya an explanatory text message that includes a location pin drop to where we are now. Within a minute, my phone rings.

"What the hell are you doing?" Riya asks by way of greeting. "How did you find this guy?"

"We can catch up later," I say, ignoring her tone, which is not remotely happy. "Right now, I need to know how long it will be before you can get a police car over here to pick him up?"

She disappears for a moment and I can hear sounds of conferring in the background, instructions called out in Hindi.

"Ten minutes," she says, and I hang up the call. Hala stares Hassan down.

"If you say one word to the police about us, or this meeting—I will go after your son and daughter. Understand?"

"Yes. I understand."

"Good. I'm sorry," she says.

"For what?" he asks.

She leans down and wrenches his twisted ankle so it's properly sprained. He yells in pain.

"For that. It's only in case you get free of the ties."

With a final tug to test the plastic binding his limbs, Hala nods at me and we hurry out of the shack and into the streets beyond, where we disappear into the crowded lanes of the slums, just as the sounds of police sirens begin to approach.

9

OUR NEXT FOCUS IS TO get to the address that Hassan spilled. It's in the south of the city, some distance from here, and it's rush hour. But we need to move now. There's a good chance that the police may interrogate that same address out of Hassan and then we'll be stuck in a race with the cops to look for evidence.

Hala takes the urgency seriously, pushing her motorbike deeper into the traffic, weaving her way past cars, rickshaws, and buses, and across one busy junction after another. On the back of the bike, I hang on tightly to Hala's waist while I send Caitlin the address so she can meet us there.

"Christ, this is not an actual chase. You don't have to drive like that," I squawk as Hala turns hard and low to the ground. We skim in front of a gaudily painted truck, so close that I can feel a whoosh of air touch my arms as we pass it. But I have a feeling my complaint is lost under the long protest of another truck's horn. The sound fades fast as Hala weaves ahead. I lean into curves with her, trying to keep the bike stable.

The address Hassan provided takes us into an industrial area, an assortment of warehouses and storage facilities that is pretty quiet now that night is beginning to fall. Not that it seems as if much activity goes on here at any time. There are very few parked trucks or vans. Hardly any people. Streetlights are nonexistent.

"Coming toward you now." Caitlin's voice comes in on the comms.

I glance over my shoulder, where her headlight sweeps the street as it moves closer. Caitlin's bike pulls up and rides alongside us. Just a few hundred feet ahead, I point to a squat blue warehouse that sits in a lot sealed off with chain-link fences. No company logos or names are visible. Security cameras sit on top of the fence posts. Big red signs warning of private security and alarms are posted everywhere. We ride around to the back and park up in a dark alleyway, out of sight of the road before we get off the motorcycles.

"Okay, so the fence we can manage, but what about the cameras?" I ask.

"You tell us," Caitlin returns. "Are they hardwired?"

I scan them with my zoom lens. "Wireless."

"So kill them," Hala says.

I've already pulled my tablet out of my backpack and started working. I use my usual software to perform a passive sweep of the wireless environment. There's a signal coming from inside the blue warehouse, and using a bit of code, I can monitor the output of data. That tells me how many devices are linked to their wireless network. After another thirty seconds, I'll get a full lock on all the devices inside the warehouse that are using the Wi-Fi.

In the meantime, Caitlin hands out bottles of water and protein bars, which Hala accepts with a disconsolate scowl.

"We never get to eat the local food when we go somewhere," she moans.

"Occupational hazard," says Caitlin, sanguine as ever.

"Even Thomas is having an Indian takeout tonight," Hala complains. "And he's in London."

Caitlin and I swap a glance and Hala shifts, realizing she may have said more than she wanted to. Caitlin shakes her head at me not to pursue it—but I can't pass it up. Opportunities to tease Hala don't come along every five minutes.

"Really?" I inquire, still tapping on my tablet keyboard. "I'm just wondering—does Thomas tell you what he's having for dinner *every* night?" Honestly, I'm trying not to grin at her discomfort.

"You know what *I'm* wondering?" Hala snaps.

"What?"

"Why it's taking you so long to do your job."

"Just because you watch TV shows where some actor from geek central casting does this in ten seconds . . . ," I huff. "Look, I can disable the entire network right now. But someone might notice that kind of brute attack."

But even Caitlin is getting antsy, coming around to look over my shoulder. Methodically, I look for devices that could be the cameras and try to verify them online. Within another minute, I've chosen the most likely ones and found my way into the camera feeds. Disabling them is satisfying, watching each streamed image drop into darkness on my screen.

"Let's move," I say. There's a strong chance that someone else has those feeds on their cell phone. Who knows if they might care enough to come and check up on the place if they noticed that the cameras were not live anymore? We can't waste any time.

Hala's already at the top of the side fence, and once she's explored, she gestures us to a piece of fence at the rear that's hidden behind industrial-sized garbage bins. She cuts open a hole right there. Caitlin and I bend down to slip through it.

"Stay in touch," she says, as we move past her.

"Of course," Caitlin says. The plan is for Hala to stay out here. She's the best at climbing, and it makes sense for one of us to be separated out, to stay nimble in case we come up against any problems inside. Meanwhile, Caitlin scans through the few windows while I check the doors for alarms. None of them seem wired to anything, so we choose one and use a small explosive charge to open the lock. Stepping in gingerly, we both wait for a moment to get our bearings. There's no beeping or flashing indicating an alarm. Slowly, we track our way forward, guided by Caitlin's low flashlight.

Closed boxes are stacked up in neat piles at the back of the warehouse. Open boxes sit out in front of them—some of them contain piles of clothing, while the contents of others gleam metallic and strange in the beam of the LED light.

We are heading over to explore when a rustling, low and constant, attracts our attention. Little tapping noises too. We both freeze, holding our breathing still. A couple of furry creatures shoot across the floor, and burrow into the cardboard of the boxes. I relax.

"Just rats," I say.

"Ugh," Caitlin breathes. "Can I just wait here?"

I have to smile. Caitlin will unflinchingly face bullets, knives, and fists, but faced with some oversized vermin, she's cowering behind me like a slab of Jell-O.

"Come on, this looks interesting," I say, indicating the boxes lying ahead of us. We both hurry forward, eager to explore—and I trip over something and fall. Caitlin reaches to grab me, but she trips too. Righting herself, she gives me a hand up.

"What was that?" she wonders, pointing her flashlight.

A taut wire is strung across the warehouse. As soon as I see it, I know why. It's some kind of deterrent, some kind of trap for unwanted visitors.

"Dammit," Caitlin says. "Booby trap?"

I nod, grabbing the flashlight from her. I walk down the length of the wire. It runs into one side of a bank of lockers on the back wall.

"This wire must be linked to something. An alarm, an explosive . . ."

"No shit. But if it's a bomb, why aren't we blown sky-high already?" Caitlin asks.

While we talk, we're both trying to break into the lockers that the wire runs into.

"Could be they set it up with a time delay," I say. "In case someone tripped it by mistake, they have time to reset. . . ."

Caitlin grabs a knife from her boot and helps me prize open each locker, one at a time. So far, each one of them has just clothes or shoes, just like lockers in a changing room. But I can still see that wire running through the back of them. I follow it along and down to the last row of lockers, low by our feet, ending with one in the corner, the hardest to reach. Caitlin inserts her knife blade into the edge of the door and levers it hard. It swings open. My stomach takes a hard dive into my shoes and a strangled sound gurgles up from the back of Caitlin's throat.

It's a bunch of explosives stuffed into a length of pipe and capped and sealed at both ends to create enough pressure to do some serious damage. Now, I've seen these before, and I've even practiced defusing them. But that was with a remote-controlled robot, or some proper equipment to hand. Both those options aren't foolproof but they often work, given enough time. But we don't seem to have that luxury. Because connected to the bomb is a timer, and it's down to four and a half minutes.

"What's that keypad?" Caitlin asks, pointing to a digital box next to the bomb.

"With the right code, it can stop the timer. And the bomb."

"Any chance of cracking it?" Caitlin wants to know.

"Eight digits. That's, like, a billion possible combinations. . . ."

"Just get out of there!" From outside, Hala's voice comes into our ears.

Her advice seems better than anything else I can come up with. Caitlin grabs my sleeve and we both run like crazy for the door. I'm fleetingly pissed off about all the evidence in here that might be lost, but I'm right behind Caitlin as she flies outside. We start bolting across the yard toward our bikes when something touches us, like a burn. Involuntarily, without thinking, we both turn and run back inside the warehouse.

Caitlin and I stand there on the threshold, staring at each other.

"What the hell was that?" she asks.

I shake my head. It felt like a searing heat, no more than a second, maybe two, but it took away all my control. Call it a reflex, or primal self-preservation, but something outside my rational mind was impelled to stop moving forward and get back. And clearly Caitlin felt the same, or we wouldn't both be standing here, inside a booby-trapped warehouse, scared to leave.

"Let's try again," I say. "We can't stay here."

We venture out once more, but as soon as we step out of the door, the same heat hits us, and I try not to let it stop me, but it's impossible to power through the pain. Both of us are compelled to retreat back to the warehouse. Caitlin shines a light onto our faces and limbs. No injury, no burns.

"What's wrong with you?" Hala growls in our ears. "Get out!"

"We can't," I pant.

"I saw this tested when I was in active service," says Caitlin. "It's an ADS."

"Can you not be an army nerd for two seconds?" I snap.

"Active denial system. It's a military weapon that heats up water and fat molecules in the top layers of skin, so it feels like a burn, and it makes you run. There are scaled-down versions in lots of countries, used by law enforcement to scatter protesters, or on boats to stop pirates attacking. . . ."

While she's talking, I'm back at the locker, watching the bomb tick down to two minutes and forty-eight seconds. I use my own flashlight to scan around the warehouse—there are no other windows or exits. So now I wave the beam around searching for something, *anything*, that could help me here. In a corner, near a rusted sink, is a power cleaner—one of those things that uses a water jet to dislodge heavy stains like oil or paint. In the meantime, Caitlin is explaining to Hala what the ADS might look like, so she can try to find it and disarm it. From London, Amber comes in too, scouring satellite images of our location in case she can see anything that could help.

I lift the cleaner to the sink and run water into it, willing the cascade from the tap to gush faster. Then I drag the machine over to the explosives. Under two minutes left.

"What if we somehow resist the urge to retreat and keep going past the ADS?" I ask Caitlin as I peer at the nozzle on the end of the cleaner. Made of metal, it forms a high-pressure jet of water, activated with a trigger handle.

"If we stay in its range, we'd be cooked," Caitlin says. "Microwaved like popcorn."

So either Hala has to find the ADS and disable it, or I need to defuse this bomb. Either solution has to happen within ninety seconds.

Caitlin helps me move the machine and plug into the closest wall socket. The clock taunts me, moving backward. 1:18, 1:17 . . . Really, I need more power than an ordinary electrical outlet can give me, something to create a burst of harder pressure. A proper bomb disposal squad would use a PAN disrupter on a device like this—something like a small water cannon. A length of shock tube, a controlled explosive charge—enough to make the stream of water it shoots cut through the pipe. I have no idea if my homemade version will hold up, but I have to try. I fire it up with fifty seconds left and aim it at the pipe. At least the pipe is PVC, not metal. The thin water jet starts to cut through, and I'm practically panting from both adrenaline and a sense of relief that this could work—when the jet stops. In fact, the whole bloody machine shuts down.

I stare at it, wild-eyed. The motor must have a safety switch that cuts off the power when the jet pressure gets too high. It's the kind of standard safeguard that manufacturers put into basic household equipment, but it's the last thing I need right now. I smash open the plastic door that houses the motor of the cleaner, pulling at wires in desperation.

"I see a guy, top floor of the warehouse next door. He's holding something," Hala says from outside. "I'm going for him now."

"Forget it, don't risk it," Caitlin instructs.

We both know we need at least thirty seconds to make it out and clear the blast zone. Even if Hala disarms the guy or scares him off, there's just no time for me and Caitlin to run.

We're down to twenty-five seconds now, so I have to make this water jet work. My fingers fumble with wires, successfully shorting out the safety switch. Within a split second, Caitlin's turned the machine back on again. My arms are shaking so badly that I can hardly aim the thing, but her hands close over mine to steady them . . . fourteen seconds.

The jet spray bursts out, covering our faces in a fine mist, but it bores through that pipe, slowly but surely. I watch the clock tick down to five seconds, four . . . And then the outer layer of pipe breaks apart, the water floods the casing, and the clock goes blank. My eyes are bursting out of my head. It takes a moment before I can gasp for breath, becoming aware of Hala's voice from outside, in my ear, desperate.

"Talk to me," she says, stressed. "Are you okay?"

Like they're made of rubber, my legs give way, and Caitlin grabs me by my arms and steadies me.

"Jessie defused it," Caitlin tells Hala. "We're fine."

I lean over, still panting from stress. Behind me, I'm aware of Caitlin taking photo after photo of the weapons and the big crates of clothing, which seem to be shirts and baseball caps emblazoned with slogans. Going over to help, I move the top layers of guns so she can photograph the ones beneath. But now Hala comes in again.

"He ran and took the ray gun thing with him, but I got pictures of it," she says. There's a brief pause and when she speaks again, her voice holds urgency. "He must have called someone. There are two cars coming this way," she says. "They don't look friendly."

My legs are still shaky, but I push myself to stagger out, Caitlin propelling me with a strong hand on my back. Hala meets us at the door. I don't need to look for the approaching cars—the distant squeal of their tires makes it clear that they are bearing down on us. We edge through the gap in the wire, one by one, then run like mad for the bikes. Hala fires hers on first, jamming on her helmet to cover her face from the arriving crew. Caitlin and I do the same.

"Hold on," Caitlin tells me as her bike roars to life. Skidding away from the vehicles which are just now screeching to a stop on the road, we all burst into the alleyway that runs behind the warehouse and emerge behind the cars, roaring past them and back onto the highway, before the men inside can do anything more than pull out guns and watch us go.

10

IT TAKES A LONG TIME for sleep to come, and when it finally does, my dreams are all about me trying to reach Kit's school in time and yet never being able to get there. I guess it doesn't matter how many miles I can run when I'm awake, or how resourceful Athena teaches me to be, there's always some deep-seated insecurity that can haunt me when I'm unconscious.

Even though my eyes are burning with tiredness, I'm relieved to wake up just before 7 a.m. I check my phone. As I scroll through today's weather and news reports for Mumbai, a message pings in from Riya.

> Meet me 8:30 a.m. Juhu police station. Pls con-
> firm

Over the time we've known each other, Peggy has often diplomatically suggested ways for me to work on my people skills.

Sometimes, I'm fine with new contacts, but other times it's not clear to me how to reach out or form a bond. Certainly, I've already experienced some rocky opening exchanges with Riya. One of Peggy's gems of advice is that offering someone a meal can often be a good way to break the ice. Keeping this in mind, I tap out a reply that's more friendly than Riya's curt text deserves:

> Good morning, Detective. Can I buy you breakfast?

Congratulating myself on implementing this piece of etiquette, I go and brush my teeth while I wait for Riya's reply. It's taking some time, so I reckon she's clearly tempted by my kind offer. That is, until my phone pings with her response:

> No

Really? Would it kill her to just be polite? I spit the toothpaste into the basin, annoyed. Then I take a breath. One of my many life lessons from the past couple of months is that it's better not to get upset by something beyond your control. I remember this excellent tip about 10 percent of the time, which is 9 percent more than I used to. That's significant progress, if you ask me. I don't bother responding to Riya any further though. Let her wonder if I'll show up or not. Instead, I take my time in the shower, get dressed in jeans, a shirt, and a jacket, then walk down the hotel corridor to Kit's room.

I knock quietly, in case Kit's still sleeping, but my mother is up and sitting with Peggy already. Both of them sip at cups of tea with delicate lemon slices floating in them. Kit's in skinny jeans and a flowing paisley shirt, which is the kind of thing that would make me look like a tablecloth if I tried it. Peggy looks just perfect in a khaki ensemble—like a fashion ad for casual chic in a warm climate. They both seem subdued, so I just come out, as gently as I can, with the question that's been on my mind:

"When are the funerals for the girls?"

"Probably day after tomorrow," Peggy says. "Often, Hindus hold funerals within twenty-four hours, but these have been delayed. Forensics and . . . things."

Jittery, Kit gets up and pads over to the desk, scooping something up in her hand. Returning to where I sit, she takes hold of my fingers, slipping a small bracelet of darkly polished, gleaming wooden beads onto my wrist. They are intricately carved with tiny symbols.

"I got these at a place around the corner," she says. "They're supposed to ward off bad spirits."

Peggy reaches for my hand to take a closer look.

"It's beautiful, Kit," she says.

"I have two more, for Caitlin and Hala," my mother adds. I can just imagine Hala's face when she gets this and is told nothing bad will happen to her ever again.

"Do they work against terrorists?" I ask. I'm trying to be funny, or at least flippant, but Kit frowns.

"I know you don't go in for this kind of thing, but energy fields exist. You studied physics, Jess, you should know that better than any of us," she says.

I'm totally ready to challenge that mash-up of new age wishful thinking and the laws of physics, but a stern glance from Peggy helps me to keep it in my head. Instead, I mutter a "thank you" to Kit, glancing sideways at her. Her shirt is open at the neck, displaying a turquoise necklace that's supposed to channel her inner energy lines. One of her many silver rings contains a magnet for balancing the ions in her body, or something. On her right wrist is a handmade bracelet of Tibetan prayer beads gifted to her by a saffron-robed monk. On her left is a delicate red thread that she got from a Hindu temple. Sometimes, it feels to me as if there's nothing Kit won't try in her quest to make sure she's got all possible sources of universal flow and blessings covered. She's always been like this. When other girls got the Harry Potter or Judy Blume collections, Kit gave me the complete works of Deepak Chopra. I'm just glad she got over the incense phase early in my childhood. The smell of that stuff still makes me tense.

Meanwhile, Peggy is filling me in on what's happening in London.

"Amber is still looking for a financial link between Imran and Family First," she explains. "And Thomas is analyzing the photos he got from Caitlin last night—the pictures of the crates of clothes and weapons from the warehouse."

"That's great," I say, only half listening.

"What's on your mind?" Peggy asks, attuned, as always, to the moods of everyone around her.

"I've been summoned to the police station by Riya, the detective on the case."

"Did she say why?"

"No."

"Well," says Kit, "I'm not surprised she wants to see you. After you got to Hassan ahead of her, she probably wants to tell you off."

"Or perhaps she just has information to share," Peggy suggests, always looking for a possible upside.

As I leave, Kit pulls me back for a hug. I go over and hug Peggy too, just so nobody feels left out. For the first time, though, I feel the stress in their embraces. It occurs to me how much they must suffer when they watch us fighting through danger. If I think about it too much, though, it'll make me soft. I turn away briskly and leave them without looking back.

On my way to see Riya, I'm told by Li and the Athena team to give the detective the details of the warehouse we broke into last night. I'm assuming the men who arrived cleared it out, but the police might still be able to track the weapons. Also, the clothing items we discovered have added a strange piece to the puzzle that I need to discuss with Riya.

Running up the front steps of the police station that she's based in, I pause just inside the front door. The building's exterior is painted in pale pink and blue, the colors slowly fading under accumulated layers of dirt and pollution. Inside, a ceiling fan chugs in lazy circles, doing very little to supplement the portable air-conditioning unit that's blasting lukewarm air into a corner. People are in and out of the place like it's Heathrow Airport, and there's already a queue waiting for attention from the lethargic cop at the front desk.

Rather than stand in line, I text Riya a message. She replies back with her usual effusiveness (**Wait there**) and within five minutes, arrives in the vestibule to meet me. Alongside her is a man in his late forties, not much taller than she is. He is slightly built, so slight that it looks like a blast from the air conditioner might send him tumbling away, but his handshake is exceptionally firm.

"Sunil Patel, detective," he says. He wears black-framed glasses and watches me without blinking.

"Sunil is my boss," Riya explains. "He's extremely experienced."

"I think that means 'extremely old,'" Sunil says.

At least he has a sense of humor. I smile and look at them both politely.

"Are you on this case as well, Sunil?" I ask.

He nods.

"Great, then I can speak to both of you." I look around for a place where we can sit quietly together, but neither of them moves. In fact, Sunil clears his throat officiously.

"Excuse me, Jessie-ma'am—it's Jessie, right? We are all big fans of Kit Love—her charity work and, in my case, her music too. I want you to go back to Kit-ma'am and let her know that we are leaving no stone unturned in our quest to find these bombers."

"And to find out who is *behind* the bombers?" I suggest.

He looks pained at my pushiness but maintains a calm tone.

"Obviously," he says, shaking his head gently in the Indian way of saying yes. "There is a bigger picture here, and we will fill in the blanks posthaste."

Posthaste. One of the many things I love about India so far is that everyone uses such precise English. And phrases that went out of fashion in London in the 1960s, and sometimes the 1860s, are still big here. Like, Indians will say "thrice" instead of "three times." Nevertheless, as delicious as Sunil's little speeches are, they are full of platitudes, and I'm not buying much of anything that comes out of his mouth. I glance at Riya. Even she has the grace to realize how dismissive he must sound.

"Well, I may have a bit more information for you," I say, eager to fill them in on last night's proceedings. Or at least a sanitized version of them, one that leaves out the part where we broke into private property and defused a bomb. But Sunil raises his hands, as if warding me away.

"We have too many cooks in this kitchen, spoiling the broth," he says. "When you interfere, you could be putting our own investigations at risk. I hope you understand that."

"Of course. But two heads are better than one," I try, since he seems to be into meaningless mottos. But he just regards me, unmoved. Thankfully, Riya steps in.

"Why don't you and I go across the street and have a coffee?" she offers.

She turns to Sunil and speaks in Hindi. Though I don't understand the words, the tone seems to suggest that she is offering to get me off their backs for both of them. He nods, gives me a fake smile along with another knuckle-crunching handshake, and heads back into the police station. Meanwhile, Riya opens the main door for me to exit down the wide steps.

Trucks, vans, cars, and rickshaws, not to mention a tired-looking donkey, fill the space between us and a small café across the road. But Riya doesn't wait for a gap in the endless flow of vehicles; she just steps out into the chaos and gracefully weaves her way through. I follow closely.

Inside are rows of densely packed tables where a few diners eat breakfast. I follow Riya to the empty counter, where we each take a stool and she orders us both chai—milky tea fragrant with spices.

"I get the feeling your boss would probably prefer me to hang out in my hotel spa and leave you alone," I say.

"Would you consider it?" she asks, hopeful.

"No."

She smiles. "Sunil's not so bad. He's just formal. But he's good at his job."

I'm glad, if slightly surprised, to hear it. Sunil didn't feel like the most progressive guy I'd ever met. But that might just have been because he was defensive around me.

"So that's why you wanted to see me," I say. "So that Sunil could tell me to back off." I am disappointed, to be honest. I'd hoped she was taking the pledge to share her findings more seriously.

"Not just that," she says, and her tone holds annoyance now. "I also want to know what information you got from Hassan. Because clearly you got something from him. But he's not talking to us. What did you do to him?"

"Gosh, nothing!" I say innocently.

"Do I look like I was born yesterday?" she shoots back. "He was quivering like a milk pudding by the time we reached him."

I try not to smile at her simile, but just the hint of amusement on my face irritates her even more. She slams a hand onto the countertop.

"Do you *really* want me to arrest you for whatever investigative methods you are using? This is India, not the Wild West. We have a refined justice system, processes that *must* be followed. You keep this up, Jessie, you are going to be investigating only the inside of a jail cell. How will you like that?"

Her dark eyes flash at me, keeping me pinned down by her gaze. Suddenly I feel nervous. But not about the investigation. Just, awkward about being around her. I look away and pick up my tea.

"Was there any sign that I hurt Hassan?" I ask.

"He couldn't walk," she accuses.

"Oh, come on," I scoff. "He sprained his ankle, running from me."

I smile at her, like I couldn't hurt a fly. I'm pretty sure Hassan is too scared that Hala will go after his kids to blame any of his injuries on us. Riya shakes her head, and a strand of hair comes loose from her ponytail, falling over her eye. For a fleeting moment, I have the ridiculous urge to push it back, but Riya herself does that, impatiently retying it.

"So, do you want to know what Hassan told me or not?" I say.

She groans. "My God, Jessie, you would try the patience of a saint. Of course I do. Tell me."

"This is where he was sent to collect his fake ID and the address of the school."

I hand her a piece of paper with the warehouse address on it. She takes it and taps the information into her phone for good measure.

"Is that everything you have?" she asks.

I hesitate. "No. But if I tell you more, you can't ask me questions about how I found out."

She makes a despairing sound. "Do you realize what you're asking of me? I am an officer of the law."

"Yes, I know it's a lot to ask. I'm sorry, Riya."

She glances at me, uncertain. "I really hate this."

While she decides, I lean on the counter and my gaze flits up to the portable TV mounted in the corner. It plays a silent loop of today's hot stories. There's a major local election coming up at the end of next week and a reporter is interviewing a politician—a tall, elegant man with delicate features.

"That's Jingo Jain?" I ask her, nodding at the television.

"Janveer Jain," she says. "Informally, 'Jingo.' He's running for office. Why?"

But I need her to agree to my terms first. "No other questions?" I push.

She's dying to know more.

"Fine," she says, through gritted teeth.

I pull out my phone and show her some of the images that Caitlin took the night before. The weapons stockpile and also the clothing. All the clothes are campaign merchandise—T-shirts and caps promoting only one politician—Jingo Jain. Riya leans in closer, studying the photos.

"These were in the warehouse," I say. "And there were lots of them. Could Jingo be involved with Family First somehow?"

She frowns. "I'd be surprised. He was one of the most vocal in condemning the attack on Kit's school. He's ex-military, ex-police. People see him as someone safe, someone who will protect Mumbai and Maharashtra state from terror."

I can see Riya chewing over the photos. Part of her wants to tell me off for going there, for being a step ahead and not sharing earlier. But she manages to hold it in. Curiosity seems to be slowly dampening her passion for process.

"I need these pictures," she says.

I nod and continue talking, telling her about the ADS that was used on me. And warning her that the place may be booby-trapped in case of a visit from unwanted guests. Like the police.

Riya stares at me, amazed. "Where did you learn how to do all this?"

"Investigating? I'm just nosy. I like putting two and two together," I say, brushing off her interest. I don't want to start the long litany of lies that my current cover backstory would entail.

"What about you?" I ask quickly. "It can't have been easy, becoming a police officer. And making it to detective."

"You mean because of the work, or because of male attitudes?"

"Both."

"Why do you assume India is worse than anywhere else?"

"I don't. It could be tough anywhere."

She nods, but I can see she's eager to get back to work and follow up the lead I just gave her. So I take out a rupee note to pay the bill for the tea—but Riya covers my hand with hers, pushing me gently away.

"You're in my city. You can't pay."

She passes some money of her own to the café owner, talking all the while.

"To be honest, it wasn't easy at times. Joining the police. But Sunil has always stood up for me, given me responsibility, pushed me to do more than I was assigned. Especially on this case."

"Why this case?"

"It means a lot to me and he knows that."

We walk to the door together and she holds it open for me. The street is raucous and bright after the cool quiet of the café. Before she can cross over to the station again, I stop her with a brief hand on her arm.

"Why does it mean a lot to you?"

She turns to face me. "Because I think we need many more of these schools, and we need to protect the few that we have. Nearly half the girls in India are married before the age of eighteen. And almost twenty percent are married by the time they are fifteen."

"Is that legal?"

"No, but it's culturally accepted . . . maybe a little less here in Mumbai. Some poorer states, like Bihar, run at seventy percent. Those girls have to stop school—if they were ever *in* school to begin with—marry a man they don't know, often much older than them, have kids, and be confined to the home. Kit's schools save at least some of these girls from that fate."

There's an impassioned note in her voice that I haven't heard before. I navigate the road with her, and when we are both outside her workplace, she starts up the short flight of stairs that leads into the police station, but then stops suddenly. From the bottom step she watches me for a moment, hesitating.

"What is it?" I say. "You can tell me."

"I was one of those girls, once," she says, biting at her lip. With the toe of her shoe she stabs at the edge of the step. "I never knew my birth parents. I lived in a crowded orphanage until I was eight. It would have been my destiny to marry someone as soon as I reached puberty, just to make room for another child to take my place at the orphanage."

"What happened?"

"I was adopted. Very few kids are, in India. There are not even a few thousand adoptions each year, but there are maybe thirty million abandoned children."

She looks down, as if she might have shared too much. But I'm glad she said something.

"Riya?" I say, and I wait for her to look up. "Thank you for telling me."

"Thank you for this," she says, holding up the paper with the warehouse address. She runs lightly up the stairs and turns at the door. Below her, on the street, I still stand watching her.

"I appreciate it, Jessie," she calls, before she disappears into the building. "But, just so we're clear—you're still a big pain in the ass."

11

ON MY WAY BACK TO the hotel, I keep replaying the conversation with Riya, especially the last part, where she talked about herself. I liked glimpsing even small fragments of who she really is. It gave me a sense of the passion that seems to make her police work a calling. Also, after circling each other like boxers in a ring in our first couple of meetings, it's good to feel that we don't have to compete all the time—that there are ways we might work together to find out who is behind this terrible crime.

Riya stays on my mind all the way through a full-blown Athena conference call, held through our secure virtual server. Kit has her feet up on the sofa in her hotel room, hugging her knees, and Peggy perches beside her. Caitlin and I are sprawled on the floor below them, and Hala sits cross-legged beside us, like a morose yogi. All of us are loosely grouped around Kit's tablet, where Li, Amber, and

Thomas are on a secure video stream from London, bringing us up to speed on their findings.

"We've unearthed more info on this Family First mob," Thomas tells us. "Along the way, we found a distressingly high number of similarly themed organizations, but Family First definitely stood out."

"How come?" asks Hala.

"Good question," comments Thomas, apparently failing to notice that Hala actually just asked the most obvious question possible. Instead, he gazes at her like she just came up with the solution to climate change. I sneak a sideways glance at Caitlin, who's clearly trying not to smirk at Thomas's lovestruck demeanor.

Thankfully, Amber chips in: "Well, apart from the obvious attack on the school and Family First's subsequent statement, they seem to be linked to a whole web of offshore companies and bank accounts, which is rarely a sign that someone means well. The accounts they file in the UK are public domain," she continues, "but they contain more fiction than the *New York Times* bestseller list. There are obvious markers in their balance sheet and P and L—"

"That's okay," Kit interrupts gently, to spare all of us any more of this fascinating insight into spotting financial skullduggery. "The question is, what do we do next?"

Li jumps into the conversation.

"We've booked Jessie and Caitlin a flight home tonight," she tells us. "Hala will stay behind and make sure Peggy's SEAL guys secure the other school before the girls are moved back in."

"Why are we coming home?" Caitlin asks.

"It's just for a couple of days at the outside," Li says. "That company that Hassan gave you, AAB Enterprises, has a link to the Cypriot Private Bank here in London. That is also one of the banks that Amber has tied to large payments received by Imran over the past year. These are very promising leads, but we've hit a dead end."

Caitlin and I both lean forward, listening as Li continues:

"To get into a bank like that, we're going to need you and Caitlin to work together. Those places use black-ops security because they cater to secretive corporations and corrupt governments. Also," Li continues, "our journalist friend Jake Graham is still sniffing around. Amber hasn't been able to get into his computer, so we need your undercover skills back here."

On-screen, Amber shifts unhappily at the implied slur on her technical abilities. A sarcastic comment rises to my lips, but I button it. There'll be plenty of time to tease Amber later. For now, Li has laid out a compelling set of tasks, and her autocratic style doesn't always appreciate random humor. The call wraps up soon after and, with Caitlin, I get ready to fly back to London.

It's still early—8 a.m.—when I arrive home in Notting Hill. It's getting close to Christmastime and sparkling fairy lights are draped over the trees and along the tops of the still-closed market stalls on Portobello Road. After a quick shower and change, I stride out toward the tube station to make my way back into the heart of the city, where Athena is based. Our rogue agency is hidden in plain sight, occupying two floors of a soaring glass-and-steel building that overlooks the gleaming bends of the river Thames. The building belongs to Chen Technologies, Li's legitimate company. It's a conglomerate that she has built from nothing into an enterprise that turns over billions each year with cutting-edge software and hardware. It also allows her to divert interesting technology to us. Athena is such a lean operation that we can use all the help we can get.

The streets of London feel somber and gray-tinted compared to India. Even the rush hour traffic seems so much calmer and quieter. Before I run down the escalators into the underground train system, I duck into a small French bakery and ignore that morning's diet recommendation in favor of a croissant that I pull apart into perfectly warm, crisp flakes, and a double espresso that helps dispel the jet lag that's starting to fog up my brain.

When I reach the Chen Tech building, I enter through an alley that snakes around the back of the structure. Apart from the myriad of usual security features that prevent anyone outside Athena getting in, Amber has recently installed a hidden camera, a new layer of security that scans my face as I approach. Only when it recognizes me does the finger scanner pad open up, low down on a wall next to an innocuous-looking garage door. Getting through another interior door, I head to an unmarked elevator that opens with a hand scan. Finally, an iris reader gets me up to the floor where Amber is based. This is a huge area, protected with one-way mirrored glass across the wide windows, and dedicated to Athena's technology research. It's also where all our weapons, IDs, and communications technology are kept under lock and key by Amber, using her indecipherable inventory system.

The muscular tones of Nina Simone belting out "Feeling Good" fill the space, emanating from a vinyl record rotating sedately on a vintage turntable. In the center of the room, remote-controlled flames dance invitingly on a raised marble hearth. On the other side of this modern fireplace, Amber sits at her semicircular desk, surrounded by computer screens. To her left is a long counter, uncluttered by any ornamentation, and behind that counter are several locked safe boxes.

"Jessie!" she says. "Good to see you." She throws me a smiling glance from beneath a carefully styled crop of hair that's currently dyed an improbable shade of electric blue.

"Are those new highlights in your hair?" I ask.

"Your powers of observation seem to evolve to ever-new heights."

"Yeah, well, I'm a highly trained special agent."

"Apparently," Amber observes.

I come close enough to perch on the edge of her desk, something that drives her insane at the best of times.

"I hear you're having some trouble hacking into Jake Graham's computer," I say.

Amber looks daggers at me and I return the glare with the most charming smile I can conjure.

"Jake is the kind of meticulous journalist who is obsessed with protecting his sources," she replies haughtily.

"Not surprising," I say. "I mean, it's not like he reports on the weather. He writes about corrupt regimes and the worst kinds of criminals."

"Exactly the sorts of people we go after," Amber agrees.

I look at her for a moment. Though Jake Graham's social justice leanings are hardly news to me, it's the first time I've really thought about him as having the same interests as us. Since his report on the shooting of Ahmed in Cameroon—the shooting that was my fault—not to mention his article about my mother singing for Gregory Pavlic, and his current stalking of Kit and Peggy, I've considered him to be an enemy. Someone to hide from and fight against. The irony is that Amber is right; Jake and Athena want mostly the same things. For the rights of women and girls, and all human beings, to be protected across the world.

Amber's bracing tones interrupt my musing.

"Without an actual lock on the Wi-Fi he uses or, rather, a lock on the router he uses for his VPN, I don't think even you'd have had more luck than me."

"So, basically, if Jake has pieced together that there's a rogue agency of women based in London bringing down traffickers and assorted scum—we won't know until the police show up to arrest us?"

Amber stands up with an exasperated sigh. Her heels tap efficiently over to the turntable, where she switches off the music.

"I doubt he has any evidence of note," she says.

"I hope you're right. And if you're not, I hope we get to share a jail cell," I sigh. "It would be fun."

"In the same way as having a root canal is fun, perhaps," remarks Amber.

She sits down at her desk and motions me to take a chair beside her. The seat is one of those lush, ergonomic jobs that keeps your posture perfect while you stare at a screen for hours. Meanwhile, Amber types like a maniac, bringing up different items on different screens.

"Do you want the good news or the bad news?" she asks.

"Good news."

"I did manage to get into Jake's email this morning."

"Well done," I say. I don't ask *how* she did it, because chances are good that I'll end up with my head on the desk, drooling from boredom. "So, what's the bad news?"

"I found out from his email that he never keeps any of his investigations on a computer," she says. "They're all on paper."

She points out the relevant messages on the screen. Notes that Jake has written to anonymous-looking email addresses to reassure potential sources that they won't be tracked through him.

"Can't be," I say. "How does he write his reports?"

"Oh, he does write his actual journalism pieces on a laptop. Because within hours, they're published in a newspaper or live on TV anyway. It's only the sources and the ongoing research and unfinished investigations that he keeps in notebooks or whatever."

Well, that sucks. I lean back in the chair, frowning.

"Don't bother," Amber says.

"Don't bother what?"

"Thinking. I've already done it for you and run the plan by Li. You're going to have to break into Jake Graham's home."

12

THOUGH ALL OF US ARE nervous about our intrepid reporter friend, I also have to hang on to the fact that my main mission back in London is still to track down more on this AAB Enterprises outfit that Hassan spilled the name of after our colorful chase through the slums of Mumbai. That means working with Li and Caitlin to get into the private bank where AAB holds its accounts. But now, I'll also need to find a way into Jake's home to see if Athena is about to be blown out of the water. It's going to be a busy couple of days, and once Amber runs me and Caitlin through the plan to access the bank, I decide to fill in the rest of the morning with a workout. Caitlin stays at Athena to check in with our private doctor about progress in coming off her meds. I'm feeling edgy and nervous, not to mention lethargic from jet lag, so I head out for some fresh air and a lengthy run along the river. My feet hit a rhythm early on; nice and steady, nothing earth-shattering in terms of speed. It's just enough to stop me from thinking, to scour my mind clean of all the noise. There's a breeze that carries the metallic smell of rain from the gathering clouds that lie crouched on top of the city. I sprint down as far as the wedding-cake spires of the Albert Bridge, then jog across it and through Battersea Park before making a big circle back to where I started.

It's only when I'm done and back at Athena, slumped gratefully in the baking heat of the steam room that connects to the gym, that my mind starts going back to India again. I'm puzzling over the warehouse—the garments printed with Jingo Jain's political slogans, and the sophistication of guarding the place with an active denial system. It makes Family First, or whoever is behind them, feel bigger and better organized than we would have hoped. While I think, my eyes trace a hundred different trails carved out by the water droplets coursing down the glass door of the steam room.

I wonder if Riya has turned anything up yet. Then I recall our conversation, about how personal this case is to her. What must it have been like for her, growing up in an orphanage? Did the people who adopted her take care of her, love her? I wonder if it would be okay to ask her to lunch or dinner; somewhere off-duty, a setting where we could be free from constantly having to worry about the stresses of the case.

But then, I think it might be better to not go there. I'm beginning to find several things about Riya—her ethics, her commitment, her sharp intelligence—attractive. And the truth is, the very idea of being attracted to someone related to my work scares me. I'm sure it has something to do with the fact that the last girl I thought was a knockout was the daughter of a human trafficking kingpin. Not only did my overactive hormones compromise my judgment but, in the end, she turned out to be a chip off the old block when it came to selling women like they were commodities. All in all, I'm not thrilled with my recent track record. Reluctantly, I decide that it would be logical to keep personal feelings at a distance, and just focus on the jobs at hand.

Twenty minutes later, I'm in the locker room, standing side by side with Caitlin in front of full-length mirrors. Both of us are getting dressed up for our next job, in navy trousers and jackets, with pressed white shirts beneath.

"I feel like your suit fits better than mine," I mutter, pulling at my outfit.

"Let me get this straight," Caitlin says in her dry drawl. "You're wearing a wig that a Vegas showgirl would find tacky, but it's your *suit* that bothers you?"

She has a point. My real hair is covered with a wig that's really expensive and realistic, but it's a dark, short, spiky cut with reddish highlights. It serves its purpose because, undoubtedly, it's only this dubious hairstyle that anyone would remember about me if they met me just once. Caitlin adjusts the tight skullcap that's covering her dark gold hair and then pulls on her own fake hairpiece—long, brunette, straight. I watch her run her hands through it as she looks approvingly at herself in the mirror.

"How come you get 'elegant' and I get 'drag artist'?" I protest.

"Maybe because you give Amber shit all the time." Caitlin grins. "And Amber chooses our disguises. You do the math."

Caitlin slips a mouthpiece over her bottom teeth that alters the shape of her jawline. Even I don't recognize her at this point. But then, with my new hairstyle and deep blue contact lenses over my naturally green eyes, I don't recognize myself either.

"You have to admit, it's kind of fun," Caitlin says, beaming at me. "I mean, in this tech-crazy world, how often do we get to play 'dress-up' like real spies?"

Being out there in the field, boots on the ground, is what Caitlin lives for. She had the worst time in the US military, but that was because of the abuse she saw on both sides, not because of the work. She's never enjoyed the endless hours pinned behind a desk that online spying entails, though she rarely complains. I shake out my shoulders and button up the suit jacket, getting a feel for it, because it needs to fit me like I wear it every day. Meanwhile, Caitlin slides on a set of aviator shades and poses in front of the mirror.

"Too much?" she asks.

"Not if you're going for a look that screams 'I'm a Hollywood actress *pretending* to be a bodyguard.'"

She sighs, removes the sunglasses, and slips them into her breast pocket.

"If you're done admiring yourself, we should get going," Caitlin says.

I follow her out of the locker area and into the tech cave, where Amber seems to be taking some kind of weapons inventory on her precious countertop. She pauses to come over and give us a final briefing. A very cool 3D floor plan projects out from her screens, and just hangs there in the space by her desk like a floating holograph. Caitlin is circling it, examining it for what must be the tenth time. She's always meticulous about this stuff. I like to think I am too, but once, twice—and I've got it.

It's the layout of the Cypriot Private Bank in London. Their headquarters is just two miles from here, housed in a three-hundred-year-old landmark building. Normally, a structure that age is a cinch to work with because the heating, cooling, and security systems have been added in piecemeal over time, without a proper plan—and that means there are often weaknesses that we can creatively exploit. Unfortunately, that's not the case here. This bank is notorious for handling offshore money for a secret roster of dodgy corporations, heads of state (usually the brutal, dictator kind), and sovereign wealth funds from countries with less-than-stellar human rights records. They're awash in cash just from the fees they charge their grateful clients to make their dirty money disappear and so, while the facade of their building remains intact and compliant with building regulations, they've had plenty of funds available to do a complete overhaul on the inside.

For us, that creates a headache. Firstly, Amber's been unable to get a lock on their most secure internal network, through which she might have tried to find any unprotected data or weaknesses in their servers. On the plus side, she's used the bank staff's Wi-Fi to get a lock on a potential vulnerability—two server ports that are unused but not properly blocked off. But she can't access those remotely. So, our job is to get an actual piece of equipment into the room where the bank houses its physical computer servers so that Amber can get into the important information flow—the data on their clients, which include AAB Enterprises.

"Let's run through the server room again," Caitlin says.

"Here it is," says Amber, moving her finger through the floating floor plan.

"And there's definitely no way in there through the door?" Caitlin pushes.

"You mean the three-foot-thick metal door opened with a biometric key and an encrypted passcode?" Amber asks sardonically. "No, probably not. That's why we've come up with the current plan. Is there anything else you want to second-guess me on?"

Caitlin smiles at her. "Just trying to help," she says.

"If I need assistance, I won't hesitate to ask," Amber replies.

"Someone got out of bed on the wrong side this morning," I comment.

Amber fixes me with an irritable glare. "Someone hasn't *seen* her bed for three days," she retorts.

"Okay, kids, let's not bicker," Caitlin says, deflecting Amber's temper. "Just check this."

Amber opens up an app on Caitlin's phone, tests that it works okay, then gives it back. Then she bustles over to me and tucks two tiny drones, the size of flies, into small padded pockets sewn into the lapels of my jacket, along with a tiny tool kit. She sniffs at me as she works.

"You smell lemony," Amber observes.

"Which is strange," I reply. "Because you seem to be the sour one."

Amber sighs. "I'm sorry to be crabby. I'm just tired," she adds.

In return for her unusual apology, I try my best to be conversational.

"Are you sure the drones won't get caught by the metal detector at the front door?" I ask.

"They're fiberglass, and the tool kit is high-tensile plastic," Amber says. "More chance of this raising an alarm." She holds up a small digital tape measure like the kind real estate agents use to figure out room sizes. Amber slips it into my pocket, then steps back and casts a critical eye over us.

"You look authentic," she says, clearly pleased with her handiwork in transforming us. "I completely believe you as Li's bodyguards."

"Really? 'Authentic' was the word in your mind when you chose *this* wig and *these* contacts for me to wear?" I demand. "I barely look human. I look like one of those avatars in a weird sci-fi game—"

"Go and get this done," Amber says, interrupting my whining. "Don't worry, you'll be perfectly fine."

Spoken like someone who'll be spending the next hour right

here, completely safe, sipping tea and listening to old-time music on her vinyl turntable, while we sweat through trying to break into a bank server protected like a fortress. With a brief nod goodbye, we move into the elevator and scan ourselves down to the parking garage, where we wait for Li to meet us by her car.

13

IT'S JUST A BIT MORTIFYING that even Li has to smother a smile when she sees me. This is a woman who could sit through any stand-up comedy set without cracking a laugh. I meet her amused look with as much irritation as I can while still maintaining a shred of respect for my superior.

"Impressive," Li tells us, perfectly deadpan. "I don't recognize the two of you. Disguises might be superfluous to our requirements, but it's better to be safe than sorry."

Thankfully, we're so close to the bank that I don't have much time in the back of Li's super-cool Tesla with my boss trying not to stare at me. When the driver pulls up outside the bank, Caitlin and I both exit smoothly, assessing the street for risks like real bodyguards would before allowing the rear door to open and Li to exit. We escort her inside the towering building, which is all carved stone and marble on the outside. Right inside the foyer, a deferential wealth manager and assistant are anxiously awaiting our arrival. They bow and scrape us into a private client lounge, an acre of neutral-toned space with lush cream carpets, expensive leather armchairs, and some kind of championship barista coffee machine. A wine cooler holds an array of champagnes and vintage wines. Another bar area houses racks of coconut water, matcha tea, and the kind of environment-slaughtering bottled water that's probably harvested by hand in the foothills of the Himalayas.

Bank managers parked behind desks are so *not* how it's done in this world, apparently. Li is ushered to a plush armchair, and the elegant manager sits opposite her. He's perhaps fifty, in a tailored suit; clean shaven, salt-and-pepper hair cut neatly and swept back. He looks like he stepped out of an ad for luxury Swiss watches; you know the ones—where a satisfied guy lounges on the deck of a yacht, smiling fondly at his designer kids, so ecstatic that their hundred-thousand-dollar graduation gift timepieces will last for six generations.

Completely poised, Caitlin plants herself by the door while I station myself right beside Li. The assistant that greeted us when we arrived, a young woman in a gray skirt suit and heels, brings over a small, gleaming silver tray. Upon it sits a solid crystal glass filled with the sparkling water that Li just requested. But Li shakes her head.

"Bring me a bottle. Sealed. And a new glass. *Two* glasses."

The woman scurries off. Even though it's Li who is behaving

(intentionally) like a prima donna, and a rude one at that, the manager apologizes profusely for his assistant's terrible service. When he's done with the self-flagellation, he starts making polite small talk. Li looks bored and provides one-word replies to his questions, upon which he casually tries tossing out a few phrases in Mandarin. Li is originally from outside Beijing, so that's her first language. Now she smiles slightly, like she's so impressed, and they chat a bit more. The water bottle appears but Li returns it again, because it's the wrong *brand* of water this time. I smirk, but only on the inside. Li is setting up her fussiness for the next stage of our attack. By the time the young assistant is back for the third time, I take the bottle of water from her tray myself, open it, pour a little into one of the glasses, and then I actually *taste* it, like it might be poisoned, before allowing my esteemed boss to get near the other glass. The manager watches politely, like he sees this kind of thing every day. And who knows? Catering to paranoid tyrants, maybe he does.

A couple more minutes go by, during which Li switches back to English and throws out three billion dollars as the amount she has ready to place with the bank of her choice. By now, her host is practically salivating. But Li shifts.

"I'd like to use the bathroom," she says.

The young assistant hurries back to escort her to the guest restroom, which is right off the client lounge that we are in. But Li does not move. She nods to me, and I whip out my tape measure and follow the girl to the room. It's a marble-clad nook with gold taps and thick cotton hand towels. Thanks to Amber's floor plan, I already know the dimensions, but I diligently throw a beam of light onto each wall and read the length and width of the room. Shaking my head, I sigh deeply.

"Mrs. Chen is highly claustrophobic," I say, and my voice just about carries to the manager in the lounge. "This is below the minimum space she requires, and there are also no windows. Is there a staff bathroom we could try?"

"Yes, but the stalls are smaller," the assistant squeaks, stressed out of her mind by my insane explanation. It's been my experience since starting work with Athena that people rarely argue if you say something that they don't quite understand.

"Are there gaps in the base of each cubicle?" I ask.

She nods. I drop my voice.

"Then it should be fine. It is the feeling of being sealed in that is the problem," I say enigmatically.

"Of course," she whispers. "I completely understand."

Honestly, it seems like it doesn't matter what bizarre needs you have if you're wealthy enough; everyone will move heaven and earth to accommodate you. The manager is up now, nodding and bowing a lot. The assistant runs around escorting the three of us out of the lounge and into the main bathrooms, which are still really nice but just a series of stalls in a long room with frosted windows at the end. Reassuringly, they are laid out exactly as Amber's building plans showed. To keep up appearances, I leave Li at the door while I measure the length and pronounce it acceptable. At the same time, I scan around the room. It would be illegal to have any surveillance within toilet stalls and, luckily, there's no camera outside the stalls either.

Relieved that we're happy at last, the assistant leaves us to it. Caitlin stands with her back pressed against the inside of the main bathroom door to prevent anyone else coming in. Together, Li and I head into the stall right at the end of the room. Standing on the toilet seat, I whip out a plastic screwdriver and attack the screws on a plate in the ceiling that leads into a vent. When the plate falls away, I hand it down to Li and she cups her hands together to boost me up.

"Hurry up," she says. I glance down at her and nod. I mean, is she worried I might like it so much up there that I'll just relax and hang out?

I crawl into the vent, which is made of shiny aluminum and is fabulously clean. The bank's air system is so new that it has the latest HEPA-type filters to reduce dust and dirt. Combined with the fact that the whole building's air is filtered, it means very little accumulation of gunk in the cooling system. I scoot my way through, using the light on my phone, take a small bend to the left, and unscrew the next plate I come to. This one is only partly over the server room but there's a one-inch gap—enough that I can see down into the space, filled with black computing boxes, flashing lights, and the noise of billions of bytes of data being processed. From inside my lapel, I pull out one of the drones and hold it above the gap. All around the server room, wireless signals are cut. But the comms in my ear still works.

"Ready?" I breathe.

Caitlin's voice comes back in my head. "Yep. Count me down."

"Ninety-nine, ninety-eight . . ."

"Cut it out, smart-ass."

I smile. "Okay. Three . . . two . . . one . . . go."

I drop the drone in through the hatch and it falls then veers upward—just a tiny fly trapped in the room. Caitlin has control of it now, through the app on her phone, and she should be seeing a video stream through the minuscule camera on the drone's back. Carefully, I balance the second drone on the edge of the gap and leave it sitting there, in case we need it as a backup. Then I turn and find my way back to the bathroom ceiling and lower myself down into the stall. Li pauses the stopwatch on her digital watch.

"Ninety-three seconds," she says. It feels like a compliment; the closest she will get to saying "well done." I screw the ceiling plate back in, then slip on the jacket that Li is holding ready for me. Outside the stalls, Caitlin is intent on guiding the drone toward the exact port that Amber needs. I brush down my suit, wash my hands, then go to look over Caitlin's shoulder at her phone screen.

"We need to hurry. Three minutes is the average time a woman takes in a restroom," Li murmurs.

Feeling the pressure, Caitlin's holding her breath, trying to dock the drone into a port deep behind a massive wall of servers. I'm itching to take over, but she's had a minute to get a feel for the sensitivities of it, so she'll do all right . . . I hope.

"It's been three and a half minutes . . . ," whispers Li.

Caitlin doesn't acknowledge. It's just so hard to get a lock on the right spot. She tries and the drone hits the wrong point and drops like a stone.

"Shit," she breathes. Pressing two keys together, like you would in a video game, Caitlin gets it back off the ground and this time, she nails it. She nods to Li and we all wait there like statues for a few more, agonizingly slow seconds, waiting for confirmation—

"You did it. Very impressive." Amber's voice comes into our earpieces.

We nod to Li that all is well, and we're out of there, following the echoing rap of Li's heels down the marble corridor. The assistant comes rushing out to escort us back to the lounge. After a few more minutes of Li's interrogation of the manager about how the bank can help her, the meeting is wrapped up. Li shakes hands and, lying smoothly, promises to be in touch.

14

WHILE WE WAIT FOR AMBER to dig into the bank's servers, we arrive back at the locker room at Athena, where I'm totally thrilled to get rid of the hairpiece and colored contacts and change back into my regular clothes. I've nearly finished dressing when my Indian phone pings. It's a text from Riya.

Info on ADS

As usual, her message hardly overflows with information, but it still makes me smile to hear from her. I doubt it would matter much if she knew, but I haven't bothered to tell her that I'm back in London for such a tiny spell of time. Instead, Amber's set me up a network just for this phone that makes it appear that I'm still in Mumbai. I glance over to the doors that lead to the showers and steam room. The sound of running water tells me that Caitlin is still washing up. On an impulse, I give Riya a quick call back. She picks up on the first ring.

"Jessie!"

It suddenly dawns on me how *great* my name sounds in an Indian accent.

"Hey, Riya. I thought I'd call you to catch up, since your texts are so light on detail."

"I think of them as short and meaningful," she replies.

"Try 'cryptic,'" I say.

She laughs, a sound like wind chimes, a sound that makes me smile. And now Caitlin comes out of the shower, drying off and casting me a quick, curious glance. Immediately, I wipe the smile off my face and, diplomatically, Caitlin turns away and starts getting dressed.

"So, what do you have on the ADS?" I ask briskly.

"We tracked it to a military base north of the city," Riya says. "It was stolen about a month ago."

"And never found?"

"Correct. It is state of the art, and very mobile. And someone signed it out of the weapons inventory," Riya explains. "That's the kind of thing that needs to be checked by a senior officer. Only four people on the base have the authority to check off the removal of weapons."

"Anyone interesting?"

"Potentially. The officer who okayed that particular movement order—and allowed the ADS to be taken off the base—is a protégé of Jingo Jain's. Jingo was the commander of that base at one time and this guy, Vikram Singh, was his second in command."

"Could all that just be coincidence?" I frown.

"Possibly," Riya replies. "But we've brought Singh in for questioning, in case."

"Well, great work," I say.

"Thanks."

There's a pause that's just long enough to be awkward. I break the silence.

"And thanks for letting me know. I really appreciate it."

"It's been nice to work with you, Jessie." She hesitates. "Maybe we can meet up in the next few days? With or without work . . ."

I feel my cheeks flush and I clear my throat, flustered. More than anything, I'm aware of Caitlin looking my way, listening while pretending not to.

"I'd like that," I murmur.

We say goodbye to each other and hang up. I move about purposefully, stashing things away in my locker, managing to avoid Caitlin's gaze, even as I bring her up to speed on the theft of the ADS that Riya just reported. Caitlin absorbs the updates and sits down to tie the laces on her running shoes. I take a seat next to her and pull on my boots.

"You're liking working with this policewoman?" she asks, a little too casually.

I shrug, brushing off her look like it's lint on my clothes.

"She's a detective, actually," I say. "And yeah, she's cool."

Caitlin looks like she's about to say something, but she bites it off and turns away from me.

"What?" I ask.

Her eyes come back to mine, thoughtful, serious. "Just—be careful, Jessie. It might not be good to develop feelings for someone related to the mission, again."

I feel my face burn. She's right, of course, but her perceptiveness embarrasses me.

"I know," I say at last. "But it's not like we meet a ton of people outside our day jobs. . . ."

She gives a mirthless laugh of agreement. "Tell me about it," she says, with a sigh.

We let a short pause drag into a silence that feels like it should be filled but neither of us seems ready to fill it. We are sitting side by side, both of us staring at the floor, which should help—not having to look at each other directly.

"Do you get lonely sometimes?" I venture at last.

"Hell, yeah," Caitlin says. "Just . . . someone to have dinner with. Someone to be with at night."

She shifts slightly, her eyes downcast, shoulders slumped. As an only child, I've never known how it feels to have a sibling, but even though Caitlin and I have known each other only a couple of years, it's easy to imagine that she's my older sister. I feel bad for her.

"You'll meet the right guy, Caitlin. You're so great. Just, like, the nicest person. Pretty smart too," I tease as she rolls her eyes at me. "I mean, you *are* getting on a bit . . ."

"I'm twenty-seven," she says defensively. "Just because you're an immature sub-millennial . . ."

"Hey! I'm trying to be understanding. Doesn't come naturally, you know."

"Trust me, I know."

At least I've made her smile, though her eyes are still sorrowful when they meet mine. But then an idea pops into my mind.

"What about a dating app?" I suggest.

Caitlin shrugs. "I guess. Have you ever tried one?"

"No, but it's still a great idea."

"If you do say so yourself," she says dryly.

"Why don't you just pick one and sign up!" I go on, trying to encourage her. "I'll tell you what. When you like someone's profile, I can hack in and Amber could run research just to make sure he's not actually a serial killer or running a porn empire. . . ."

Caitlin stares at me.

"That's what friends are for, right?" I ask, trying to be supportive.

Caitlin groans and puts her head in her hands for a long moment.

"We're just not normal people anymore, are we?" Her voice is small and muffled through her fingers.

Well, I can't really argue with that, so I stay quiet for a bit, thinking, till something comes to me.

"Listen," I say. "I know we're not 'normal.' And sure, every day we put ourselves out there so far that we could lose everything. But at least I know why I get up in the morning. Don't you?"

Caitlin sighs, turning to give me a hug. I can't tell whether I've made her feel worse or better, so I just hang on until she's ready to let go.

. . .

Out in the tech cave, Amber's record player is still turning but it only lets out a soft squeak because the album on it has finished playing. Amber hasn't even noticed, because she can barely drag herself away from the treasure trove of disturbing data that she's managing to excavate from the Cypriot Private Bank servers. But she has to give me some attention, if only to get me organized for my next mini-mission. Once that's done, she races back to her desk, and only when I hit the button for the elevator does she bother throwing me a quick smile and a cheery "good luck."

My first stop is the parking garage under Chen Technologies. I emerge at the private floor. Li's car is still there, as is Amber's scooter, a dinky blue Vespa with a shopping basket on the front. But there's also a van emblazoned with the logo of one of the main domestic power supply companies in London. The keys are in the ignition. It looks realistically unwashed. How it got here and who brought it, I don't know. I am sure it must be someone else who forms part of Li's network, but she chooses to keep us all separate and unaware of each other, which makes sense when I think about it, given the risks of getting caught. Just from the sheer volume of work that Amber gets through, I know she must have a whole team of helpers, but she is always our only contact on the tech side of things.

Getting into the van, I take a moment to get familiar with the stick-shift gearbox and the general layout of the dashboard. Then I tap an address into my GPS and rev my way up the twisting exit ramps of the garage and out into the London traffic that slowly trails its way down the Embankment.

Jake Graham's home is located in Wimbledon, a leafy area of London best known for its Grand Slam tennis tournament. It takes me about fifty minutes to get there, weaving through the traffic over the Albert Bridge and through Battersea. Jake lives with his wife and two teenage boys in a small, detached house on a quiet backstreet. I pull up across the road and scan over the building. Both he and his wife are at work, and the kids are not due back from school till after four. But there is a cleaning lady who apparently comes over twice a week.

I jump down from the van. I'm wearing dark green overalls and a baseball cap supplied to me by Amber. Both are embroidered with the energy company's logo. In my right hand, I hold an iPad in a thick cover. In my left, I hold my company ID, complete with a phone number that a suspicious homeowner can call, so that Amber can use her cut-glass accent to assure them that I really am an employee of South West Power.

The outside of Jake's house is free of CCTV cameras, with only an alarm box on the brickwork outside the upstairs window. I keep my head down, anyway, so that my cap covers my face in case of any bored or nosy neighbors. I ring the front doorbell twice, and it repeats a tinkling chime that feels completely suburban. I watch through the frosted glass panel in the door as a shape approaches from inside the house.

A small, muscular woman opens up. Pale eyes, pale hair pulled back from her face. She's in jeans and a sweater, covered with an apron. She's also holding a microfiber duster cloth and a can of furniture polish, so it doesn't tax my powers of deduction to feel sure that this is, indeed, the cleaner.

"I've come to read the meters," I say. "Gas and electric."

I hold out my ID and her eyes flicker onto it briefly, but she's not terribly bothered and just holds open the door. I suppose that this is one of the safer parts of town and I am a nonthreatening young woman. The cleaner bustles across the hall and throws open the door to a small utility room. Inside, a tumble dryer spins a load of laundry in relentless circles and there, on the wall opposite, are the power meters. She doesn't stop to watch me do my fake read of the numbers, but carries on back to the kitchen, where I hear the tap go on. The laundry room has a small window but it's locked. Casting about, I find the key neatly placed on a shelf beneath it. Quickly, I unlock it and put the key back. Just in case I don't get what I need right now, I'll be able to come back in later.

I pad out of the room and call out. "Sorry, would you mind if I use your loo?"

The cleaner comes out of the kitchen, but leaves the tap running in there. A yellow washing-up glove on her hand drips water.

"Upstairs, first door on the right." She seems a tad annoyed. Maybe she just cleaned it.

"Thanks. Won't be long."

I hurry up the stairs and open and close the bathroom door—but I'm still outside it. I take a hasty glance around. There are obvious bedrooms running off the long hallway, but right at the end is a closed door that feels right. I stride down toward it, my steps mercifully silent on the thick carpet. The door's unlocked, thank goodness, and as soon as I step inside the room, I can see I've hit pay dirt. Jake's office is compact and filled with books and magazines, not to mention towering stacks of old newspapers piled on the edge of a wide, wooden desk. Digital subscriptions don't appear to be his thing. To my left, a small window looks onto the road. To my right, a university degree hangs on the wall, along with a couple of framed newspaper clippings and pictures of Jake meeting political bigwigs. But my attention is drawn wholly to the long wall behind his desk.

It's a chart, but on steroids. The first thing I notice is a head shot of Kit, positioned top and middle. A clipping about Peggy, with a quote of hers highlighted in pink marker, is next to it. From there, hand-drawn arrows radiate out—to other story clippings and a picture of Ahmed, the warlord I killed in Cameroon.

Still more arrows lead to city names written out in capital letters—BELGRADE, CAMEROON, LONDON, TOKYO, MOSCOW, BEIRUT. Some I know all too well, some I've never even been to. There's a bunch of stuff that means nothing to me and a lot that does, but I can't process it because I'm under extreme time pressure here. Lifting my phone, I snap photos of the chart from all angles. There'll be time to analyze it later. Turning my attention to the desk, I stick a tiny microphone under the foot, just in case Jake takes calls in here.

Next, I flip through the notebooks on his desk, taking more photos of the pages. The one that's open is filled with notes and clippings about the attack on Kit's school. Flipping through, I find more charts, and a transcript of a call he's had with a source, in which he's trying to find out who Family First are. It's all fascinating, but spurring me on is the sense that time is passing fast. I need to leave. I'm about to get out of there when my eye is caught by a grainy picture sticking out of another notebook on the desk.

Outside, the birdsong from the trees on the street is temporarily drowned out by the sound of a car pulling up out front. I glance out the window briefly and then do a double take, appalled. It's Jake, getting out of the driver's seat and strolling up to his own front door. Quickly, I open the notebook—the picture is of Caitlin—probably the same photo he showed Kit. Her face is covered with a scarf, up to the eyes, but that doesn't seem to have helped disguise her from Jake; amid the densely scrawled handwriting on the well-thumbed pages is her real name printed out in block capitals. I snap a photo of the page, then put the notebook back where it was. Downstairs, the front door opens and closes. The low tones of Jake's voice greeting the cleaner float up to me. I open the door, just a crack, but all it reveals is the sound of Jake's footsteps tramping lightly up the steps.

I close the door and think. If I come out, pretending I couldn't find the bathroom, it would look like I'm worthy of suspicion, incredibly stupid, or both. It would also mean that Jake would get a good look at me—and he has seen me once before, at the Cameroon embassy with Peggy. Even while I'm having this internal flash debate, I've lifted the window frame. I'm on the second floor, but there are substantial wisteria branches clinging to the redbrick walls, crawling high up the house. I step out the window and use the branches to slow my tumble down into the front garden. Regaining my footing, I stride as fast as I can out the garden gate and across the road to my van.

I fumble the key into the ignition. Inhaling and exhaling deeply, I breathe, calming my racing heartbeat. The engine turns over and I pull out into the road. Using my rearview mirror, I cast a look back at the house. The open window of the study slams down hard, giving me just a glimpse of Jake, still standing behind it. I bang a fist on the steering wheel and curse under my breath. I get the sinking feeling that Jake made it upstairs in plenty of time to watch me go.

15

"EXPLAIN THAT TO ME AGAIN," Li says.

We are in the situation room, and while I sit squirming in my chair, Li gets up and paces the length of the table, pausing only to look down at me like an empress deciding whether to behead a displeasing subject.

"Which part?" I mutter.

Beside me, I feel Caitlin shift, feeling bad for me. Across the table, Thomas studies his nails and Amber keeps tapping on her computer, trying to give the impression she's not even listening to this semi-interrogation.

"The part where you stayed in the house long enough that the reporter who is investigating everyone around you saw you jump out of his window and drive off," Li snaps.

"He didn't see me jump," I protest. "By the time he got a glimpse of me, *if* he did, I was getting in the van."

Li takes a breath in through her nose, holds it for a few seconds, and then lets it out through her mouth. It's a relaxation technique she's recommended to all of us over time. It doesn't seem to be helping her a huge amount just at the moment.

"At least he didn't call the police," Amber chips in, trying to be helpful.

Li rounds on her. "I think that what you *mean*," she says savagely, "is that Jake didn't call the police from his *study*, where we have a bug listening to the room. We don't have a tap on his home phone. He could have called them from there."

I swallow. I highly doubt Jake did call the police, and anyway the van I used is off the road now, spirited away to wherever it came from. It's probably newly spray-painted already. But I don't feel that Li is in the right mood for me to share these uplifting thoughts with her at this exact point in time.

Thomas chimes in: "To be fair, Li, I should have figured out that Jake was on the move. He didn't follow the schedule in his calendar, and I should have kept closer tabs. . . ." It's sweet of him to try to take some of the blame and help me out. But Li's not interested.

"Anyway," I say, mounting my defense. "I stayed back so I could find out what he has on Caitlin. And he has her name. That's important for us to know, isn't it?"

Li just holds up a tired hand as if to stop my stream of thought as she sits down next to Amber.

"That is not all he knows," she states. "Thomas has done a quick analysis of the photos you brought back from Jake's house."

Relieved that we're moving on, Thomas sits up straighter, bringing up his presentation on Jake so that it fills the expansive screen before us. First up is a slide with head shots of the six of us—the three Athena founders, and the three Athena agents. Colored arrows move between the photos in unfathomable ways that remind me of the chaos of Mumbai's traffic.

"Green arrows indicate the connections Jake has already made between members of Athena. For instance, between Kit and Peggy."

"What are the yellow arrows?" Caitlin asks.

"These are connections Jake could make soon with the right intel. For example, he saw Jessie outside the Cameroon embassy with Peggy, but may not have remembered yet or thought it important. He also has your name, Caitlin. You may show up as Peggy's assistant during your stint at the US embassy, and most certainly your military experience will be clear."

He goes on to a more complex graph of our missions and Jake's findings. Li rubs at her temples like her head is starting to ache. Thomas notices and skips on to a quick summary.

"Jake has enough to suggest that Kit and Peggy are working outside the rules to bring down people like Gregory Pavlic, if he wants to think along those lines. The fact that he broke the story about the girls we rescued in Cameroon doesn't help. Also, the fact that Li connects to Kit and Peggy through their work for the UN, back in the day."

I stare at him, appalled. "So, basically, we're screwed?"

Even Amber seems stunned: "Surely Jake can't believe that either Kit or Peggy is capable of taking down a Cameroon warlord or a human trafficker?" she comments.

"Sorry to be devil's advocate," says Thomas. "But I disagree. Kit or Peggy could easily have hired mercenaries to do that work, and in Jake's mind, the photo of Caitlin could support that theory."

Caitlin looks up, her face pale. "What are we going to do, Li?"

"We'll find a solution," she replies curtly. "Everyone has their price."

"I don't think Jake's the type to roll over for money," I say, doubtful.

"You are correct," Li intones. "But that is not what I meant. Everyone has something that is of great value to them, that speaks to their principles. We will find that out about Jake and solve this."

I glance at Caitlin. She looks as uncertain as me about that inscrutable path forward. But Li survived a tough childhood, torn from her parents during China's cultural revolution. Whenever she chooses to turn her laser gaze onto a problem, it usually crumbles eventually. But this feels like it might be beyond even Li's capabilities.

"For now, you both have to focus on Family First," Li instructs. "Luckily, we already have some leads from the Cypriot Private Bank."

"Shall we patch in the team in Mumbai?" Caitlin asks.

"Kit and Peggy are visiting the homes of some of the girls' families at the moment, offering their condolences," Thomas says. "But

I've got Hala on video link now. . . ."

He brings up Hala's face on the big screen and looks up at her, his face breaking into a wide smile. "How are you?" he asks.

I glance at Caitlin. I'm not sure about her, but the last time Thomas asked me how I was, it was only because I'd almost been killed.

"Good, thanks," says Hala.

Li nods to Amber to start her briefing, and we all sit forward to listen, but even as Amber opens her mouth to speak, Thomas chips in with *another* question:

"Are you liking where you're staying?"

Hala looks vaguely embarrassed and tells him it's fine.

Li favors Thomas with a look that just *dares* him to try another bit of small talk. He subsides, his cheeks flushing—but I can't let it go.

"Is the power shower strong enough, Hala?" I ask.

Caitlin chuckles. "What about the sheets and towels? Nice and soft?"

"That's enough," says Li. "Amber, can you remind us why we are all having this meeting?"

"This company that Hassan Shah gave us, AAB, is indeed linked with this repulsive Family First enterprise. Do you want to know how I traced that connection?"

Amber glances up with a touch of pride in her abilities—but Li rains on her parade, waving her on.

"Just give us the highlights," she requests.

"Well, the Cypriot Private Bank has now realized there's been a breach of their servers and have started to plug the holes. But not before I downloaded nearly two hundred thousand documents. We've found out that all sorts of shell companies link back to Imran. He appears to have been a key operative for Family First. At least, his payments go back to early in their history."

"His name comes up on the bank documents?" I ask.

"Well, not quite. He has long used the Cypriot Private Bank not just as a bank but as a trustee—an entity to act in his place—to run his companies in Pakistan. That's how we know it's him. But that same bank is also a trustee for a company I traced to *this* man in India. . . ."

With a click of her mouse, Amber mirrors her laptop onto the colossal wide screen of the situation room, probably devastating Thomas by reducing Hala's video link to a small box at the bottom. The photo that comes up is of an Indian man, with a long, refined face, and thick iron-colored hair swept back from his forehead. He wears a pale blue jacket with an elegant Nehru collar.

"Jingo Jain," I say.

Amber nods. "Exactly. The man whose election swag you found in the warehouse. As you probably already know, he had a distinguished career in the Indian army, served as police commissioner in Mumbai some years ago, and is one of the front-runners in the state's elections, which happen early next week."

"Is he right wing?" Li asks.

"Definitely," confirms Thomas, before Amber continues.

"Having said that, Jingo has gone a bit quiet recently on what he used to call 'traditional family values.' He was certainly very vocal in condemning Family First's attack on our school. But he is on record from a few years back saying that he wanted women excluded from universities, reserving places for the men that 'deserve' them. He's also lobbied in the past for the legal age of marriage to be dropped to fifteen."

"Does he have daughters?" Caitlin asks, genuinely curious.

"Two sons, both in their twenties. One is in the military, the other runs an insurance business. Both seem clean."

"So, is there a direct link between Jingo and Family First?" Li wants to know.

Amber frowns. "Still looking. But I did find one big donation from a Family First shell company to a far-right politician in Pakistan. If Family First are pursuing political avenues as well as terror, I'm sure there will be a connection to Jingo somewhere."

"Then I need you and Caitlin back with Hala in Mumbai," Li says, looking at me. "Check on the schoolgirls and make sure they are safe. And then, since Jingo is the most solid lead we have, find a way to lean on him and see if he's involved with Family First. With these elections coming up, you have to find out if anything else is planned."

It's raining in Mumbai. But this isn't polite British drizzle; this is amped-up, torrential precipitation, fat drops of water drumming relentlessly out of a steel-gray sky. I've fallen asleep on the couch in

Caitlin and Hala's apartment—all this travel back and forth is taking a toll—but the sound of the rain wakes me. I stretch and come out to the balcony, where Caitlin stands watching the water cascade down onto the street. Dusk is beginning to settle soft shadows over the city. Below us, the usual mishmash of vehicles fight each other through a crush of gaudy street stalls, limp and battered by the rain. Lights come on in a temple on a distant hill, and streetlamps glow orange in the gathering gloom.

"Wow," Caitlin says. "This place is really something."

And then, as suddenly as it began, the rain stops—as definitively as if some huge tap in the heavens has been turned off. Within seconds, people start to crowd back out into the street.

"Good timing," Caitlin says, consulting her watch. "We need to head out to meet Hala."

We follow each other down the stairs and onto the road, negotiating oozing puddles and overflowing drains. It's a short drive on the motorbike to the second school, the one in Bandra that all the girls have now been moved into. As we approach the place, we can see guards within the building and outside, hired from the private security firm that Peggy's ambassador friend recommended. Additionally, two policemen in khaki uniforms maintain an official presence, standing on each corner of the block.

Hala is parked outside the school perimeter, waiting for us. She lets us into the iron gates of the school and we walk toward the building through a playground shaded by trees. Before we get very far, two tall men step out like shadows. They are in light combat gear, and holsters sit across their broad chests. These are Peggy's ex-SEAL guys. Our final layer of defense against another attack by Family First. We shake hands.

"I'm Luca," says the taller of the two giants. He has short, curly hair, and a couple of days' worth of stubble coat his chin and throat. He jerks a nod toward his companion, who is clean shaven with night-vision glasses perched on top of long, tied-back hair. He raises a hand in greeting.

"That's Ethan," Luca continues. "We call him Ethan for short."

Maybe that kind of thing passes for hilarious banter in the military. In any event, Caitlin seems to find it funny.

"Anything you need, and I mean *anything*, you holler," Luca says. "Peggy Delaney saved my life once and I'll never forget it."

The three of us look at each other in surprise. I mean, I know Peggy spreads trust and loyalty everywhere she goes—but saving a SEAL's life? I'd like to hear that story.

"Really?" I say. "How?"

But Luca's eyes just crinkle into an enigmatic smile and suddenly he's as tight-lipped as the Mona Lisa. He turns to lead us into the school.

"How are the girls?" asks Caitlin.

"They're back on their class schedule," Luca says. He directs Ethan to keep a close watch on the outside of the building, then he turns to shepherd us through the inside and run us through all the security measures in detail. Caitlin walks beside him while I tag along behind them, next to Hala. As they go, I can hear them start to talk about Iraq and their respective military careers. Maybe it's just me, but shared laughs seem to be flashing between the two of them pretty quickly.

Before we get very far into our tour of the building, though, my phone rings. It's Riya, and she doesn't waste time with pleasantries. In fact, she sounds totally stressed.

"I need to see you," she says.

"What's up?"

"I can't discuss it on the phone."

She gives me the name of a bar where we can meet in an hour.

"They have a terrace," she says. "I'll meet you there."

I confirm, then hang up and relay the contents of the call to Caitlin and Hala.

"Riya's been open with the information flow this far," I finish. "And it sounds like there's a real problem."

"Then you should go and see her," says Caitlin. "But, Jessie—be careful." She gives me a quick smile—a look that makes me wonder what she thinks I should be careful of. My safety or my feelings.

"Of course," I reply, feeling just a little defensive. "You don't have anything to worry about."

16

I HAIL AN AUTO-RICKSHAW AND give the driver the address of the meeting place that Riya has suggested. At the first red light we encounter, I find myself surrounded by little kids begging for coins. They swarm up to me, leaning into the tiny back seat of the rickshaw, holding out their hands, crying, pleading.

The driver barks at them to leave, but they hang on, pushing to get something before the lights change.

"Don't look at them," the driver tells me.

I try to ignore them at first, but I just can't. They are tiny children, with no shoes, unwashed, uncared for, painfully thin. One girl, who can't be more than eight or nine, carries a baby on her hip. I'm not stupid. I know they are most likely owned by a street gang or pimp or trafficker who will take whatever money I give them. But still, as the light turns green and horns explode around me, I pull out a handful of rupee banknotes and pass them around as the driver takes off. Then I turn to watch as the children run back to the sidewalk. My eyes sting with sudden tears, but I blink them back, swallowing hard.

Within a few minutes, though, the rickshaw driver pulls in at the curb and deposits me outside my destination, turning my mind back to Riya. Stepping up to the door, I immediately judge this bar as one of those places that's trying a bit too hard to be cool. It sports a granite exterior, a supermodel doorman, and only a discreet metal plate on the door confirms its name. Having said that, it's a strategy that seems to work for them, because inside, even relatively early in the evening, the place is heaving with bodies. A long bar runs down the right-hand side of the room. On the left, a DJ presides over some serious mixing equipment and loud fusion music. Filling the rest of the space, a crush of people mills around, talking and shouting at each other over the din. I make a quick scan of the room for any sign of Riya, but it's dark enough that I could have worn my night-vision lenses. Weaving my way through the tightly packed clusters of people, I aim for the glass doors at the back of the bar. I slide them open and step out onto a wide wooden deck overlooking the sea.

Out on the terrace, it's still pretty busy, but certainly less jammed than inside, probably because the interior is air-conditioned, while here, the night heat feels like something you can touch—sultry and heavy. But a breeze from the sea relieves the intense warmth a little; an ebb and flow of wind that gently touches my hair and face. Riya's not out here either, but then, I am several minutes early. I make my way right up to the wooden railing that marks the end of the terrace and take a moment to look out at the ocean, glittering under a crisply outlined moon. The smell is not salty or fresh, but humid, with a base note of something rotten. Maybe it's the engineer in me, but I'm getting the sense of a sanitation system and water supply network stretched to their limit in this city where tens of millions of people are crammed together with an overused infrastructure.

I pull out my phone—my current "normal" phone, the Indian number that Riya has—to check for messages, just as a hand touches my arm. I turn to find Riya behind me.

"Sorry I kept you waiting," she says.

"No problem—I was early," I say. Riya looks a lot more relaxed out of her suit. She's in faded jeans and a collarless blue shirt that opens at the neck to display a silver pendant on a leather necklace. Her dark hair is pulled back, and even off duty, her face is free of makeup, which is just as well, because it probably couldn't improve anything about her features anyway.

In her hands are two drinks—she offers one to me.

"Pomegranate soda," she says. "Unless you want something stronger?"

"This is perfect," I assure her, taking a sip. I kind of remember from Li's nutrition sheets that pomegranates are a superfood, but on first gulp I'm not loving it. On my scale, it's somewhere just above cough syrup, but at least it's cold. Again, I find myself strangely nervous around Riya. I grip my drink, focusing on the cool touch of the glass under my fingers.

"Do you come to this bar a lot?" I ask, casting around for conversation.

"I'm not really a bar person," Riya replies. "I like this one because of the view. I like looking out at the ocean."

"You find it relaxing?" I suggest.

"It's a good touchstone," she replies. "It reminds me that life has been going on for millennia and our everyday hassles are not the big dramas we like to pretend they are. Our lives are nothing more than specks, really. Specks in time and space."

"That's comforting."

She laughs. "Maybe cops shouldn't try to be philosophers," she says.

I watch her until she looks away.

"Listen, Jessie, I called you here because I feel something's going on, but I'm not sure what," she says. "I just feel . . . uneasy about what's been happening over the past two days."

"What *has* been happening?"

She frowns. "Well, first, I wanted to follow up the lead you gave me to the warehouse. But Sunil took it over and sent another team out there."

"Did he find anything?"

"It was mostly empty—he said there was nothing much there to help our case or to relate it to the attack on Kit's school."

"It might be true that it was cleared out," I tell her, thinking about the men who arrived and chased us off the premises.

"Fine," she concedes. "But it must be linked to the school attack.

Hassan gave you the warehouse address and he is clearly involved somewhere. . . ."

I acknowledge, but it's still not enough to warrant the stress she seems to be feeling.

"Anything else bothering you?" I ask.

"Well, yes. After that, it felt like Sunil got back on track with the investigation. Because the campaign caps and shirts had Jingo's name on them, Sunil sent me to interview Jingo Jain himself."

That sounds like a reassuring move from Sunil, more meaningful. And yet Riya still looks disturbed.

"Did you talk to Jingo?" I ask.

"This morning," she confirms. "It was weird."

"Weird, how?"

"Usually, I would take someone with me, ideally Sunil. He's senior and Jingo is a big deal in this city. But Sunil said he was busy and asked me to go ahead, alone. So I did."

Waiting for her to continue, I feel a sense of misgiving. If Jingo laid a hand on her, or even *looked* at her, I'll find his home and teach him a lesson he'll never forget. . . .

"Jingo was expecting me. He was perfectly polite and correct," she continues, perhaps reading the unspoken concern on my face. "I asked him a lot of questions about the attacks, about Family First. He claimed he had never heard of them before this and said many times how sad he was about the attacks."

She stops to take a drink, delicately. I do the same but manage to sip at my soda with a graceless slurp through the straw. I hope Riya can't hear it under the music and the chatter of people around us.

"Did you ask him about the ADS and the guy at the military base who signed them out?" I ask.

"Yes, and Jingo seemed shocked that it happened. Claimed to know nothing." She peers out across the ocean, as if recalling the conversation in her mind. "All his answers stacked up."

"So which part was weird?" I probe.

"After I was done with my questions, he went into this whole speech about how he's heard exceptional reports about me, about what an asset I am to the police force. And that it was his intention, once elected, to offer me a series of quick promotions."

"What?" I ask, taken aback. "What does that even mean?"

"I asked the same thing. Honestly, I was shocked," she says. "And he quickly reassured me, saying he thought it would be good for Mumbai to have a woman in a high-up leadership role. And he asked me if I wouldn't want to make a *real* difference, instead of worrying about small cases."

"Small cases?"

"Cases like the school attack. Family First. He said any cop could follow those leads and do that job. But that it would be much better for me to rise in the ranks and be a role model for women." Riya gives a laugh that's not remotely amused and shakes her head.

"So—to be clear," I say, dropping my voice, "he was bribing you to get off the case?"

She looks at me, her eyes wide and focused. "Indirectly, yes, I felt he was. I mean, he tried to make it seem honest and real, but this guy has a very poor track record on women's rights," she says.

"I know," I tell her. "I did some research on him."

In the back of my mind, I'm sure that's why Sunil skipped the meeting with Jingo. He must have known Jingo was going to try to persuade Riya to drop her investigating. She looks at me, reading my thoughts.

"Sunil may actually have been busy," she says, but her voice drops and so do her eyes, away from mine.

I decide to just spit out what I'm thinking. "Do you think there's some kind of cover-up going on?"

"Within the police?" she says, looking away. "Absolutely not."

Well, I didn't mention the police directly. But she did. It doesn't make me feel good. It feels like she's keeping quiet about something, maybe out of misplaced loyalty to Sunil.

"You don't want to believe Sunil is cozy with Jingo?" I suggest.

"I'm not naïve," she says firmly. "But anyone faced with a request from a powerful politician to send me alone might have done the same. It's expedient. It doesn't mean he has any involvement."

That could be true but I'm less kindly disposed to Sunil than Riya is, and considerably more wary of his motives. But I decide it's better to move on and so I ask another question:

"Did you tape your conversation with Jingo?"

She shakes her head. "As soon as I arrived, he asked me for my phone and placed it in a box by the front door. Far from his study, where we met."

"And that didn't make you suspicious?" I wonder, surprised.

"It made me completely suspicious. And that's why, early on in the conversation, while I was still asking about the ADS and whatever, I pretended to have a coughing fit and asked him for some water and some tea." She glances at me with an embarrassed smile.

"I'm not following," I tell her.

"When Jingo stepped out to order the tea from his cook, I did something terrible," Riya explains. "I put a thumb drive into his desktop computer and downloaded the hard drive."

Well, I wouldn't have believed it. Riya, the stickler for due process, sneaking out evidence on the sly.

"Then what?" I ask.

"Then, he came back and I went on with the interview," Riya says. "And when we were done, I asked him about one of the beautiful paintings hanging on the wall behind him. He turned to look at it and I quickly pulled out the drive and took it with me."

"Impressive," I tell her, smiling.

She shrugs. "It was pure instinct. And not something I'm proud of."

"Why?"

"Because what I did completely ignores police procedure and legal boundaries." She turns away from me and leans on the railing that looks out over the ocean. "If everyone just does whatever they think is right, wouldn't the world be in complete chaos?"

That's exactly the question that Kit, Li, and Peggy chewed over before starting Athena—an agency that devotes most working days to breaking the rules set by judicial systems. The irony is that now

Riya looks back at me like she's waiting for my answer to her ethical dilemma. If only she knew who she was asking for advice.

"Here's the way I see it," I tell her. "The terrorists and criminals we're looking for don't follow those procedures or any rules. So, all you're doing is trying to level an uneven playing field. Jingo tried to *bribe* you."

"So, it's okay for me to leave behind my moral code? Why doesn't that make me feel better?"

She looks away again, her dark eyes focused on the inky line far out to sea where the water meets the horizon. I do the same. For a long moment, neither of us speaks, but I am very aware of her arm right next to mine on the railing.

"It's strange that you are the only one I can talk to about this," she says finally.

I hesitate. "Isn't there anyone at home who'd understand? Husband? Boyfriend?"

If Riya notices how clumsy that little probe was, she doesn't show it. She shakes her head, but still doesn't look at me.

"I'm never going to make my parents happy by finding a suitable young man. It's just not who I am," she says simply.

"I understand that," I say.

"Do you?" Her gaze meets mine, earnest.

"Yes."

For a long moment, we just look at each other, and the seconds seem to stretch out painfully, pleasurably. Suddenly, Riya leans toward me. I hold my breath as her lips brush my cheek and linger there for a moment. My face burns. The scent of her is all I can process. Then her hand slips down my arm, a touch I feel in every nerve ending. Her fingers pause at my waist and lift up the edge of my shirt. Her hand touches my skin as she slips something into the pocket of my jeans.

"That's a copy of Jingo's hard drive," she says quietly, into my ear.

Then she turns and weaves between the crowds of drinkers, between the mass of people who are now dancing inside. Within moments, she disappears out the front door of the bar and into the night.

17

AMBER PICKS UP MY CALL but she's not happy about it.

"I'm trying to get to sleep," she complains, before treating me to an audible yawn. "If you need something from me, it had better be chick lit recommendations."

"Really, Amber? I always imagine you reading science journals in bed."

"That's what you imagine when you think of me in bed?"

I actually feel myself blush at that, but the moment passes quickly because Amber starts huffing unhappily.

"My goodness, now *Li* is pinging me every five seconds. What's going on?"

"I uploaded the contents of Jingo Jain's home hard drive to you just now. I copied Li so she'd be sure to get on your case as well."

"So kind, thank you," says Amber, with weary sarcasm.

I can hear the sounds of movement as Amber gets up to check her computer.

"I've got the drive copy here, thanks. How did you get it?" Amber asks, sounding more awake now. "I don't remember breaking into Jingo's house being on today's agenda."

"It was given to me by Riya."

"How thoughtful of her," Amber says. "By the way, I checked her out thoroughly. Her whole story about the orphanage and being adopted is true."

"Good to know," I reply.

"I did it because you clearly didn't think it was important to do a proper background analysis on her. . . ."

"I'm kind of busy out here," I return. "I rely on you for that stuff, tech genius. If I thought Google searches would be adequate for everyone I meet, I'd do them myself."

"Just make sure your *brain* is doing the thinking, not any other part of your anatomy," Amber mutters. "When it comes to Riya."

"Of course," I reply indignantly. She's right, though; I need to take her advice. But still, the impulse to needle her takes over. "Hey, Amber—you're not jealous, are you?" I ask, teasing.

"No, but I am tired," she says. "Is there anything else I can do for you now that you've ruined my chances of sleep?"

"One more thing, since you ask," I say. Briefly I fill Amber in on my suspicions about Sunil, especially since he sent Riya to see Jingo for the express purpose of warning her off the case. "Can you dig around Sunil for me? Personal background, any weaknesses that

Family First or Jingo might be exploiting?" I ask.

"I already did. Give me a second . . . ," Amber says. I can hear her mouse clicking as she looks for the right file. "Sunil Patel . . . lifetime officer, excellent record. Divorced, one daughter, aged twenty-two, recently graduated with a law degree. His ex-wife runs a textile business."

I process that. There's nothing about Sunil that looks particularly dodgy, unless he hates his wife and daughter being educated and independent. Amber is busy murmuring to herself—a sure sign she's fallen deep into the hard drive contents already.

She surfaces for just a moment. "I'll dig into this," she says. "Anything specific you're looking for?"

"I just want links. To Family First, and whoever is behind Family First."

"Don't we all?" says Amber. And then she hangs up.

While Amber gears up to work through the night, I get to drift off for my first full night's sleep in ages, in the comforting embrace of my hotel duvet, feather pillow, and silent air-conditioning. Over in their apartment, Caitlin and Hala get some rest too, and we all meet for breakfast at a buzzing street café that Kit takes us to. Peggy has gone off to a meeting with someone she knows from years ago at the justice ministry. I don't know whether she has a particular agenda, but I do know that part of Peggy's travel is always reserved for building relationships and keeping alive contacts that might help us on our current mission, or future ones.

"*Masala dosa*—a typical South Indian breakfast," Kit announces as she and Hala carry over plates from the service counter, to where Caitlin and I have saved a table the size of a postage stamp. Each of us has a big, round, lace-thin pancake filled with spiced potatoes. On the side is a dish of pale coconut chutney, and a bowl of sambar, a spicy lentil soup.

"Beats eggs and bacon," I say.

"But not hummus and zaa'tar," notes Hala sorrowfully. "That's what we had every day when I was growing up in Palestine."

We all listen, intrigued. This kind of reminiscence from Hala is rare. But she says nothing more.

"Speaking of home," Kit asks her, a little overcasually. "I don't want to pry, but is there any news from your brother?"

Hala hasn't seen Omar since she escaped from Syria years ago. But in the past year, he got back in touch, trying to get asylum in the UK. His request was denied because of evidence linking him to extremists in Afghanistan.

"The pictures Peggy showed us *were* of Omar," Hala says quietly. "But he was infiltrating that group to get information against them."

"Why would he do something so dangerous?" Kit asks.

It's clearly difficult for Hala to talk about, but she is deferential to Kit and all of the Athena founders. There's a very deep respect ingrained in her for anyone who's from an older generation than she is. She would never use the offhand, sarcastic tone with them that she generally treats me and Caitlin to.

"Revenge," she answers simply. "They killed our parents. I hope one day he can tell what he knows to MI5 or the CIA. If he gives them enough, maybe he can come and live with me."

Kit's eyes touch briefly on mine. We're both thinking that her idea seems like an awfully long shot.

"Yes, maybe," Kit replies gently.

In any event, it's good to hear Hala sharing a little more. Her face softens as she thinks about Omar, although her eyes show how desperately she wishes they could see each other again. Caitlin pulls her into an impromptu hug before Hala smiles and pulls away, like she's irritated, even though she's not.

For a few, precious minutes, it feels like we are at a real family meal—all of us sitting together, not talking about work. But the pleasure of that doesn't last long. Before we are even halfway through breakfast, Amber buzzes me a message to say she's found some good information on Jingo's hard drive. We pack up our uneaten food and head back to the hotel so we can call into Athena more securely.

On our video link, Amber looks exhausted, although her eyes are bright as she brings us up to speed. Li sits beside her.

"So, the same shell company that funded Imran in Pakistan showed up on Jingo's hard drive," she says. "But there's no evidence of any money going to Jingo."

Caitlin frowns at me. That's a letdown.

"However, that shell company put shares in a medical company in Jingo's name."

"That could be a payment-in-kind," Kit suggests. "But for what?"

Amber nods. "Thomas is looking into the medical company now. There are links to Chinese entities and illegal drug shipments, no surprise there. And they have a few laboratories under their umbrella, one of which is in Mumbai. I'll get you the address in a second."

"Well done, Amber," says Kit.

"There's more," Li chimes in. "Encrypted on the drive were emails to Jingo from someone signing themselves X."

"A link to Family First?" I ask, hopeful, but Li shakes her head.

"I doubt it. The emails are . . . personal. Intimate. *Graphic*," she stresses. "Jingo appears to be having an affair. The most recent email was only two days ago."

"We don't know who the person is," says Amber. "But we sent her a text offer in the style of social media ads she seems to have clicked on before. And she clicked, letting us install the app we needed to track her GPS."

"And?" Hala asks, impatiently. "Where is she?"

"In a house around twenty minutes' drive from Jingo's home."

The consensus is that going directly to that house is pointless: to create any kind of leverage against Jingo, we would need to catch him there. So Hala and Caitlin head over to Jingo's home to keep tabs on his movements, and also to see if anyone interesting comes in and out. If Jingo was brazen enough to call Riya into his house to subtly bribe her, maybe there are others who might be summoned and who might give us the break in this case that we need.

In the meantime, I'm tasked with going over to the lab that Amber mentioned. The whole medical angle feels a bit out of left field, but it's worth exploring. We've agreed that I can feed the

Mumbai police the name of the medical company and some of the people that Amber found associated with it. But I'll keep the lab address to myself for now, because we'd like to have a look around before the police go barreling in there. Of course, Riya has the same information from Jingo's hard drive, but I imagine that, to get all the clues available from it, she will endure a much longer, more bureaucratic process than Athena's. It's very unlikely that any police team can work as fast as Amber.

As we all part ways to get on with our day, the first thing I do is call Riya, purely because I'm supposed to give her the name of the medical company; not because I'm wondering if that intense moment between us at the bar last night meant anything. Her phone rings, but she doesn't answer. I try texting, just to request a call or a quick meeting. I wouldn't want to put the information I have into a written message. While I wait for a reply, I collect Caitlin's motorcycle since she and Hala have hired a car for the stakeout at Jingo's place. Before I set out, I check the whereabouts of the lab that Amber gave us. The shortest route to it runs pretty close to the police station. Since there's still been no reply from Riya, I decide to stop by her workplace, deliver the information I have for her, and then go on to the lab.

It's insanely busy outside the police station in Juhu this morning. Several squad cars are parked outside, and people mill around, arguing with uniformed officers. Some of them hold placards. From my sweep of the local news this morning, it seems like election fever is gripping the city ahead of voting day, which is the day after tomorrow. Demonstrations and marches have been springing up. I'm guessing that the police have broken up at least one of these and that the bedlam outside is the result.

It seems intelligent to park my motorbike farther down the street, away from the chaos. I'm just removing my helmet, and about to take off my leather jacket, when I see Riya emerge from the police station. She slips on sunglasses, runs lightly down the steps, dodges the protesters and the barrage of traffic, and heads out to an unmarked car parked on the sidewalk across from the station. I hit redial on my phone, hoping to catch her before she leaves. But she just glances at her phone, declines the call, then gets into the car.

Well, that's annoying from the perspective of the investigation, but it also leaves me with a depressing feeling of personal rejection. Was I imagining that there was some kind of spark between us last night? But now my phone pings. It's Riya.

Stuck in meetings

Yeah, right. Putting my helmet back on, I zip up my jacket and rev up the motorbike. Before she leaves, Riya puts on a baseball cap—inside the car, where it's not exactly sunny. It's troubling. Together with the sunglasses, it looks more like an attempted disguise. Within seconds, I'm weaving my way into the morning traffic to follow her. The traffic is bumper-to-bumper, but finally we turn onto a highway where the cars are moving. My one consolation is that, so far, we are heading in the same general direction as the lab. Frankly, I feel a bit daft just taking off after Riya like this, so I'm not planning to waste too much time on it, but I can let it play out for a short while. I cruise along far behind her, changing lanes frequently so that she won't spot me.

It's not long before she slows down, making a turn into a smaller street. I settle the bike behind two gaunt cows being walked along the side of the road. Ahead of me, Riya pulls into a tired-looking car rental office bearing the proud signage "Kwality Kars." Amber would break out in hives at that spelling. The establishment has only five cars, all of them generic white Toyotas, parked out back. I watch from my vantage point down the street as Riya chats with the young guy at the desk. Within a couple of minutes she is outside, pulling the cap down over her eyes and having a glance around before slipping into one of the rentals.

I feel my pulse quicken. At the same time, a bitter wave of disappointment rises up inside me. She must be up to something if she doesn't want her own car seen wherever she is heading. I snap some photos of Riya getting into her fresh vehicle and then I'm off again, behind her. This time, the ride takes only seven minutes and I'm more than a little stunned by where we've ended up.

Riya stops on a main street outside a row of dilapidated shops, and then walks down a few blocks toward a single, detached building. She looks around her as she reaches the place, like she's worried to be seen. There are no signs on the building, but on my GPS street map, that block is identified as "India Laboratory." Exactly the address that Amber gave me to investigate.

18

I FEEL LIKE I'VE BEEN punched in the stomach. What is Riya up to? Has she been lying to me all this time? Watching from a safe distance, I track her as she paces around the side of the building to a heavy metal door with a keypad on it. She pushes at the door, but it's clearly locked. The whole place is quiet. No sign of anyone coming in or out, no sign of activity through the windows. Right at the back is a weed-infested patch of tarmac that could probably act as a parking lot. But although it's a working day, there are not even any cars parked on it, like you might expect from a place full of lab technicians or researchers. Only a single white van sits there, alone, unattended. On it is the logo of a cleaning company.

I move the motorbike, trying to protect it from the scorching sun by parking under a tree that cascades feathery green fronds into the road. Then I pull off my helmet. Riya has disappeared around the back of the building now, and I hurry to follow her. She's checking out the white van, trying to open the rear doors, and not having much luck. All of this reassures me somewhat, dampening down my suspicion of her. It's not like she has a key to the place, or knows the way in. I decide to accost Riya directly and get to the bottom of things. When I stride boldly around the corner, into the parking area, she stares at me.

"What are you doing here?" she asks.

"You gave me the hard drive. The info on it led me here," I say, just a little indignant. "What are *you* doing here?"

"Same," she says briefly.

"Really?" I ask, wanting to believe her. "I figured the police would take longer to work it out."

"They would," she says dryly. "Which is why I stayed up last night and figured it out myself. Is that why you were calling me earlier?" she continues. "To give me this address?"

I wasn't going to share it with her, but there's no point in antagonizing her, so I nod. "Among other things. Don't you have a warrant to get inside?" I ask.

She looks at me a long moment, her eyes tired. "I didn't ask for one. I took the drive illegally. Normally, I'd trust Sunil with what I did, but since he sent me to talk to Jingo, I'm just unsure whether to go to him with every lead. I covered my tracks coming here too."

I can understand her hesitation.

"So, what's our plan?" I ask, scanning the building. It's only two stories high, made out of concrete blocks, with small windows set into the gray walls at regular intervals. Bland, utilitarian. Not one of the windows is open, and all of them are barred.

"*Our* plan?" Riya asks with a quick smile. "That's presumptuous."

"Let's be honest—you're going to need all the help you can get from someone with brilliant skills."

"I guess until she shows up, I'll make do with you," Riya returns.

"You're very funny," I tell her.

"And you're very arrogant," she replies. "What about the roof? I see a chimney or something up there."

"Looks more like the top of a furnace, or incinerator, maybe for medical waste. . . . Let's look for the back entrance. There must be a place where they take in supplies or whatever."

We both walk around to the other side of the building. Sure enough, there is a garage-sized door. But it has no visible handles or locks, only another keypad by the side of it. It doesn't respond to my attempt to slide it up either. Great. I look up at the walls, trying to figure out where the power supply to this door is. There's a small chance that cutting the electricity would mean we could drag it open manually. Meanwhile, Riya walks back toward the parking area, frustrated.

"You know, that van back there doesn't belong to a cleaning company," she says.

"How do you know?" I ask, following her back to the vehicle.

"The telephone number on the side is fake," she says. "I tried it. And look at this."

She points through the front window and we both peer in. On the floor, peeking out from under a pile of garments, is something that looks very much like the butt of a pistol. Jammed into the pocket by the driver's side is a sophisticated walkie-talkie kit. And nothing else. No cigarette packets, gum, newspapers, religious icons on the dashboard—none of the normal, everyday stuff that you would expect from people who might use this vehicle to go from job to job, if they were actually cleaners. There is one more thing in the front, though. We both spot it at the same time and exchange a look. It's a small remote-control unit, the kind you use to open garage doors. I lean down to unlace my boot.

"What are you doing?" she wants to know.

I just smile while I pull out the shoestring and rapidly tie it into a firm loop right in the middle, a loop that looks like a tiny noose. Riya watches as I hold the long ends of the string apart and work the shoelace—and the loop—into the top corner of the van's door.

"Didn't they teach you this in the police academy?" I ask.

"How to steal cars?" she returns. "I must have been sick that day."

Moving the shoelace back and forth, I make it slide down so that the loop is inside the car where I can maneuver it into place till it hooks onto the end of the lock mechanism. It's an aging van, with an old-style lock that you push down or pull up with your finger. With a quick tug on the loop, the door lock pops up. Riya opens the door, raising an eyebrow at me.

"I really wonder about your past, Jessie," she says, taking hold of the remote.

"I'm just resourceful," I assure her. "And I watch a lot of 'how to' videos."

"So do I," she says. "But usually things like 'how to make fresh pasta.' Not 'how to be a criminal.'"

Eagerly, she presses the button on the remote, and the door slowly rises open. Riya pulls her gun out of its holster before we step in. Just because the place *looks* deserted, doesn't mean it is. If nothing else, the driver of that van might be inside.

We've entered through a delivery door that leads into a storage area. Stacked white metal shelves fill the room. There is nothing on them, except a couple of empty cardboard boxes and a carton of disposable gloves. Creeping farther on, into the main part of the ground floor, we find a couple of large science labs, but they don't feel like a place that's processing blood tests for the general population. The long workbenches and white laboratory sinks look much the same as the storage area—empty and abandoned. Riya runs a finger through a thin film of dust on the lab benches, showing that they've been unused for some time.

But from the floor above us, there's sound. We freeze, both of us glancing up at the ceiling. Footsteps perhaps? Silently, I lead Riya back toward the storage area, toward a staircase we passed back there. When we get to the stairs, she takes my arm and draws me back behind her, indicating that she's the one with a weapon. I do have a knife in my boot but decide that this isn't the best time to show off about it, so I fall back and follow her as she moves silently up the concrete steps.

We reach the second floor. Ahead of us, the space is mostly open plan, with regular lab tables and stools. At the back, two men in jeans and T-shirts move around. Crouching low, we stay back near the stairs and watch them. One man is around fifty, gray-haired but stocky and muscled—clearly someone who takes his gym time seriously. The other is taller and younger with a head of thick, swept-back hair. The young one is passing documents through a small paper shredder that sits on one counter. The older guy wears long protective gloves and works at the other end of the space, moving in and out of some kind of walk-in refrigerator that sports a thick door and a digital temperature gauge.

"Can you see what he's doing?" Riya whispers.

"He's getting stuff out of the fridge—little tubes. He's packing them." I don't dare to lift my head any higher, but not getting a proper look at the action is driving me nuts. It certainly appears that these two are busy clearing out whatever is being stored in this lab. As if to bolster my theory, the younger guy comes walking back out to the benches closest to us. Quickly, I pull back and hold my breath, and feel Riya do the same. Ever so slowly, her hand comes up to her jacket pocket and she removes a compact mirror. She holds it out and uses it to watch him.

Not twenty feet from us, the young man opens drawers and pulls out more paper. Leaving the drawers open, he goes to the back and starts shredding them. In the meantime, the other guy opens the door to an incinerator and starts tossing tubes and vials into it. I lean out and use my phone to snap some pictures of both of them.

"We have to do something," Riya whispers. "They're destroy-ing evidence!"

Before I can answer, before I can even *think*, she stands up, strid-ing into the room, her gun out in front of her. I stay in my place, crouched down, and listen, horrified, as she crosses the room.

"Police," I hear her say. "Put your hands where I can see them."

The only response to that is a series of gunshots.

19

I SCRAMBLE UP FROM MY hiding place by the stairs, trying to find Riya and trying to stay low at the same time. She's hiding on the floor behind a lab table, still holding her gun. I scoot over to her, drawing another shot from the younger man, before the older guy yells something and the shooting stops.

"Are you hit?" I ask. She shakes her head. I can tell she's spooked by the near miss, though. Her breathing is fast and shallow, her eyes wide. The footsteps of the gunman move closer, slowly, surely. Two things about this situation freak me out. First off—faced with an armed police officer, these men didn't surrender. Even worse—since Riya didn't shoot them when she could have, they've probably figured she's a soft target.

In any event, if we just wait here like sitting ducks, we'll both be splattered across the floor of this lab in about three seconds. I propel myself out from behind the lab bench and barrel into the legs of the younger man, tackling him to the ground. His gun hits the floor as he does, skittering away, out of reach of both of us.

Clambering on top of him, I use my legs to keep him pinned down and on his back while our arms and hands flail at each other, looking for contact, for grip. A bullet fires toward me and I roll over, lying flat next to my opponent.

The *other* guy's waving a gun now. Riya emerges, shooting at him so that he drops, taking cover near the incinerator before chancing another shot from back there. Riya scoots forward, trying to get closer, and I hear her shouting out a frantic stream of Hindi. A reply crackles over her police radio. But I don't have time to process, because I'm scrambling to get back on top of my guy. Even though he's lying on the floor, and I'm back on top of him, his strong arm keeps me at a distance. With his free hand, he aims a fist at my jaw, which I mostly dodge, then jams his huge palm up against my chin. My teeth rattle together and he makes me bite my tongue, but apart from that, his stupid move helps me. Because at least one of his hands is busy. I punch down on his nose, then his eye. Only then do I have a split second to pull my pocketknife out of my boot. I flip it open and hold it against the hipster stubble that coats his throat.

"Stop moving and turn over," I say. He rolls onto his front. "Put your hands behind your back." He obeys.

In the meantime, Riya is crouched behind her lab table, and the gray-haired guy is out of sight, hiding out by the incinerator. She keeps talking to him, probably trying to convince him that there's no way out. With a cable tie, I bind the hands of my captive, retrieve his gun from under a counter, and I signal Riya to keep the conversation going. Then I creep across the room so I can get to the other guy from behind, where he won't expect me.

Suddenly, her police radio fires up—a rapid stream of Hindi and English mixed with earsplitting amounts of static. I use the noise to cover my footsteps, and quickly move up behind the older man, placing the weapon I retrieved from his friend against his back. It's enough to paralyze him. I take the gun out of his hand and pass it to Riya, who turns to keep her weapon trained on my captive.

From outside, the whine of approaching sirens floats into the lab.

"You called for backup?" I ask her as I tie the hands and feet of my new captive. My eyes are scanning the tables and counters between the refrigerator thing and the furnace—I'm trying to trace the path the older guy was taking. The heavy door of the fridge lies open, and the inside, lit with eerie LED lights, is empty. But the box that he was packing sits just below the counter, on the floor. He must have put it down here when the bullets started flying. It's a sturdy metal container covered in skulls, crossbones, and warning stickers.

"What is this?" I ask him.

"Please, I don't know," he replies, his voice shaky. "I was told to get rid of it."

Riya comes closer to look at it with me but, behind her, something catches my eye. It's the younger man. He's up and running for the door. Riya turns and bolts after him. I hear them clattering down the stairs. Briefly, I consider helping. But she's armed, he's not, *and* his hands are tied. I'm quite sure she can handle it. So, I turn and grab some long disposable gloves from a box on the counter, and flip open the metal container. Within it, cushioned by specially made foam inserts, are several smaller boxes, each sealed, each marked with the same labels—a bunch of codes that mean nothing to me. Outside, police cars screech into the street and the parking lot. I hesitate for only a second, then I pull out just one of the smaller boxes. I wrap the box in as much gauze and cotton as I can find, then put everything into a sterile glove and tie that all up with tape and shove it into my jacket.

Leaving my captive tied up on the floor, I go to the front window and glance down at the parking area. The young guy is sprawled on the ground, surrounded by armed officers. An unmarked car pulls up and Riya's partner, Sunil, emerges. I notice that Riya doesn't hang around to talk to him though. She disappears back into the building, fast. I hurry to the top of the stairs to meet her.

"Why did you call for backup?" I demand.

"Are you serious?" she asks. "What else should I do? I was fighting two armed men, with you, a civilian. I nearly got you killed!"

Before I can answer, Sunil's voice barks up the stairs. I follow Riya down, and we are both treated to her boss's annoyed stare following us as we descend. He sniffs and turns to give orders to two uniformed officers behind him.

"Seal this place off with tape. No one goes up there till we know what we are dealing with."

"There's another guy up there," Riya says.

Sunil sighs and gives further instructions in Hindi to the officers, then turns a stern glare onto me next.

"How did you get mixed up in all this?" he wants to know.

"Following my own lead," I say.

"Why?"

"Why?" I shoot back, unfazed. "Because that's what Kit hired me to do."

"What lead? Where from?" he demands. I don't even glance at Riya. The last thing I want is for him to suspect her of helping me in any way.

"You might want to get everything in this lab down to the station for processing as evidence," I reply. I'm just trying to dodge his question, but the look on Sunil's face reminds me that there's possibly nothing more antagonistic than telling a senior police detective how to do his job.

"What lead did you follow?" he repeats, slowly. As if I'm too daft to understand him.

"I'm sure you'll find your answers," I say, sweeping my arm to indicate the lab. "If you have any more questions, arrest me," I continue. "Otherwise I'm done here."

Behind Sunil, Riya gives me a pained look at my aggressive tone. But I really want to get out of there and find out what I'm carrying around buried in my jacket. And I'm gambling that Sunil didn't get where he is by wasting time teaching lessons to mouthy young women. Still, he *does* look as if he'd like to handcuff me and throw me in a cell. But instead, he turns to Riya, and takes his irritation out on her.

"I told you to come to me with *anything* you find," he berates her.

"I know, sir."

"But *you* know better, it seems. One whole *year* as a detective, and *you* are the Sherlock Holmes of this force. . . ."

"I felt so sure . . . ," she begins.

"You *felt?*" he yaps. "Don't feel. We are not in the psychic business. We are not some Bollywood film where the heroine *feels* the answer. This story does not end by you running into danger and being a hero."

Ouch. I try to give Riya an encouraging look, but her eyes are downcast.

"I'm sorry, sir," she mutters.

"Did it occur to you," Sunil continues, "that I might be piecing together this part of the puzzle already?"

She looks up at him, surprised. "No, sir."

He grunts, like she just proved his point. "You know, detective work is slow and painstaking. This hotheadedness is not an asset."

"I understand, sir," she replies.

Sidling slowly toward the door, I decide this is a good time to get out of here. Sunil notices my shuffling and turns and fixes me with a pointed stare that I return with a quick smile. But he doesn't stop me from exiting. I turn to take a last look at Riya to send her a silent message of support, but she doesn't meet my eyes.

Outside, I walk quickly past the cops in the parking lot and run across the street. Getting back on my motorbike feels like freedom. But I'm still very aware that I'm carrying around a little package of god-knows-what in my pocket. I drive as carefully as I can through the traffic tumult of central Mumbai, calling in to speak to Thomas along the way.

"Tell me," he answers.

"I've got something I took from the lab."

"Where is this 'something'?" he inquires.

"In my pocket."

"Good grief," he says. "Is it sealed?"

"Yes. I need to find somewhere to take it for testing," I tell him.

"Just sent you an address," he says. "Want directions piped into your comms unit?"

Well, that was quick.

"Yes, great," I reply. "But, Thomas? It can't be some random lab—who knows what's in this thing?"

"Random?" repeats Thomas, sounding mortally offended. "This is one of the city's most sophisticated university research labs," he continues. "Peggy knows the owner and I've just asked if they will both meet you there."

"How did you manage all that so fast?" I wonder, relieved.

"It's called the art of anticipation," Thomas explains patiently. "I knew you were scheduled to explore a lab this morning. That meant an outside chance you'd find something that needed testing."

"Thanks," I say, impressed. "You're the best."

"I'm sure Amber would disagree," he says. "Anyway, good luck. And let me know how it goes."

• • •

If the lab I just left was eerie and downright dangerous, the one I pull into feels like a happy contrast—calm, safe, bright, efficient. I pull up to the front door and am immediately greeted by a shy young woman in jeans and a lab coat, who looks like she's been posted there for the express purpose of meeting me. She does not engage in any small talk but immediately directs me to a back entrance. There, right inside the doors, I find Peggy herself, accompanied by an imposing man around Peggy's age.

"This is Ajay," says Peggy, introducing me. "He owns this lab and has been a dear friend to me since the days when I was leading trade delegations to India."

Ajay chuckles. "More years ago than I care to remember," he says. I hold out my hand to be polite, but he does not shake it.

"Apologies, ma'am," he says. "I do not mean to be rude, but we do not know what you are carrying, or to what contaminants you may have been exposed. We must take all necessary precautions."

Peggy shoots me a worried glance as we follow him inside. Around us a small team of people in protective aprons, masks, and gloves gathers, and they walk with us down a series of corridors.

"Where are we going?" I ask.

"We have labs that are level three biosafety areas," he tells me. "Until we know what gift you have brought us, it is better to be safe than sorry."

We are shown into a room that features a secure area on the other side of a glass-and-steel wall. That section seems to be accessed through a series of small chambers that look like air locks. One person is already in there, standing around in what looks like a full hazmat suit.

"How does all this work, Ajay?" asks Peggy, always curious.

"Our staff enter without any clothing," he says. "They go through to a shower room, then into a changing area where they then dress in decontaminated scrubs on the other side."

Ajay has me follow exactly that procedure. I step into a closed chamber, remove everything I'm wearing, underwear included, then pass through the shower, and help myself to scrubs. The little box is the only thing I can take with me, wrapped up as it was when I left the lab.

Once I'm into the sterilized side of the lab, I'm instructed to leave my mystery package on the counter. Then Ajay directs me to come back to his side. On the other side of the glass, we watch the suited technician painstakingly remove the gauze and protective packaging and unseal the small box. Inside is a tiny metal vial.

"We will take it from here," Ajay says.

"How long do you need to analyze it?" I ask.

"That is hard to say until we know what it is. Ideally, we must run it through a full centrifuge-type process that separates out the tiniest particles. It takes time, many hours. But we will run it overnight, so there should be news in the morning, if not before."

"Thank you, we so appreciate this," says Peggy. Ajay turns to me.

"I am afraid we will also have to incinerate all your clothing as a precaution," he continues. "You can keep these scrubs and wear them to go home. But before you leave, we will take swabs and blood tests. Just to be sure you have not been infected."

Well, that little speech makes me anxious. I pull Peggy aside.

"Riya, the police detective, was also with me at the lab," I say.

"Then I think you need to ask her to come in and go through the same protocol," Peggy says. She steps over to Ajay, letting him know that he has one more person to decontaminate.

In the meantime, I text Riya, trying to make it clear that this is important. She messages me straight back to say that she will come over at once. I write back:

Good. I'm sure Sunil will understand

Her reply flies in:

He doesn't have to. I'm suspended

20

"MY PARENTS ALWAYS WANTED ME to become a doctor," Riya notes as we sit side by side on a long row of chairs, waiting for the results of our medical checks and blood tests. Ruefully, she looks down at the green medical scrubs that we've both been wearing since our clothes were tossed into a furnace. I'm not much for fashion, but I was gutted to lose my leather biker jacket. It was a vintage piece that Kit had bought for me in Portobello market.

"How'd they feel when you joined the police?" I ask.

"They weren't thrilled about it," she replies. "But I've been obsessed about fighting for justice since I was a child."

Her fingers tap nervously on the arm of her chair.

"I'm sorry you got suspended," I venture.

"It's my own fault," she says softly. "I broke into a lab without a warrant. And Sunil doesn't even know the part where I met you in a bar and gave you a thumb drive full of information that I stole from a politician's home. None of it is really standard procedure."

"Standard procedure can be overrated," I say.

"Trust me, I'm learning that," Riya returns. "But I'm a police detective. Not some rogue agent. Or private investigator, like you."

I try not to smile at that. Riya's police training and instinct to circumvent process might actually be a great combination if she worked at Athena. But right now, she's completely angst-ridden about losing her place by Sunil's side.

"How long did he suspend you for?" I ask.

"A week. And it goes on my record," she sighs.

The sound of footsteps ringing down the hallway makes us both look up. It's Ajay, brandishing two sheets of paper and wearing a reassuringly wide smile. Peggy left the lab before Riya arrived. She and Kit have things to do, plus there's no need for her to come into contact with anyone from the police.

"Ladies," Ajay announces, "you will be delighted to know you are both all clear. No sign of contamination, pathogens, or anything else."

Riya and I exchange a relieved smile as we shake hands with Ajay. He escorts us to the back door of the clinic.

"Make sure to keep me informed if you develop any reactions or symptoms," he says. "But I suspect everything will be fine."

We both thank him as I collect my motorbike and Riya hails a cab.

"What are your plans for the rest of the day?" I ask her.

Her eyes turn away, to the street, watching the constant blur of passing traffic while she considers.

"I'll go home to get some clothes," she replies. "Then, I suppose I'll stay at home. And think about the fact that Family First is busy plotting terrible things while I sit around and do nothing."

"Well, at least you're not feeling sorry for yourself," I say. She hits my arm in response.

"What are you going to do?" she asks.

"Once I'm out of these scrubs? I was going to eat lunch. Are suspended cops allowed out for lunch?"

"I believe it's acceptable." She smiles.

"But before that, I have one little thing to do . . . just routine. Want to come?"

"Something to do with the case?" she asks.

"Yes," I say. Her eyes stay on mine as she hesitates. "What are you thinking?" I ask.

"I'm thinking that Sunil told me not to come to work," she replies. "But he didn't actually say anything about staying off the case."

I don't want Riya to come with me to my hotel, in case we bump into Peggy or Kit. So under pretense of saving time, I let her go home in a taxi to get changed, and arrange to pick her up outside her apartment an hour from now so that we can travel together to my errand.

As soon as I reach the hotel, I throw on some cargo pants and a shirt, and let Peggy and Kit know I'm back. Then I check in with Hala and Caitlin.

"How's the stakeout on Jingo going?" I ask.

"Like watching paint dry," Caitlin complains. "Hala's gone out to get us some lunch. Jingo hasn't left the house. Amber intercepted an email from his girlfriend, though. He has a date at her place later tonight. I'll need you for that."

"Sure thing," I confirm.

"How are you?" Caitlin asks. "Your morning sounded more exciting than ours."

"You'd rather be shot at in a lab filled with horrible poisons than hang out in your car eating Indian food?" I ask.

"I think here, it's just 'food,'" ponders Caitlin, missing my point.

There's a knock at my door, so I hang up with Caitlin. I check the peephole—it's Kit. Opening up, I find her in a subdued but graceful flowing tunic that falls low over matching pants. It's an Indian-style ensemble that looks elegant but tells me that she's heading to another funeral or set of condolence rites. Without saying anything, I just offer my mother a hug. She clings on, emotional. When she pulls out of the embrace, her eyes search my face. Her hand comes up to touch my jaw, where a slight bruise is forming from the glancing blow I took in this morning's fight.

"What happened?" Kit asks.

"Did Peggy not bring you up to speed?"

"She did. But I mean, what happened to your chin? What's this bruise?"

There's a good reason we don't share that level of detail all the time. Kit is clearly stressed and anxious. I have no idea how to deal with her questions. If I ignore them, she'll get upset. If I address them in too much detail, I'll freak her out.

"Jessie?" she persists.

"You know how these things go," I say lightly. "Half the time you're watching us through our lapel cams."

I'm not super keen to share with my mother the intimate details of how I feel every time I dodge a bullet or a knife. How I attacked the guy this morning. How I wasn't 100 percent sure I wouldn't be hit when I ran out into the path of his gun. Those details alone could drive her back to the solace of vodka, for all I know.

"Mum, you're just feeling fragile because of the girls who died. It's understandable . . ."

"Are you even wearing the bracelet I gave you?"

I wonder at how desperate Kit is, that she's clinging to the superstition that her magic wooden beads will save me. Maybe that's what we all do when things feel shaky. Cling to whatever we think we can control. I look at my naked wrist, then remember.

"I'm sorry, Mum. I had to give it to the lab. They incinerated it. Procedure."

Kit nods. "I suppose that's safer," she says, but she doesn't look like she really believes it. She seems seriously upset. I'm relieved when there's a knock on the door of my room.

"That'll be Peggy," Kit mutters. "I have to go."

Riya's wearing jeans and a white blouse, maybe not the best ensemble for traveling on the back of a motorbike. But the afternoon is warm and muggy, and I keep our speed down as we head toward Bandra. Riya hangs on tightly on the turns, and a few times, she directs me onto side streets that help us cut the route shorter. As we drive down quiet residential roads, with lush vegetation on each side, we pass many older villas with verandas, wooden shutters, and arched windows. I slow down so we can take everything in. It feels good to be together, without any pressure, without anyone else.

When we finally get closer to Kit's school, we park nearby. Riya stays on the bike for a long moment after we stop, and I stay there too. Her arms remain around my waist. Gently, I bring my hand up to cover hers, and for a moment our fingers intertwine. I feel as if my heart might stop—and it nearly does but in a different way when a low, male voice says my name, inches from my ear.

I spin around and find myself face-to-face with Luca, the former Navy SEAL. He raises his hands with a grin.

"Sorry, didn't mean to scare you," he says. "Ethan clocks anyone who parks on this block and your bike showed up, so I came out to see if we had anything to worry about."

"No, it's just me," I say, trying to get over my inner fluster caused by the handholding with Riya. "I need to see the headmistress for a few minutes," I say.

"Jaya? She's in her office," Luca says. "Come on, I'll take you over."

In the meantime, Riya has swung off the motorcycle and

removed her helmet. I introduce her to Luca, explaining to her that Kit has hired private security to watch over the girls. We both follow him across the street and into the school grounds.

"The girls are back on their timetable. Nothing strange has come up on our watch yet. I feel good about security," Luca tells us. "We're still not letting them out in the playground though."

"Sounds smart," I comment.

"You bet." Luca nods.

On the front steps of the school, I pause and take a look around again. The building is set back from the street, but the road that runs outside it, the one we parked on, is really busy. Beyond the road, over on the other side, low apartment blocks rise up; the top layers of them overlook the playground. Colorful scarves, saris, and shirts hang from lines on each level of the blocks, like festive bunting. Posters for various political candidates are plastered haphazardly over any free wall space and a lot of telephone poles. Trees are scarce, but satellite dishes and complex tangles of wires are everywhere. It looks like some of those apartments are using those wires to cadge electricity off others, which is not the first time I've noticed that happening in this city. When I turn back, Luca's tying on a paisley-print bandanna.

"Like it?" he asks.

"Very cool." I feel like I've seen a similar one recently. "Where'd you get it?" I ask.

"Caitlin gave it to me," he says with a grin.

That makes me smile too. Caitlin has a stack of these and wears them herself once in a while. Now that she's passing them around to certain handsome SEALs, I'll have something to tease her with to pass the time at tonight's stakeout.

We walk inside but before we get very far, Jaya herself ricochets out of her office and into the large foyer, bounding toward us.

"How wonderful to see you," says Jaya, shaking hands all around. "I hope all is well?"

I assure her that everything is fine.

"How can I help you?" she asks, turning to lead us inside. Luca raises a hand to say goodbye and disappears back to his post. Not wanting to waste time, we both step in to walk beside Jaya. I nod to Riya to go ahead.

"It's just routine, ma'am," Riya says. "We have a couple of pictures to show you."

"Not a problem," says Jaya. "Let's step into my study."

Inside the office, the blinds filter out the harshness of the afternoon sun, but the room still feels cheerful. A couple of saggy armchairs look well used, and there's a desk covered in paperwork, china cups, and biscuit packets. Jaya offers us tea, coffee, snacks—but we politely decline, eager to cross this task off our list and be on our way.

"What did you want to show me?" Jaya asks.

I hold out my phone and flick through the pictures of the two guys from the lab.

"Have you seen these two men before?" I ask. "Take your time."

While Jaya peers them, I take in the walls of her snug office.

They are covered in artwork made by the pupils, showing what they want to be when they grow up. Riya joins me and our eyes range over them. The scale of the girls' ambitions makes us both smile. Some want to be astronauts, others scientists, doctors, explorers, songwriters. . . . For a moment, I feel—well, not pride, exactly—but appreciation. That Kit has offered these young women the chance to learn, to study, to aspire to be something in addition to wives and mothers. But inevitably, it sharpens the loss too, of the eleven girls who have had their lives and their dreams snatched away by Family First.

Jaya scoots behind her desk to retrieve wire-rimmed glasses, then she returns to study the pictures again.

"They do look familiar . . . ," she says.

Riya shoots me a concerned look. "Are you sure?" she asks the headmistress.

Jaya sniffs, uncertain. But she keeps studying the photos. Before long, she gives a decisive snap of her fingers and looks up at us.

"I've got it. They're the doctors. I didn't recognize them without their white coats on."

Tension floods through me. From Riya's brisk, urgent tone I can tell she's stressed too.

"What doctors?" she asks. "Where?"

"They came here. To both schools, in fact," Jaya says, looking first at Riya and then at me.

"Why?"

"It was only for the vaccines," she explains, keen to reassure us.

"This was long before the attack. Maybe two weeks before . . . Here, let me look up the date. . . ." She bounces behind her desk and Riya follows, on top of her like a ton of bricks.

"Never mind the date right now. Please. What vaccines? Injections?" Riya demands.

"TD. Tetanus and diphtheria. There have been so many diphtheria outbreaks in the city that when they offered them to us, I decided it would be safer to get it done than risk the girls falling sick."

Riya almost collapses on the desk, as if her legs have given way. Her gaze turns to me, and it's filled with fear.

"Jessie?" she breathes as Jaya stares at her, then whips a questioning look over to me.

"Don't worry," I say. "We'll figure this out."

That's what comes out of my mouth, but inside, I've hit full panic mode. Those men at the lab, the ones Jaya recognizes, are not doctors. Or if they are, they are not trying to make anyone well. Nor does it seem likely that they work for any legitimate vaccination clinic.

"I have to tell Sunil," Riya says, her tone desperate. "He has them in custody. He can push them for information."

"Someone please tell me what's happening?" Jaya interrupts.

I look at her. "We have to get blood tests done on every one of the girls."

21

JINGO'S HOME IS RELATIVELY MODEST for a man of his political stature; a compact, white bungalow with a decent-sized garden in the front. Palm trees and bushes fill every part of the yard except for a thin, paved pathway that leads down to imposing iron gates that separate the plot from the street itself.

The early-evening light is golden, the heat less intense than it was during the middle of the day—but I can't enjoy it. I sit in our rental car, keeping an eye open for Jingo, and all I can think about is the schoolgirls. What was in those injections that the two lab goons put into them? It's been nearly an hour since Caitlin arrived at the school to change places with me. Between them, she and Luca are watching over doctors from Ajay's lab as they take blood samples from each girl for testing. They will rush the results, but every minute seems to drag as we wait.

"Cait?" I ask over our comms. There's a brief pause before she responds.

"Jessie, we're on it," Caitlin replies patiently. "First batches of blood got back to the lab thirty minutes ago. They should have something for us soon."

In the side mirror of the car, I watch Hala, far down the street behind me. She's standing at a colorful street cart hung with garlands of marigolds. I watch her pull out some rupees and offer them to the vendor. He chats with her while he slices the tops off two bulging green coconuts, puts straws into them, and hands them over. Cradling them in her arms, she comes back to the car and hands one to me.

"Coconut water has electrolytes," is her sales pitch.

"I don't want it, thanks," I say.

"Did I ask?" is Hala's charm-filled reply. "Drink it."

I drink. The freshness of the cool liquid on my tongue feels like relief. Hala watches me while she sips too. If nothing else, it's calmed my breathing, just by making me swallow a lot. And the truth is, I was getting thirsty.

"Better?" she asks.

I nod my thanks. The sun is slowly sinking behind houses and the last, crimson rays glitter on windows and sparkle on the windshields of cars in driveways. It's coming up to seven thirty; about the time that Jingo should be leaving for his 8 p.m. extramarital rendezvous. Sure enough, within a few moments, his front door opens and he gets into his car. During the day he has a driver hanging around, but I have no doubt that he prefers to do this kind of excursion on his own. Hala watches him pull out, then waits for several other vehicles to pass and fill the space between us before she follows.

As we drive, Caitlin's voice comes in over the comms:

"Blood tests are still in progress, but so far they're showing nothing."

I'm relieved but also doubtful. "Are you sure?"

"I mean, they do have the diphtheria and tetanus antibodies," she says. "But nothing else. So, it looks like they were clean vaccines."

"Did they check for everything?"

"All the basics," Caitlin confirms. "A couple of the girls are low on iron; normal stuff like that. But there's nothing sinister that cuts across all of them. This is just first-round, basic testing and they still have more detailed tests to do. Stuff that takes longer. But it's a good result to start with, Jessie."

Hala looks at me with a brief smile of relief.

"Feel better?" she asks.

"A little," I say, trying not to scowl. But the truth is I don't feel completely relieved about the girls. I'm still wary. The men who had access to them just shot at me in the lab this morning, so something is up. We just don't know what it is yet, what clue or information is hanging there, just outside our reach. I look out of the window, keeping my thoughts to myself while Hala negotiates the traffic. It is great the blood tests were clean, and yet . . .

"What's the matter?" Hala says.

I don't have an answer for her, but out of the blue, I come up with the word that sums up how I feel right now. Dread. But what I'm dreading and why, I really have no idea.

Up ahead of us, Jingo turns into a side street and parks his car. We stay on the main road, hidden by the constant flow of pedestrians and traffic. This is not the address we tracked on the cell phone. But it seems that Jingo's just taking precautions. When he exits the car, he's wearing a cap and glasses, which create an effective disguise. He walks back in our direction, onto the main road, making sure to look around him discreetly. But he can't see us. Hala has tucked our car behind a busy street stall selling hot fried samosas. Jingo hails an auto-rickshaw and we watch him get in and instruct the driver.

We continue to trail Jingo for another ten minutes or so, through streets that twist and turn, finishing up on a residential street that feels quiet and wide; expansive and expensive. The rickshaw stops about a hundred yards ahead of us. We park and watch. Jingo pays the driver and waits for him to leave before crossing the road and heading into the driveway of a detached house, enveloped by overgrown bushes and trees.

"Let's go," says Hala.

As we exit the car, I put in my night-vision contact lenses. They have the added benefit of turning my own green eyes a murky shade of brown. It's not a full disguise, but it's something. Immediately, I can see Jingo's outline, small in the distance, going to the back door of the house, which opens and shuts briefly to let him in. We circle around toward the house, trying to decide the best way in.

Once whitewashed, the exterior of the place is now faded, coated with layers of peeling paint. But the structure itself is beautiful—a wooden, two-story home with plantation shutters at the window frames and a porch that winds around the sides.

"I can't see any cameras," Hala says, glancing at me for my opinion.

"Me neither," I reply. Maybe Jingo realizes that the smart way to cheat on his wife while upholding family values is to not leave any digital evidence that he was ever here.

We pad quietly up to the house. The rooms are dark except for one on the ground level, and one on the floor above. We check out the downstairs room first, through the window. It's empty and a subtle glow of lamplight illuminates an expansive living room filled with beautiful paintings and antiques. A fireplace, set ready with kindling and logs, completes the country club look.

"He must be upstairs," I whisper. Hala nods, pointing up to a very low light issuing from a room on the top floor. It's to the rear of our position in the grounds below. We walk around to the back door that Jingo used to come into the house. It's not a hard lock to pick, and it leads us directly into a clean, tidy kitchen.

Moving stealthily past, we both pull up neck scarves to cover our mouths and noses, then climb up wooden stairs that are worn with age, and also creaky, even at the edges. I signal Hala that we might as well go faster. If they hear our feet on the groaning steps, it's best not to leave much time for them to panic about it.

Quickly, we run. Hala goes ahead of me, turning at the top of the stairs and opening up the only room with a thin bar of light under the door. I have a knife at the ready, while Hala has her phone out, taking video. Jingo is certainly in a compromising position but, funnily enough, it's not with a woman. A young man, slim and with a delicate, beautiful face, looks up at Hala and me. So much for Family First's anti-LGBTQI+ stance.

Jingo takes a moment to process and then he's up, snatching his pants from a chair next to the bed. But before he can get a leg anywhere near them, I push him back onto the mattress and show him my knife, keeping it close to his throat. Hala is busy turning his young companion toward the wall so he can't watch us, pulling his arm back behind him so that he feels it will break if he moves. He whimpers but complies.

With my free hand, I rummage around in Jingo's trouser pocket. Inside is his phone. I message my own burner handset from it, then text back a little attachment that will give us access to everything on Jingo's handset at all times. Then I turn my attention back to Jingo himself, keeping a knee pressed to his chest. He watches my blade, gleaming in the lamplight. Dim lighting is supposed to be kinder to people, but he looks older up close, his eyes wide and strained, his body lean and pale, without much hair on his chest and legs.

"Tell us about your links to Family First," I say.

Jingo hesitates, then clears his throat, like a politician about to give a speech. "As I have said on record, I am shocked by their terror tactics and condemn them in the strongest possible—"

He stops talking when I carve a line in his chest, drawing blood just from the top layer of skin.

"Let's stop wasting time," I suggest. "Does a company called AAB Enterprises ring a bell?"

Jingo watches, dismayed, as the blood rises to seep out from the cut on his chest. He begins to shiver now, perhaps from the pain, but more likely from my question.

"They paid you," I continue. "By putting shares of a medical company into your name."

"Not in my name," he says. His eyes slide away from mine.

"My mistake," I reply. "The shares are in the name of your shell company. You know the one—it uses the Cypriot Private Bank as a trustee."

Jingo looks at me again, his eyes wider now and more anxious. "Who *are* you?" he asks.

Well, obviously, the information flow is only going to go one way here, so I ignore that question.

"We have enough to send you to prison right now," I say. "Not to mention pictures and video that will make you a beacon of hope for the LGBT community in India. So, do you want to talk, or play games?"

On that, the young man tries to make a break from Hala.

"Give me those pictures!" he mutters, going for her pocket, looking for her phone.

Hala doesn't take kindly to that. She kicks him behind the knees so he hits the ground, and cuffs him on the head, twice, till he falls flat. He lies there, arms spread out, too fearful to move, but she keeps her boot on his head for good measure.

Watching his boyfriend get a little beaten up seems to affect Jingo and loosen his tongue. His breath becomes ragged, audible shreds of sound that follow the rise and fall of his thin chest.

"I need immunity. I want to know I'll be safe."

"You're not really in a position to bargain," I point out.

"What are you hoping?" he asks, his voice shaky. "To stop Family First?" He smiles but it's not a happy look. More like a wide-eyed grimace. "Their power base is growing internationally."

"Who is behind them?" I ask.

"A few, very powerful men."

"Names?"

"You think they give me their business cards?" He laughs mirthlessly. "They are deep in the shadows."

"Where are they based?"

Jingo hesitates. "Here. Pakistan too."

"Who do *you* report to?"

"Nobody. All communication, from the start, has been through low-level bankers, lawyers. . . . Even with them—it's not like they deliver checks by hand or come anywhere near me. It would look bad for me and make their strategy too obvious. They fund me very indirectly, because we believe in the same things."

"Do you really?" I ask, puzzled. "How would they like a picture of you and your lover here? I mean, they're bound to notice it when it hits the front page of the *Times of India*, right? And right before the election."

"I'll make you a list of everyone I know that's connected," he offers. I let him up and switch on my recording app.

"Spell out all the names," I instruct. "And give me where you met them and when. And any addresses you have."

He rubs his temples, trying to gather his thoughts, and starts talking into the phone. When he's done, I put the knife back at his neck and address the bigger issue that's troubling me.

"What does your medical company do? What goes on at India Laboratory?"

He looks surprised at the question.

"I've never even been there. I don't know and I don't care. It turns over ten million dollars a year. It's just a payoff from Family First, a way to get money to me without transferring funds into a bank account."

"What else is planned against those girls at the school?"

"Nothing," Jingo says, his voice breaking. "I'm set to win the election. The truth is that the bombing of the school last week boosted my numbers and made me the front-runner. I doubt Family First needs anything else. Now, I've told you everything I know," Jingo rasps. "I want to see you delete those pictures."

"They're on a remote server," I say. "Where they will stay till you've given us more."

The color seeps out of his face, making him look ghostly.

"What more?" he asks.

"Find out what was being manufactured or stored at the India Lab. And why it was being destroyed. I need detail."

Jingo gives a pained sigh. "I'll find out what you need to know.

But I have to be subtle. Give me a day or two."

"No," I reply. "You have till eleven a.m. tomorrow. At one minute past eleven, those pictures will hit the desk of the editor of the *Times*. And then they'll be uploaded to the internet."

He looks like the hope has drained out of him. But he nods in agreement, so I let him up and he reaches for his shirt. His hands are shaking so badly that he can't get his buttons done up. Hala hands him a burner phone.

"We'll be watching you," she says.

We get out of there like we're chasing a land speed record, just in case Jingo thinks to try to follow us or call for help. Even as we rev our car away, back into the heart of the city, Hala calls Jingo on his new burner phone. He picks up straightaway and she reminds him once more that he works for us now. He agrees, his voice heavy and hoarse. However, the word of a man like Jingo is probably worth less than a couple of rupees, so Caitlin heads over to watch his house. She'll make sure he spends the rest of the night at home and keep tabs on anyone who might come in or out, in case he calls on Family First for help. Meanwhile, I check in with Amber.

"I've sent you Jingo's list of contacts that he spilled."

"Oh, lovely," she says, genuinely excited. "I'll get on it right away."

"And I gave you access to Jingo's regular phone," I say.

"Yes, got it. Thomas is already watching every call, message, and email," she confirms. "Right now, he's texting his wife to say he's done with his campaign meeting and heading home."

"Campaign meeting, yeah right." I sniff. But then I notice a message on my Indian phone. "Listen, Amber, I've got to go. Let me know what you find."

The message is from Riya. Naturally, I had my sound alerts turned off while we were busy breaking into Jingo's pleasure palace, so I didn't notice it come in.

The message is weird, though. Just a location pin that opens up to a block right behind a hospital in Juhu. Nothing else. I try calling Riya but the phone just rings and rings before going through to her voice mail. I text her back, asking for more, but no reply comes. I show it to Hala.

"Is it a live tracker?" she asks. "Does it mean her phone is there?"

I shake my head. "No, it's static. Like, she's sent me this address."

"If someone else has her phone this could be a trap," Hala says.

"Or she could be in trouble."

Hala considers. "Direct me," she says. "We'll go together."

22

THE HOSPITAL SPRAWLS OVER A couple of city blocks. There's definitely a lot of coming and going at the emergency room. But, for the most part, the place has quietened down for the night—presumably visiting hours are over.

While Hala parks the car off a side street nearby, I try calling Riya again. Still nothing. The location pin guides us away from the main entrance of the hospital to a road that runs down the left side of it. Bypassing the hospital itself, it leads us around the back, past massive waste bins, past a delivery bay, and into a back alley that ends in a fifteen-foot-high chain-link fence. Beyond the fence is a section of the hospital that is mostly unlit. And, wouldn't you know it, somewhere in there is where the pin lands.

"What would you do without me?" Hala says, grabbing hold of the fence. Her feet seem to find tiny bits of traction on the small holes in the wire—but she moves so fast that even when I get to watch her, it's hard to figure out how she manages it. Within ten seconds, she has scrambled to the top. She pulls a small coil of black rope from her pocket, drops the climbing line down to me, and helps me up. Getting down the other side is a lot easier because I can hang down by my arms till I'm only ten feet off the ground. Hala jumps first, landing with grace. I follow, stumble, and dust myself off as we tread our way carefully toward the pin location. Now that we are over the fence, the alleyway leads into a dilapidated building, streaked with grime, and sporting a number of broken windows. There's a sign above the threshold. Hala flicks on a flashlight so we can read it:

Post Mortem Center

Hala looks unhappily at me. It doesn't make me feel great either. But more than my vague dread of walking into some kind of hospital morgue, I'm filled with worry for Riya. What could have happened to her? A breeze picks up, rattling dry leaves on the trees that line one side of the alley. On the other side a nondescript car is parked; an old Honda. The engine is still ticking slightly as it cools down, leading me to the brilliant deduction that it was parked here very recently. I take a picture of the license plate before we creep inside the front door and past an entrance hall where the wall paint peels down in tired flakes. Beyond that is a gloomy corridor that leads into rooms that look like morgues and labs. Neither of us is eager to explore down there unless we really have to. We turn to scope out the opposite side of the corridor. That passageway leads to an exterior door, which in turn leads out into an open courtyard.

Hala switches off her flashlight—because the exterior door is propped ajar and someone is outside it, hanging around. We edge closer as male voices, low and urgent, float over to us. We get within a few feet of the open door, then pull back as a burst of light suddenly floods the courtyard, illuminating the outlines of three men. One of them has opened a large furnace, and flames dance up inside, hissing into the night air. He shuts it again, making a comment to the others. Not far from them on the ground are two long objects wrapped tightly in layers of dark cloth. They are each about the size and shape of a human being. My heart drops, thinking about Riya. But both the bodies are tall and hefty—they feel more like men.

The fizz of a match inserts another small point of light into the dark, as the guy who opened the furnace now lights a cigarette. He's dressed in a stained hospital uniform, as is the man next to him. They take turns pulling on the cigarette until the third guy, who's in a rumpled suit, gets impatient and turns to them. He's wearing a germ mask over his mouth and nose, and dark-framed glasses. Even in the dark, I recognize him.

"That's Sunil, Riya's boss," I whisper to Hala. I give her a desperate look.

She gets it. Even though she's been taking photos with her phone, we need a better sense of what's going on here. She leans in, whispering in my ear.

"I'll get them to move."

"Okay." But I stop her before she turns to go. "Do you have gloves?" I ask.

Of course, she does. Those pockets of hers are a treasure trove of handy items, perfect for those nights when you unexpectedly end up hanging around mortuaries trailing dodgy police detectives. She fishes a thin pair of silicone gloves from her cargo pants, hands them to me, then disappears back into the morgue. In the meantime, I lean in, closer to the open door, so I can hear what's going on—not that any of these men seem particularly chatty.

Aggressively, Sunil picks the half-smoked cigarette out of the other guy's mouth and tosses it onto the ground, stamping the heel of his shoe onto it for good measure.

"Get going," he barks.

"Yes, sir," replies the uniformed man. He opens up the furnace and heads for the wrapped bodies on the ground, gesturing to his pal for help. In my head, I beg Hala to hurry up with her chosen diversion. The two guys lift the first bundle, struggling under its weight. With grunts and groans they shift it toward the furnace, before managing to drop it on the ground with a graceless thud that makes even Sunil wince.

"You idiots," he says. "You're morgue workers. I thought you throw bodies in here all the time."

"We've had a long day, sir," says the smoker, slyly. "This is over-time. We are tired."

Irritated, Sunil pulls a bunch of rupee notes out of his pocket and peels off a stack, then waves them at the men—actions that show up beautifully in my lenses and on the photos I'm taking with my phone.

"Here's a bonus. But hurry up," he clarifies. Then he looks off to his left.

"What's that smoke?" he asks the men. The two of them look up, eagerly taking the opportunity to lower the wrapped body to the ground once more.

It's Hala's smoke bomb. It's silent but it creates a ton of smog— so much that people are rarely tempted to ignore it. I watch them all panic, easing on my gloves and pulling up my face scarf while I wait.

"Go and check," Sunil instructs the men. It's like the two of them are competing for Laziest Employee of the Month. They slope off so reluctantly that Sunil is forced to follow, herding them toward the smoke, pulling out his gun as insurance. That gives me the chance to stride up to the furnace. It's obviously a place for incinerating remains. I look unhappily at the wrapped bodies on the ground. I really don't want to do this. But I have to.

Gingerly, I pull back the covering over their faces and the sight makes me recoil. Holding my breath, trying not to heave, I snap more pictures. It's hard to describe, but whatever it is that killed them clearly caused them to suffer. Their eyes bulge from their sockets, and the dried remains of spewed blood and foam crust around their mouths. Covering them up again, I toss my gloves away and move back inside the morgue, where Hala arrives to join me.

"What did you find?" she whispers.

Before I can answer, Sunil's voice rises out in the courtyard. He's back with his apathetic morgue workers and he's giving them quite the tongue-lashing. Under pressure, they hustle the first body into the furnace and then start hauling the next.

Since it looks like their work is nearly done, Hala and I hurry back through the reception area and out to the alleyway.

"I need to get into the car," I tell her. I'm assuming that junk heap outside the morgue does belong to Sunil. If he is on the take, he's certainly not splurging his extra cash on a sensational set of wheels. I'm carrying a tool set that has a couple of options for me to lever my way into the vehicle, and Hala offers up another—a long, thin bit of plastic, similar to a ruler. I take that one and nod my thanks.

"Stay over there and cover me," I say, pointing to a large waste bin near the fence. With a parting good-luck pat on my shoulder, Hala disappears while I get to work breaking into Sunil's car. I get myself onto the floor of the Honda's back seat just moments before Sunil hurries out of the morgue.

23

FROM MY CROUCHED VANTAGE POINT in the back of the car, I watch Sunil approach. His spare frame is huddled into his jacket and he frowns as he glances about him. He pulls off the germ mask he wears, tosses it onto the ground, and unlocks the driver's door. I drop low. He sits heavily into the car and takes a moment. A big, exhausted sigh fills the interior, creating a patch of breath steam on the windshield. Sunil lifts his glasses off his nose, rubbing at his eyes tiredly.

I shift up from the back, reaching around to place a knife blade at his throat.

"Put your hands on the wheel," I say.

He does so, but he clearly recognizes my voice, because he turns his head, just a little, to try to catch a glimpse of me.

"Not you again," he complains. "I've had enough of you stalking me."

Sunil clearly believes there's no other way I'd have found him here, and I don't want to drop Riya in a pile of shit and get her fired. So I keep quiet, but that infuriates him even more.

"Tomorrow morning, I will put a restraining order on you so fast your head will spin," he threatens.

"Go ahead. Arrest me now," I suggest. "Take me down to the station. I'll be happy to explain what I've seen here tonight."

Sunil makes a grunting noise that sounds almost like a laugh.

"I'm attending to police business," Sunil says.

"*Please*," I say with a disbelieving snort. "Pulling out wads of cash and paying people off to burn bodies? Not much due process there."

"Can you put that knife down?" He sighs. "As irritating as you are, even you strike me as intelligent enough not to slice the throat of a police detective."

I move the knife back but keep it out and ready. Gingerly, Sunil shifts in his seat, turning so we can see each other better.

"May I?" he asks, pointing to a pack of cigarettes sitting on the passenger seat. I stare at him, amazed. What, like we're buddies now, hanging out over a smoke?

"No. I hate the smell," I say. "And you'll die an early and painful death."

Sunil sniffs unhappily. "That's what my mother told me when I joined the police," he says with some measure of irony.

"Speaking of early and painful deaths, what happened to those men?" I ask, moving on. "They were the same men you arrested this morning at India Laboratory."

Sunil nods. "We questioned them. They wouldn't talk. They were scared."

"Of what?"

"Reprisals from whoever they work for. That is what I surmised," he replies. "So, I had them transferred to a prison nearby for more *intensive* questioning."

His eyes meet mine, giving me the unmistakable impression that "intensive" is a polite term for some kind of coercion.

"But when they were taken out of the police van," Sunil continues, "they collapsed, right there on the street. Before the uniforms escorting them could even get them inside. They died on the spot. Within a couple of minutes."

"They were killed?"

He chews at his bottom lip, scowling. "Yes and no. I mean, they were not shot or stabbed. But they both died of some internal disease at exactly the same time."

"That doesn't strike you as unlikely?" I ask.

"It strikes me as something to be concerned about," he returns.

"What disease?" I push.

"Nothing the prison medical examiner could identify. But he felt it might be contagious, so I was asked to dispose of the bodies."

"At night? For cash?" I ask.

"We cannot afford a panic in this city," he says evenly, "and even less can we afford an actual outbreak of some unidentified virus. The Centers for Disease Control in the US opened an office here.

But it has a handful of people to cover an area populated by hundreds of millions. There are no meaningful resources for this kind of thing. So, in the real world, this is how it gets dealt with. Orders of the police commissioner himself."

Part of me doesn't want to believe him, but part of me knows he might be telling the truth. In a world where law enforcement is always overstretched, and oversight is lax, shortcuts happen. Sunil reaches for his cigarettes, and lights one, without asking me this time. He drags on it like it's the taste of relief. With his first exhale of putrid smoke, a real shudder passes through his thin shoulders.

"Why are you telling me all this?" I ask.

"Because I'm not covering anything up. Except," he adds, "for the cover-up I just explained to you." He has the grace to look embarrassed about the irony, at least.

"Where's Riya?" I ask.

"I suspended her. After your joint antics today." He seems unconcerned about her. "Why?"

"No reason. I need her home address," I say.

"I'm not going to hand out the address of a police officer. I don't trust you," he says.

"I'm devastated," I reply, deadpan. "But back to Riya. I'm really concerned. She's not answering her cell phone."

I cough from the acrid cigarette smoke that's filling the car. Like a real gentleman, Sunil winds down his window and flicks his half-finished cigarette outside. Then he picks up his phone and scrolls down. "Here," he offers. "This is her home number. That's all I can give you."

I get out of the car and he starts the engine and reverses back. But before he drives away, he stops to say one more thing.

"If you speak to her, tell her I asked about her," he says. "She's a good cop. And she'll be even better if you leave her alone to do her work."

I call the number that Sunil gave me before Hala and I even make it back to the car. It's an immense relief to hear Riya's voice when she picks up.

"Jessie! Are you okay?" is the first thing she says.

"Fine," I reply.

"Are you sure? I've been terrified something happened to you since I sent you that address."

"Why aren't you answering your phone?" I ask.

"It's smashed. And your number is in it."

"Smashed? How?"

She hesitates. "Listen, can you come over to my place? Something is happening but I can't figure out what."

Before we hang up, Riya gives me her home address. Hala refuses to let me go there alone in case Riya is in trouble or being coerced into something.

"Well, it's better she doesn't see us together," I say.

"I know," Hala replies. "You can go in without me. I'll wait outside in case you get into trouble."

While she waits, Hala will update the team on the developments with Sunil. I'm doubtful that what we saw is enough to press charges against him. Who knows what extracurricular work a police detective can get up to in this city without consequences? But Sunil's late-night bonfire still felt like it involved getting rid of evidence.

I chew on all this while Hala does the driving. Nighttime softens the edges of Mumbai. Small fairy lights wind around temples and trees. Naked lightbulbs illuminate men taking cups of tea or liquor at street stalls. Car headlights sweep past the prone bodies of the homeless lying under scraps of tent on the street. I look away. There never seems to be a time when the city is completely asleep, but it's getting late enough that at least some of the main roads are not so jammed with cars. It doesn't take long to reach Riya's home— a long, thin apartment block in Andheri West. Hala pulls the car into a driveway that leads up to the block and parks up by the entrance to an underground garage that seems to serve its residents.

"Switch on your comms if you need me," she tells me. "I'll be here."

"Thanks," I say. "Keep your doors locked."

"Are you afraid for me, or the idiot who tries to mug me?" she says, with a glimmer of a smile.

I smile back and close the door.

Coming into the building foyer, I find only a bored-looking porter downstairs. It's easy to walk briskly past him and head into the elevators, where I follow Riya's earlier instructions to go to the tenth floor. She opens the door almost as soon as I knock, as if she's been standing around waiting. Behind her, the television plays some American superhero show. For a moment, I just take Riya in. In jeans and a soft green shirt, she looks fine, unhurt, not jittery. I feel the fear and tension that I've been carrying around all night drain out of me.

"Well, listen," I say, coming inside. "Thanks for sending me over to a morgue while you hung out at home and binge-watched trash TV."

I smile and she laughs but then winces, doubling over in pain.

"Don't make me laugh," she breathes. She straightens up, slowly, her face creased with pain.

"What happened?" I ask, shocked. "Riya?".

"I'll explain." Walking gingerly, she leads me into a galley kitchen, where a kettle is just starting to boil on the stovetop. She reaches up to get cups off a shelf, but she stops mid-movement—even that is too much for her. I grab the cups, switch off the stove to kill the insistent whistling of the kettle, and take her arm gently.

"What happened?" I ask again.

In reply, she lifts up her shirt and I flinch. Her stomach and torso are covered with red marks—early bruises, by the looks of them. I've suffered so many over the past year or two that I've gotten to know these marks intimately well. The bruises look like they were inflicted very recently, no more than an hour or two ago.

"Let's get you to a doctor," I say. "What if you broke a rib?"

She waves off my concern. "No, I broke a rib once. This is not like that. I think I'm fine."

"Well, you need ice," I tell her.

"I've been using the frozen veg," she says, indicating a defrosting packet of sweet corn on the countertop. There's a small freezer on top of the fridge behind me. I pop some cubes out of a plastic tray, wrapping them in a damp tea towel. She takes it and holds it under her shirt.

"Who did this to you?" I ask.

"I don't know. I was home, and it was driving me crazy, being stuck here, not being able to question those men we arrested at the lab. Anyway—late in the afternoon, I called in to speak to Maneesh, one of my colleagues."

She putters about while she talks, going for the kettle. I take it from her and make some tea, while she continues her story:

"Maneesh is a good guy, we get on. I asked him if these men had confessed anything. And he told me they were dead. Both of them. He didn't know much more than that, so I told him why I thought it was important to the case. I asked him to find out more."

She leads me back out to the living room, where I leave our cups of tea on top of a day-old newspaper that sits folded on the dark, polished coffee table.

"And then?" I ask.

"He called me back, right before I messaged you. He'd over-heard Sunil taking a call from the police commissioner, and he thought Sunil was going to the morgue. And so I decided to go over there myself and find out what was going on. Confront Sunil if I had to. But I never made it. I sent you the location pin to start with, thinking that I'd call you on my way, to explain. But when I went down to the basement garage, as soon as I got near my car, two guys jumped me. One put a hood on me and held my arms, the other one punched until I collapsed on the ground."

I feel sickened at the idea. "Did they do anything else? Hurt you . . . in any other way?"

"No, nothing like that," she says, but her eyes don't meet mine. It feels like she's holding something back, but I plow on with questions.

"Did they say anything?"

"They warned me to stay off the case. Or I would die." She shrugs. "That was all they said."

"In English?"

"In Hindi," she says.

"Did you see them?"

"No. I mean, the guy punching me had gray sneakers on—I could see his feet, looking down, where the hood opened."

We both know that's not much to go on.

"What happened at the morgue? Did you find anything?" Riya asks. I recap my encounter with Sunil, both by the furnace and later in the car.

"So everything he said holds up?" she muses.

"It seems that way," I admit. "But there's still something rotten going on here. I just can't figure out what it is."

Again, her eyes drop, away from mine. I pass her some tea and she holds the cup. There's a long pause. We both watch slim tendrils of steam curl off the top of the liquid and disappear into the air. She sips at the tea and shifts a little.

"What are you keeping from me?" I ask, out of the blue.

She looks at me. "What?"

"When I asked you if they did anything else to you . . . it felt like you were hiding something."

She puts the cup down and pushes back her hair, out of her eyes. Then she ties it back. Then she gives all this attention to a loose button on one of her shirt cuffs. Lots of fidgeting and zero eye contact. My gut fills with misgiving.

"It's not what you are thinking," she says. "They didn't really touch me other than the punches."

"Then what?" I ask.

She gets up and opens a window, even though just that movement must be painful, then sits back down beside me. Outside, thunder simmers, crouched and grumbling. The scent of coming rain hangs there between us; metallic, intense. Then, suddenly, she reaches over me to switch on another lamp, and the light is soft and warm, and the sudden, fresh scent of her is right there, all around me. I don't know how it happens, but I just lean across and touch my lips to her neck. Her skin is warm and soft against my mouth, and I close my eyes and kiss her again, just there. Riya's hand comes up to caress my face, to look at me, and her eyes go to my mouth. Without thinking about it, I move closer, toward her mouth, to kiss her.

Riya pulls away, fast.

I sit back, away from her, wishing that the ground would open up and just swallow me whole. Anything to get me out of there.

"I'm sorry," I say, flustered. "I'm an idiot. I don't know what I was thinking. . . ."

Her hand goes to mine, taking hold of my fingers.

"It's not that, Jessie," she says. "Really, it's not. It's just that—they *did* do something else to me." She reaches for her cup but her hand shakes so much that she puts it back down.

"They gave me an injection," she continues. "That was when they told me I would die if I didn't drop the case. I don't want to kiss you, Jessie, because I don't know what I have, how it's transmitted, or when it will kill me."

24

THE SORROW IN RIYA'S EYES, the belief she has in her impending death, breaks my heart. My first thought is that she needs an immediate blood test. But there's no reply at the lab, and so I take the liberty of calling Ajay on his cell phone. He answers sleepily and listens while I explain my concern.

"We have the blood you both provided to us when you brought in the vial. But Riya will need a new test, since this just happened," Ajay says. "My people are working, but the technicians don't answer the phones at night. I'll come over, let you in, and we can take her blood for analysis. For safety, we should get yours checked again too."

Over our comms, I explain the plan to Hala. She heads home while Riya and I take a taxi to the lab, where Ajay arrives just minutes after us. He takes Riya through the whole decontamination ritual again just to be super safe. Once our blood tests are done, I drop Riya home and finally, around 1 a.m., I make it back to my hotel.

Up in my room, I'm too keyed up to sleep. I run a bath and try soaking in it, breathing, trying to release the tension in my neck and shoulders. Getting into bed, I close my eyes, which are gritty with tiredness, but sleep evades me like a shadow I can never put my hand on. I pull up the sheets and turn onto my back. Thin slats of streetlight filter through the blinds on the windows, painting bars of pale yellow onto the ceiling above me.

I check my phone again, hoping for some word, some outcome. Ajay promised that his team would work around the clock on those samples we brought in from India Laboratory, and also on the next round of blood tests for the girls and now Riya. But those tests involve advanced equipment and they will take time. Staring at my phone won't make that time go faster. What does come up, though, is a message from Amber, on my Athena handset. It's marked green, meaning it's not super urgent, but I call her up on our video link anyway, wanting something to think about other than Riya, the schoolgirls, and what might be floating around in their bloodstreams. Amber answers straightaway, and Li comes into the picture, settling into the chair beside her. In front of them both are numerous boxes of Amber's favorite Thai takeout.

"So, those contacts Jingo gave you are indeed relatively low level. But terribly helpful," Amber says. "One of the lawyers is Muslim—and Muslims form a minority in India but a majority in

Pakistan. That made me focus on him and, sure enough, he has a bigger office in Pakistan, in Lahore. And that office has links to both Imran and a General Khan in the Pakistani army."

It feels like progress, but I can't see what kind of progress yet. "How does that help us?" I ask.

"I won't bore you with the details," says Amber.

"First time in history," I cut in.

"Very amusing," she continues. "Without real evidence, we're working on the theory that this general could well be one of the top people in Family First. So far it's panning out."

"Can we bring him down?"

"If our investigation continues to stack up, then yes."

Li chips in. "But, Jessie, that would take weeks and months, waiting for local governmental and secret service process to complete. That still leaves us vulnerable to Family First in India, especially if they elect a candidate like Jingo, and especially if his medical company is involved in something underhand."

"Got it. So you want me to go full steam ahead," I confirm.

"Yes, but I've reviewed your sleep data for the past week," Li adds. "It's highly unsatisfactory. I recommend you try to meditate now and get a few hours of quality sleep."

"I'll do my best," I reply, resisting the urge to salute.

Li makes it sound so easy. I hang up and spend some time riling myself into annoyance at Li's placid logic, which leaves pretty much no room for emotion, tension, or stress. Then I try using a meditation app on my phone. I remember doing a lot of deep breathing but I don't remember falling asleep until an insistent knocking on my door wakes me. I force my eyes open against the bright sunshine pushing its way in through the window blinds. Shuffling to the door while grasping for the hotel robe, I open up for Peggy to sweep in. She looks so perfectly put together that I can only imagine she's been getting ready since dawn.

"The lab has something for us, but they won't discuss it on the phone," she says. "Can you be ready in ten minutes? We'll go over there together."

Clutching an iPad, Ajay is standing outside the lab door to greet us as soon as we arrive. If he wasn't wearing a different suit and tie, I would have sworn he'd just stayed there all night, standing to attention and anticipating our arrival. It strikes me that I've yet to meet an Indian who believes in nine-to-five work hours.

Peggy greets him warmly and we all move at a fast clip through the foyer and into an elevator made of glass that rises up through the building, giving us a cool view of the labs that are arranged out from the center of the building like spokes on a wheel.

We emerge onto the top floors, a light-flooded oasis of white corridors. A younger man meets us as we leave the elevator. He holds open a lab door and we enter to find an impressive array of equipment lining the counters, and high ceilings studded with LED lights.

"My name is Raj," the doctor introduces himself. "Ajay asked me to oversee this case and put myself at your disposal," he adds.

"I've also heard personally from the Indian ambassador in London that I should make myself fully available."

Good old Peggy and her contacts. Never more than two degrees of separation from someone useful and, we hope, trustworthy. It feels like Raj is looking for us to reciprocate on the introductions, but Peggy just thanks him effusively and once she is finished, we both watch him, waiting for information. He gets on with it.

"The vial you brought in from India Laboratory—by the way, not a real lab, with any real credentials—contains a toxin."

"What kind of toxin?" Peggy asks.

"It's a neurotoxin. But it is made very difficult to detect because it is so tiny. You see, the toxin is encapsulated in a nanoparticle," he explains. "This has the effect of making it untraceable with regular blood tests. Even the centrifuge is not stable enough on particles so small. But we used an electron-transparent support on the vials you brought in, and it showed up."

He turns to a desktop screen and jiggles a mouse around to wake it up. What he shows us is a computer-generated image that looks like an egg.

"The toxin seems to be a virus, and a virus generally looks like this—a shell with DNA inside. The shell is sticky. It seems that whoever made this concentrated the virus into a nanoparticle to make it more potent."

Peggy's worried eyes flick to mine, then back to Raj.

"Are the girls carrying it?" Peggy asks him.

Raj looks at Ajay, who steps forward, with his iPad at the ready. On it is a list of names and, I presume, test results.

"I am sorry to say that the girls are all carrying it," Ajay confirms. "When we knew what we were looking for, we knew how to find it. The good news is that your blood test was clear, Jessie."

"Thank God," Peggy breathes. But I'm not relieved.

"What about Riya?" I ask.

Ajay hesitates and my heart sinks. "She has it too."

Take a breath, Jessie. *Think.*

"So why aren't the girls sick, if they're carrying a powerful virus?" My voice sounds unnatural in the unfamiliar atmosphere of the lab.

"Good question," replies Raj. "The protein moiety that allows the virus to work is currently 'hidden' by a molecular structure attached to the nanoparticle."

Seriously? How is it helping to talk to us like we're advanced medical researchers? I look at Peggy in frustration, and Peggy gently asks Raj if he could explain it in a simpler way. He apologizes, embarrassed, then quickly goes on:

"Basically," he says, "there is a structure sitting on the nanoparticle that is preventing it from passing through the blood-brain barrier. That's the border that protects the brain from foreign substances."

"So, the girls are safe?" I ask.

"At this moment, yes. Right now, the virus is dormant. *Until* the structure is displaced. That would expose the moiety, so the nanoparticle *could* pass the blood-brain barrier."

"And then?" Peggy asks.

"And then—the toxin would attack the brain. There is no cure.

And it would probably work very quickly. Within seconds. Possibly a minute or two." He hesitates. "Quicker would be better. It would be a traumatic way to go."

Peggy places her hand on the lab bench behind her, looking for support. For a moment, a tense silence settles on the four of us, there in the clean, white lab. I pull out my phone and show Raj the pictures that I took of the bodies outside the furnace. Even he blanches at the sight of them.

"Could it look like this? The virus attack?"

He nods. "It's hard to know the exact symptoms, but yes. That looks like something brain-related."

Peggy paces the room. "You said that the protein thing . . ."

"Moiety," says Raj.

"Thank you," says Peggy. "You said it needs to be displaced for the virus to work. What could cause that displacement?"

"Any one of hundreds of triggers," he says.

I think about the two guys who I just watched get incinerated at the morgue. Somehow, they were "triggered" with perfect timing before they could give any information to the police. And now over a hundred girls and Riya are exposed to probably the same thing. My hand slams down onto the desk before me, hard enough to make Raj jump.

"Like what?" I demand. "You have to give us a list, a full list, of every possible trigger."

He's taken aback but answers, spreading his hands.

"It could be something in the food supply, the water . . ." He trails off.

Well, that's a huge task to manage on its own. "What else?" I press.

"Another particle could be introduced through a ventilation system, or into the general air supply; something that could be inhaled. . . . Basically, it has to affect the girls internally. But it wouldn't have the slightest effect on people who aren't carrying the toxin."

It's just too vague. There's nothing I can catch hold of. My desperate look meets Peggy's frown. She shakes her head at the doctor.

"We really need a list. What else could trigger it?"

"Perhaps we are not explaining this well," Ajay interrupts with a sigh. "The science around virus delivery has grown exponentially in the past few years. And that's the science we know about, not the top-secret work that governments get up to, that terror groups could steal."

Raj nods. "We don't have a corresponding sample, or a list of characteristics, for this particular particle. It's specifically engineered."

"So, there must be a specific trigger?" I ask, almost pleading.

"Yes, that's true. It won't be any one of a hundred things; it will be one specific thing. But it's not like we can just guess or do one single test to find out. There are any number of ways it *could* be triggered, depending on the nature of the particle. It's never happened before, but there's even a theoretical possibility that something like a microwave could trigger it, if the particle is engineered that way."

"So, tell us how the particle is engineered," I snap.

"I should be able to do that," Raj says, eager to be able to finally toss us some hope. "My initial tests have been to figure out *what* this virus is meant to do, not *how* it does it. That alone often takes days. We've done it in under twenty hours."

"And we are extremely grateful." Peggy nods, waiting for more.

"There is good news," he says. "Once we pull apart the structure of this nanoparticle, the chances are very high that we can defuse it. We can construct a new particle which conjugates with the first one but has a targeted antiviral."

I glance at Peggy. I'll literally give this guy my life if he'll stop talking like he swallowed a medical dictionary.

"Do you mean you can make an antibody?" Peggy clarifies.

"In a manner of speaking," Raj says.

It's like I can breathe again. There's hope. Some hope.

"How soon can you do it?"

"If we work round the clock and everything breaks in our favor—twenty to thirty hours. But that's never been done before. It would be miraculous. But worst case, double that."

Maybe it would be a miracle, but it feels like an eternity. Peggy puts a calming hand on my arm.

"That's a day or two," she tells me. "We can work with that."

"Then, if you have no more questions," Raj says apologetically, "I will get back to my team and I will call you the moment I have anything that could possibly help."

25

PEGGY AND I GET BACK to our hotel just after 8:30 a.m. and, with Kit in tow, we join the Athena team in London by video. Hala and Caitlin link in by audio from outside Jingo's home, where Hala has just arrived to take over from Caitlin in watching the place.

"We have one clear focus over the next several hours," says Peggy after she's summarized our visit to the lab. "To figure out what the trigger for the nanoparticle might be."

"Thomas is leaving messages at all of the top research universities here in London," says Li. "He'll find any brain virus or neurotoxin experts and track them down in person as soon as he can."

"Well, it *is* four in the morning over there," says Kit, with understanding.

"Oh, I'm having him hunt down their home addresses and

phone numbers," says Li briskly. "We can't wait for London to open for normal working hours. Meanwhile, I have calls in to my contacts in nanotechnology in San Francisco and in Beijing."

"Needless to say, I'm researching too," says Amber.

Kit asks Caitlin about the school, since she's been spending the most time there.

"Those girls are well protected," Caitlin tells us. "But I'll talk to Luca and Ethan right now about tightening up security and what other kinds of safeguards we can place around the girls."

"Hala, anything from Jingo ahead of his deadline?" asks Peggy.

"Not yet," says Hala through a mouthful of something that's presumably her breakfast. I'm still waiting to find the stressor that would cause her to lose her appetite. "I got a text ten minutes ago saying he's working on it," she continues.

Peggy turns to me. "Jessie? Go and meet with Hala. In case you need to strong-arm Jingo again."

The call ends, leaving me alone with Kit and Peggy in the hotel room. Hastily, I get up to go to Jingo's, trying to move past the helplessness I feel inside. But I have to ask permission for something first.

"Someone needs to tell Riya what's going on," I say. "What she's carrying."

"Perhaps the lab would be best placed to explain it?" Peggy suggests kindly.

But Kit's looking at me. "You've become friends with Riya?" she asks. She doesn't try to imply anything more to the relationship.

I nod. "She's a very good detective. We trust each other." I look away from Kit's keen gaze. "Anyway, I feel like I should be the one to tell her," I add.

Kit and Peggy exchange a glance and then nod.

"Thanks," I say. "I'll call her to find a time. I don't want to leave my post, in case Hala needs me."

"I think that's sensible," Peggy says.

I leave Kit's room and try Riya's home line while I'm making my way out through the lobby. She picks up on the first ring.

"I got a new cell phone," she tells me. She dictates the number and I save it into my own cell. It gives me something to do while I figure out how to approach this. I decide to be businesslike.

"I need to talk to you later," I say. "I went to the lab earlier today and we should go over what they said."

There's a long pause before Riya answers.

"You don't have to worry, Jessie. I just called them."

I swallow, hardly daring to ask.

"They told me what was in the vial," she says. "And they told me that the nanoparticle is also in my blood sample."

There's a terrible silence, and all I can hear is my own breathing. "I'm sorry," I say, inadequately.

"Don't be," Riya replies. "And don't worry, I'm fine."

"I'll come over, as soon as I can," I tell her.

"No, I just . . . I just need some time on my own. To get used to the idea. Okay?"

"Okay. Riya?"

"Yes?"

I'd like to tell her she's amazing, that she's a good cop, that I care about her. That she doesn't deserve any of this. But I can't put into words the fear and pain rising in my chest.

"Jessie?" she asks, waiting.

"Nothing. I'll call you later," I say.

The truth is that thinking about Riya leaves a heaviness in my heart that makes it hard to function. And I have to stay sharp. I have to find solutions. To that virus and also to the puzzle of what havoc Family First are planning to unleash. Sprinting out of the hotel, I collect my motorbike and rev it as fast as it will go, weaving my way down to the street where Jingo Jain lives.

I park the motorcycle several cars behind the vehicle that Hala is sitting in. Her car keeps a substantial distance from Jingo's home too, a distance we can maximize because we each wear contact lenses that give us a nice zoom view of the house. I join Hala, slipping into the passenger seat and handing her a sweet milky coffee, while I sip on my own macchiato.

"Hey," she says.

"Hey. Listen. We need to think about getting into his house and persuading him to find out more, faster."

Hala agrees. "Want me to circle around the back of his place and find a way in?"

Right now, we can only see the front of Jingo's home and it doesn't look promising as a subtle way to enter. I give her a nod, but before Hala can exit the car, an old Honda pulls into Jingo's driveway.

"Hold on," I say. "Let's see who we have here."

"I think that's the same car from last night, at the morgue," says Hala.

Sure enough, the driver's door opens and Sunil gets out. He tucks in his shirt and straightens his tie, looking around at the street for any sign he's being watched. That gives us a nice view of his face for the snapshots we're taking through our lenses. Then he knocks and disappears into Jingo's house.

"I can't believe this," I growl. "Well, actually, I can. This asshole has been stonewalling us and Riya from the start. I just *knew* he was in Jingo's pocket."

"Jingo or Family First?" Hala asks.

I shrug, because that might be the same thing. Either way, it's a huge problem. "We have to get him removed as a detective. I have the pictures from last night, where he's paying off the guys at the morgue. And now these photos . . ."

Hala nods.

"Maybe Riya should report it?" I go on, thinking through options. "She could start the case with Internal Affairs, or whatever the police disciplinary department is over here?"

I don't have time to finish that thought because the front door opens again. That must have been the quickest meeting in history. Jingo has come out to the porch to see Sunil off. Jingo's doing all the talking, looking relaxed in an open-necked shirt, his hands thrust casually into his pockets, while Sunil nods and scrapes like the toad he is, practically backing into his car.

"I'll follow him," I suggest.

Hala nods. "Take the bike."

While Sunil negotiates his old banger of a car back into the road from the driveway, I have plenty of time to pull on my helmet and hop on my motorbike. Giving Sunil a very healthy lead, I ease the motorcycle out with low throttle and minimal noise, and trail him, leaving four or five cars between us. We travel along for around twenty minutes, half of which is spent waiting for two angry bus drivers to stop fighting over a collision and clear the road in front of us. Sunil, policeman or not, makes no attempt to intervene, only shoves in earbuds.

Hala checks in with me on the comms. "Where's Sunil heading?" she asks.

"Beats me," I say. "He's driven right past the usual turnoff for the police station. He's listening to music or something."

"Maybe he's on a phone call?" Hala asks.

"If it is a call, he's not saying much. I'll keep you posted."

Switching lanes so as to avoid getting caught in Sunil's rearview mirror, I toy with calling Riya and bringing her up to speed. But she calls me first. I pick up the call on my hands-free.

"Riya, hi. I was just thinking about you."

"Jessie, I had the strangest call, a few seconds ago. From Sunil. He wants to meet."

I feel the hairs prickle on the back of my neck.

"Where? Why?"

"He said now. At Bandra Terminus."

"The railway station?" I ask.

"Yes."

"Riya, I'm trailing him right now. He just had a meeting with Jingo Jain, at his home."

Riya lets out an audible breath that sounds like despair. "So he *is* mixed up in this?" she asks.

"It looks that way. I'm sorry," I tell her. "Did he say why he wants to meet?"

"No, he was very short on the phone. He did say one more thing, though," she says. "He asked for you to come too."

Bandra Terminus is a large train station, all columns and arches topped with a sloping tiled roof and a small watchtower on the top. Outside, lines of black and yellow rickshaws and taxis pull in and out from the curb, fighting their way through layers of vehicles that are three deep from the sidewalk.

At the fast-food restaurant across the street from the station, the smell of grease and oil feels like it's soaked into the walls. I check that my comms unit is working, deep in my ear, and that my team can pick up sound from me and my surroundings too.

"All good here for me and Li," Amber says.

"Same here for us," says Peggy.

"Check," says Caitlin, and Hala gives a quick confirmation as well.

Within minutes, Riya walks into the restaurant, looking for me just as we have planned. I wave from the stool where I've been perched and we both hurry straight out, dodging the passing cars and bikes on the road, heading over to the station.

"It's a good thing you're here, Jessie; you can stop me from killing Sunil," she says by way of greeting. "If he thinks he's going to threaten us off the case, he has another thing coming."

"Take a breath," I tell her.

"I can't take a breath," she says, turning to me. When our eyes meet, it's like the fierce anger drops away suddenly, replaced by disappointment. "I'm still in shock. It's not who he is."

Clearly, she's struggling with believing the worst about her mentor. There's no reason to add my two cents and make her feel worse.

"How are you feeling?" I ask, indicating her torso.

"On the upside? Every time I think about the brain toxin I'm carrying around in my bloodstream, I forget the pain of the bruises."

She tries a brief smile but neither of us finds her attempted humor amusing. But it makes me stop walking. Something in what she just said, about carrying around the virus, freaks me out. I grab hold of her arm, holding her back before she can head into the station.

"What is it?" she asks.

I pull her along with me, away from the terminus, ducking into a small street off to the side.

"Jessie, what are you doing?"

"Just come with me," I reply. My heart is beating a million miles a minute. "What if Sunil has the trigger that sets off the virus?" I ask. "Those men from India Lab died on his watch yesterday . . ."

"But he wasn't there."

"So *he* says. But do we know that for sure?"

I watch her turn it over in her mind. "I suppose it's possible. He might have wanted them dead before they could spill too much information," she muses. "Information that might implicate him . . ."

We walk down the side road, which is crammed with shops catering to the train passengers, and I install Riya in a cramped store selling women's clothes. She hangs around pretending to be interested in the rolls of fabric piled up right in the back. The front of the place is busy and lively, with plenty of women choosing cloth, unwinding long, colorful saris, and generally hanging around chatting. Sunil would never find her there. I promise to keep in touch and turn away to head into the station alone.

The thunderous clatter of an arriving train forms a wall of noise. Scores of people wash in and out onto the platform below us, like waves onto a beach. I locate the steps that lead down to where Sunil has asked us to meet. This platform is off to the side and feels unused and empty. On the tracks, an old engine squats, listing tiredly to one side. As I descend, Sunil steps out to beckon to me, then quickly disappears back into the shadows behind the stairs.

"Where's Riya?" he says as I reach him. "We don't have much time."

"She doesn't want to see you. She's feeling . . . betrayed," I say.

Poor Sunil looks hurt. "Betrayed?" he repeats, shocked. "By me?"

I shrug, because I could care less about his feelings. I'm alert, wary—scanning Sunil's hands, his pockets, his face for a sign of malicious intent. But he seems tired and dispirited, not to mention awkward and nervous.

"You'll report back to her at least?" he asks, talking quickly.

I nod.

"First off, tell her she's back on duty, with immediate effect."

Is he serious? The gall of this guy. Riya's not around to listen to threats so now he's trying to *buy* her allegiance? I'm getting steamed but I try to keep my mouth shut. Ripping into Sunil might give me a moment's satisfaction but it's not likely to help our case. Still, the detective's next words take me by surprise.

"There's a cover-up going on," Sunil says firmly. "Within the police."

While that's hardly news at this point, I wasn't expecting *him* to spill his guts about it, especially to me.

"No kidding," I say. "Care to elaborate?"

"I told you last night that the police commissioner had me deal with those bodies to avoid a panic. Well, it's the kind of thing that happens, but now I don't believe that is the real reason he wanted them gone."

"What *is* the reason?"

"I just found out. From Jingo Jain. He's a politician. . . ."

"I know who he is. You went to see him?" I ask. Like I have no idea.

"Just now. I went for one purpose," Sunil says urgently. "To bug his landline. I've tapped his cell for the past two months and—nothing. But something is building here. The lab you found with Riya contained a toxin."

"What toxin?" I ask. It's annoying to have to ask about stuff we're already on top of, but I need to find out what *he* knows.

Sunil almost grinds his teeth with frustration. "Our forensics had to send it out for specialized analysis. No matter, the suspicious thing is that the two men who were handling the toxin are now dead, before they could speak. And now . . ."

He trails off, frowning at the floor.

"And now?"

"I just intercepted a call on Jingo's home line. Family First plan to kill the schoolgirls at twelve noon today with some kind of bioterror attack. But I don't know how. On tonight's television news, Jingo is to wear his army uniform and prepare a speech unifying the nation against the attack, and by tomorrow, he will be the obvious winner even as the voting opens. Next, they want to push him toward a run for prime minister. "

"Election tampering?"

Sunil nods. My head is spinning. I don't know what to think of him, what to believe.

"And Jingo knew this all along?" I ask.

"From the call, I would say this last part came as a surprise to him. But he didn't argue."

I look at my watch. Twelve noon is an hour and a half away. Eighty-nine minutes, to be precise. I stare at Sunil. His eyes meet mine, unwavering, as he speaks.

"I called you here because I think you and Kit-ma'am may have resources that we don't have. I need your help—and Riya's—to stop this, because I don't know who I can trust in the police anymore. Jingo was once head of the police force and he may have friends all over the top ranks."

I hesitate. Sunil pulls out his wallet and flips it open to a picture of a young woman in a university gown and cap.

"This is my daughter," he says, and his face softens. "Jingo would have her and all young women married instead of at university. He would take away her chance to practice law, and have her stay home, dependent on the man she marries. He is a monster and I've been looking for a way to stop him and whoever funds him. But now I need your help."

26

THE FIRST THING I DO is get hold of the recording of the call Sunil intercepted between Jingo and Family First. I upload it to Amber, then return it to Sunil. He doesn't feel that Jingo has any idea what form the attack will take, but I'd prefer to get Amber's confirmation about that. While I wait for her analysis, Li tells me that I can go ahead and tell Sunil that I have photos of Jingo that could be used to blackmail him. Obviously, I don't tell him how I got them, not that I feel Sunil much cares.

"Photos of him with a lover?" he asks.

That surprises me, that he guessed the content of the photos.

"You knew he was having an affair?" I reply.

"No. But for the last few minutes, my phone has been pinging nonstop. Here . . ."

He swipes into the news notifications on his phone, showing

me. I flick on my own local news app. An array of breaking news greets me—all of them Jingo-related headlines:

> Military Hero Falls Victim to Fake News by Liberal Left
> Jingo Jain: Photoshopped Images "A Low Attack on My
> High Character"

Similar headlines continue to pop up, overlapping each other. No one even has these photos yet, but it seems clear that Jingo and/or Family First have decided to come out ahead of our threat to expose him.

"I can prove the photos are real. And we have video . . . ," I begin, indignant.

"Even if we can prove the photos are real, do we want to spend the time we have bringing down Jingo?" asks Sunil.

In my ear, Peggy comes in: "Jessie, he may be right. There's no guarantee that discrediting Jingo will protect the girls," she says.

On that, I agree with Sunil to let the blackmail angle drop for now. In my ear, I'm being further instructed by Peggy to bring Sunil up to date on the virus and the fact that there is a trigger. He stares at me, openmouthed.

"What trigger?" he asks me, appalled.

"We don't know yet."

Sunil lets out a choice string of curse words in Hindi. Don't ask me how I know that they are swearwords; it just always seems to be the first vocabulary I pick up, whichever country I get sent to. I don't feel right telling him that Riya is carrying the toxin—that should be her decision to make. I call her and direct her to meet with Sunil, leaving them together outside Bandra Terminus while I race back to Ajay's lab. Before I head off, I text a piece of software to Sunil and he obligingly opens it when I ask.

"This gives me access to your phone's microphone. So I can hear you if you learn anything from Jingo, or if you need me."

"Millennials," Sunil grunts, grudgingly impressed.

On the way to Ajay's lab, I check in with Thomas. The reality is that I don't have time to listen in to Sunil's phone, so Thomas will be on that. Watching over everything Sunil gets up to is also extra insurance for us. Since we've decided to trust him, it doesn't hurt to keep tabs on him. Thomas confirms he has access and that he will keep me updated. It takes me fifteen minutes to reach my destination. I drop the motorbike right outside the front door and run in, hurrying my way through security and up to the top floor.

I burst out of the elevator just as the lab door opens.

"They told me you were coming up," Raj says politely. His pleasantries fade away when faced with my wild-eyed stare. I hurry him into the lab where we met not two hours ago.

"Those girls are set to die—to be triggered—in fifty-nine minutes from now," I tell him.

He makes a gasping sound and pulls at his beard. "We can't even decipher the particle we have in that time," he says.

"What about somewhere with better equipment?" I ask.

"Stanford might have something," he offers.

"Stanford University in California?" I ask.

Raj shakes himself, crestfallen. "I know, stupid idea. It would take a day just to get the samples to them." He's clearly panicking and not thinking very well under pressure. I try to calm him down, not to infect him with my own stress.

"Isn't there some general antivirus we can give them?" I ask.

"No. We can kill bacteria with high-dose antibiotics. But not an unknown virus. And we can't risk giving the carriers anything by mouth. Even an antibiotic or antiviral could be a trigger, if this particle is set up for that."

I know he's trying his best, but it's not helping us. What he's saying is that anything and everything near the girls could be fraught with danger. If we split them up, that danger will multiply, because our control of their immediate environment will be diluted.

"How's the deconstruction of the particle going?" I ask as I head out the door.

"As well as it can," Raj replies. He really doesn't want to commit to a time frame but I pin him to the spot with my gaze till he provides one. "No guarantees, but I think we can crack this within twenty-four hours."

I glance at the countdown timer that I've set up as my watch face. Fifty-five minutes left. Within me, frustration rises with such force and heat that I feel like kicking in a wall. Instead, I thank him and run.

If this nightmare has to happen, it's a small mercy that the main places we have to travel between are concentrated within a relatively small area of Mumbai, because just crossing the city in its entirety can take two hours or more. But from the lab to the school in Bandra, it's less than twenty.

Still, I rev the bike harder as I ride along the road that runs down to the sea. Forced to stop at a red light, I edge forward, trying to push past the thronging traffic that floods the street in front of me, blocking my progress, but I can't find a way through. Desperate to contain my panic, to avoid the phantom ticking of the countdown in my head, I turn to look at the water, gleaming in the sun. The waves lap in, creating lacy edges of white froth at the shore as they push themselves over the backwash. It's soothing, primal, true. The water exists free of chaos, choices, dilemmas. Right now, I wish that could be how our messy lives are. Ahead of me the opposing traffic finally pauses and, before the light can even change, I'm speeding over the junction. At the school, Caitlin has the gate open, ready for me. I pick her up onto the bike behind me and we roar up the driveway.

"What's the update?" I ask as we disembark and head inside the building.

"We got rid of the private security firm in case they were infiltrated," she says. "Only Luca and Ethan are in here now. They have complete surveillance around the school and a bunch of cool weapons—don't ask me how they got them. And Hala just got here. And then there's you and me."

"Five of us guarding a hundred girls? Feels a bit light," I suggest.

"Yeah, well, think of it as 'lean,'" she replies.

She leads me through the foyer and back toward where Jaya

has her office. The door hangs open and the room is empty as we stride in.

"We've put together our own list of things that could potentially activate the virus, and we're trying to cross them off, but damn," Caitlin says, discouraged, "with every expert Amber and Thomas talk to, there just seem to be more."

On the main wall, next to the girls' art about their dream careers, Caitlin has pinned up a list. New triggers are scrawled into an increasingly tight space at the bottom, while most of the top ones are ticked. Caitlin whips through them:

"We cut off all food and water deliveries yesterday morning, and got rid of existing stocks, in case the supply chain was compromised."

"How are you feeding the girls?" I ask.

"Ethan went out with Jaya to buy supplies from an hour away, spread across a bunch of different stores. But right now, we're not giving them anything by mouth, no medicine, nothing until . . ."

She trails off. Until the deadline comes and goes, she means. The thought of it makes us both check our watches. Thirty-two minutes to go. We leave the office to continue our circuit of the inside of the school.

"What if it's an airborne trigger?" I ask.

"The air-conditioning vents are clear," replies Caitlin. "There's no tampering with the units that we could see, but we've switched them off, obviously. The guys have sealed off the vents and grilles that lead into the classrooms and dorms. In the basement there's nothing but an old cooling unit and some gas heaters. They're clean but Ethan pretty much took them apart anyway."

"And you've scoured the place for any other kind of device?" I check.

"What, like a bomb?" Caitlin asks. "Sure. We've checked every nook and cranny, tested for any trace of explosive residue, any places of ingress, the works."

We keep moving through a corridor hung with more artwork and with photos of famous female scientists. It feels like we are pacing, marking time. And yet, it's hard to know what more we can do except be on our guard and wait, ensuring the girls are isolated from any possible contaminant.

"We're keeping them all in the dining hall for now," Caitlin explains. "The teachers were sent home yesterday as a precaution, and we don't have much in the way of supervision for the kids."

"Have they figured out what's going on?" I ask.

"No. I mean, they know something's up, because they're all moved into one room. A few of them have been getting nervous, asking questions. But Jaya's keeping them calm and busy."

As we approach the dining hall the sound of young voices bubbles up, chattering, bickering, laughing. It sounds strange—*wrong*, even—to hear laughter when terror and death are bearing down on us. And yet, there's relief in it too; the sound of life. A few of the girls have started singing at one end of the hall, and more of them join in. Ahead of us, right before the entrance to the dining hall, Jaya's stocky outline leans against the doorframe, watching the girls, unseen. As we peek inside from the corridor, some of the girls are up and dancing, a perfectly coordinated set of moves that make the others laugh and clap. Jaya looks back at us over her shoulder as we approach.

"It's a dance number from one of our most popular Bollywood films," Jaya explains. "Normally, I would be in there telling them not to waste time."

Her voice breaks. I draw her back from the doorway so that the girls won't see her and become alarmed.

"Jaya, it is time for you to leave," Caitlin says. "We can't put you at risk."

Jaya sniffs wetly and Caitlin rummages in her jacket pocket, finding some tissues for her to blow her nose into. When the headmistress is done, she shakes her head emphatically.

"I am not leaving. These are my girls. This is my school. I will not abandon it."

She turns back to watch the girls, cutting off any further discussion. I look at Caitlin for guidance on how to handle her, but now Luca comes striding down the hallway toward us.

"I have a breach," he says. "That young police detective is outside. The one you were here with before."

"Let her in, fast," says Caitlin. "She's carrying the virus too. The last thing we need is for her to be out there exposed to anything Family First wants to throw at her. . . ."

Luca sprints out, and I'm right behind him. Meeting Riya at the gate, I hurry her back up to the school building while Luca brings up the rear, sweeping the school grounds and the street with his gun. Once we're inside, Luca goes back to his post, leaving me and Riya alone in the foyer. It's a large entrance area, painted in pale blues and greens. On one wall, a welcoming mural painted by the girls brightens the space. On the opposite wall, near the front door, neat rows of pegs hold school blazers and backpacks. Just seeing them there reminds me of the girls that we need to protect. I'm antsy, my foot tapping up and down on the wooden floorboards, as I watch Riya.

"You can't stay here," I tell her.

"Why not?"

"You need to keep away from the other girls. If Family First trigger them, they'll trigger you."

"Twenty minutes from now," she says softly. I look down, away from her gaze. "Sunil told me the deadline," she adds. "Before I told him I have the virus too."

Despite myself, I feel a lump rise in my throat. I take a breath to steady my voice.

"Riya, please, let me try to protect you at least—"

"Really, Jessie?" she interrupts, frowning at me.

"Really what?" I ask.

"Tell me I didn't misjudge you all this time," she says. "Tricking your way into my crime scene. Brawling with those men at the lab. I thought you were a fighter. But now you sound like you've given up."

I almost smile at the tone of challenge in her voice.

"I'm still fighting, but we have to think about the worst that could . . ."

The rest of the words collapse in my mouth before I can even form them. Who am I telling about the worst that could happen? Just looking at her—high cheekbones, expressive eyes, and, somehow, a small smile forming at the sides of her mouth—makes me so deeply sad. Tears sting at my eyes suddenly and I hit the wall with my palm, forcing them back.

Without warning, Riya grabs me in a hug that is passionate, intense, laden with too many emotions for me to grasp at. It's like she understands everything I'm feeling, all the things I can't put into words. I feel her lips on my cheek, my neck, my forehead. Her eyes are closed as she kisses me. I hold her close, taking in the feel of her, the scent of her. The moments stretch out, like they might just last forever and yet, suddenly, it's over so fast. She pulls away, and reluctantly I let her go.

"You know what I figured out since I found out about this toxin?" she asks gently.

"What?" I say. Despite my best efforts not to cry, I feel tears on my lashes. Riya's finger comes up to brush them softly away.

"We can't worry about failing, Jessie. We have to figure out how to win."

27

LUCA GIVES RIYA AN EARPIECE that will give her a communications link to all of us here in the school and I introduce her briefly to Caitlin. Then I leave her in Jaya's office to sift through the last few days, to go over all the events since the bombing of the first school and think about any evidence or events that could help us identify the trigger. Even though we are under the impending pressure of this deadline, I'm hoping that maybe by sitting still for a few minutes, Riya can come up with some clue that Family First have left us, even inadvertently.

I look into classrooms as I go back to Caitlin. The spaces echo back at me, silent, deserted. Only the computer room buzzes with life. Inside, Caitlin and Luca watch a set of three monitors. He's still wearing Caitlin's bandanna, and I don't think I imagined that her hand was holding on to his when I walked in. But she's standing up now, arms crossed. I keep my eyes on the screens.

"This looks good," I say. The streets outside the school appear live before us.

"I've had this set up since we got here," says Luca. "Using the Wi-Fi, it's a cinch. And just today, I've added lasers. If anyone breaks the beams coming onto the school grounds, we'll know about it."

All of this technology would usually make me feel safer, and yet, as Luca talks, I suddenly get a pit in my stomach. I ask Caitlin to step outside, and take her into an empty music room. She sits on a piano stool while I put in a call to Amber.

"Sixteen minutes left," Amber says as a greeting. Really, what does she think? That maybe I forgot to watch the clock over here?

"Listen," I say, urgently. "The guys have all this camera and laser stuff set up for surveillance. It's all running on Wi-Fi."

"I know what you're thinking," replies Amber. "Someone could tamper with the Wi-Fi and that might somehow activate the toxin?"

"Exactly."

"We didn't add it to our list for a reason. It would take equipment that's not commercially available to even begin to mess with those kinds of waves. . . ."

"Is that equipment available somewhere, in some form?" I ask.

Amber hesitates. "Barely. And it's mostly untried, even by the military."

"I still think it's safer to cut all Wi-Fi signals," I say.

Li comes in now. "Jessie, that would leave you without any visual security beyond the eyes and ears you have between you.

You'd be much more exposed to an attack. . . ."

"It also cuts out vulnerabilities," I argue. "What if they're using the Wi-Fi to watch us? Or to mess with our phones? What if there's some way to concentrate a signal to be a trigger?"

"That's science fiction," Li says. "Or, at least, unproven . . ."

She trails off. Li's business, her legitimate business, is to know all about tech that is months, and sometimes years, away from being usable. If she had said "impossible," I would have left it alone. But "unproven" suggests that there's some evidence that it *is* possible, and that idea doesn't thrill me.

"I agree with Jessie," Caitlin chips in. "Wi-Fi should be considered a contaminant, even if we can't figure out how or why. Family First have already shown us they have access to super-sophisticated virus technology. Let's not take a chance."

Li hesitates barely a moment. "Fine," she says. "Cut everything."

While Luca takes care of killing the Wi-Fi, Jaya continues to watch over the girls, and Caitlin and I continue our patrol around the building. We head upstairs and walk through the bathrooms and dorms. Bedsheets are stripped and every mattress has been shredded. All the drawers that store clothes and personal stuff belonging to the girls are open. Even the shower drains are covered over with metal sheets, hammered in with nails. I give Caitlin a surprised look.

"Overkill?" she asks.

"No, I'm impressed. Better to go overboard than have regrets later." I shrug.

"Ethan, do you copy me?" Caitlin says.

Ethan's voice comes in on a radio unit in Caitlin's ear. Not our Athena comms, but one connecting the three of us agents with Ethan and Luca—and now, Riya too.

"Copy."

"Coming in," Caitlin says.

We run up a final flight of stairs that leads to the attic. High up, I notice a mirror in the corner of the staircase that clearly reflects an image of me and Caitlin approaching back into the attic space. It seems that, even in the absence of Wi-Fi or clever surveillance apps, Ethan has some kind of security covered, as homemade as it is.

The attic runs the length of the building and is barely high enough to stand in. Both Caitlin and I have to crouch to walk through it. Ethan must be bent double when he stands up. But right now, he and Hala are sprawled out on the floor, on opposite sides of the room. Between them, they are covering the front and back of the school with a pair of sniper rifles.

Two more unmanned rifles sit on stands, aimed out of the remaining east and west windows, which look over onto the streets on the right and left sides of the school.

"Anything?" I ask Hala. If she had noticed something worth reporting, we'd know about it by now, but asking her the question gives me something to say, at a time when it feels frivolous to greet each other with the standard "Hi" or "How are you?"

"Nothing. I'm just scanning, one side to the other, all the time," she says.

I lean down to look through one of the free rifle scopes. The school is surrounded by so many buildings. Most of them are at a distance, but still close enough to feel threatening. Is Family First hiding out in one of them, watching us the way we are trying to watch them? I zoom in and pick up one balcony after another on the buildings. Random images crystallize in my lens. A line of laundry strung across; an old man outside, smoking; a woman washing her child's feet in a bucket. I zoom back out for a wider view—and the harsh sunlight glitters back into my eyes, refracted from a hundred different windows and surfaces.

Caitlin and I run back downstairs, where Riya is coming out of Jaya's office, looking for me.

"It's Sunil," she says, waving her phone. She flips on the speaker. I know Amber and the rest of the team will be getting this conversation too.

"Family First called in a warning ten minutes ago that the school would be attacked at noon," Sunil says. "The police are marshaling a response unit to come over to the school and evacuate the girls."

"They said the *school* would be attacked, or the girls?" I ask.

"The school. Hence, the plan to evacuate," he replies.

"When will they be here?" says Riya.

"Maneesh saw a commando response unit, fully armed, heading straight out from Juhu station, just a few minutes after the call. Which is strange, because the only police commando unit I know of is called Force One. They are based in the north of the city, much farther from you. They haven't been used in years, yet today they seemed to be ready and waiting," Sunil says, clearly stressed.

"Because they were expecting the call from Family First," Riya says.

Sunil's voice is strained. "That's what I am afraid of. I'm heading toward you now too. I told them you are there—that we have a detective on site in the school. Whatever I can do, I will do—but be careful. I believe the police commissioner himself is giving the orders here. Because no one is listening to me."

He ends the call. Caitlin looks at me.

"Doesn't make sense," she says. I know what she means.

"If Family First want to make sure the attack happens without interference, why warn the police?" I wonder.

"And why is a rapid response unit ready so fast?" Riya broods. "Honestly, we are not usually that organized."

Luca has joined us and looks completely pissed off at the details that he's picking up.

"The police? This is bullshit," he says, stressed. "We've spent the past twenty-four hours creating a perfect shell around these girls, cutting off any possible contamination. And now cops are going to come barreling in here, opening doors, spreading radio waves, bringing in weapons. . . ."

He's right, it is a nightmare. Our secure, sealed-off bubble is about to get blown out of the water. And who knows which one of those cops might have been persuaded to work with Family First in exchange for a handy retirement fund, or medical treatment for a sick family member? There are infinite ways that people become vulnerable to criminals waving cash. Or, as Riya seems to fear, perhaps this entire police operation is the handiwork of Family First.

"Let's stay calm."

This suggestion comes from Riya. Which is an irony that's not lost on me.

"Going back to the task you gave me, Jessie," she continues briskly, "there are only two things I could think of that might link to what's happening here. One—we missed something at the lab that day."

"The lab was empty except for the vials with the nanoparticles," I say.

"Or, secondly, we haven't properly explored the weapons you found at the warehouse," she says. "We logged all those using the photos you took."

She brings up a list on her phone screen. It's a police inventory of every item found in the warehouse that Hassan led us to a few days ago. It feels like a lifetime away and it doesn't feel like it means much, but I need to trust Riya's instinct. I need to do *something*.

Taking a breath, I run my eyes down the page, past the itemized list of Jingo's campaign caps and T-shirts, and down to the catalog of guns and explosives we found in the crates. I rack my brains. Which of these things could be fashioned into a trigger for this specific virus? What could touch all the girls and finish them off?

"Holy crap," says Ethan from his post upstairs. "The cops are driving toward us. I have two vans, approaching from the east."

Downstairs, here in the foyer, it's just me and Riya with Caitlin and Luca. The girls and Jaya are on the same ground floor as us, but they are down the long corridor that leads through to the dining hall. I step away from my teammates for a moment. Because, even in the chaos of the police arriving, and with all the panic and commands flying around, I'm still thinking about the list that Riya showed me. The inventory of stuff from the warehouse. In my head, I replay that night now. Trying to remember if there was anything else in the warehouse. Because, amid our current state of panic, something is bothering me, teasing at me, crouching right outside the edges of my conscious mind.

Ethan's voice comes in again. "There are eight special forces–type cops. Getting out, lining up near our perimeter, getting a pep talk."

Luca and Caitlin look out from the nearest window.

"I can't believe this is happening," breathes Caitlin.

"I can take 'em all out," Ethan says. "Just an idea . . ."

Li and Kit and Peggy simultaneously echo into our Athena comms.

"No one starts a shootout with the police. Is that clear?"

"Clear," Caitlin says.

"Clear," replies Hala.

Caitlin instructs both Luca and Ethan not to engage. They confirm.

In my peripheral vision, I see Luca peer out of the window again. I see Caitlin sneak a glance at her watch. I feel Riya standing right beside me, watching me. But I make myself ignore her, I make myself forget about the police and the countdown and the fact that there are only seven minutes left. I try to think about that night at the warehouse. I close my eyes for three precious seconds, maybe four. And then it hits me. There was something *outside* the warehouse. My eyes snap open, wide.

"I think I know what the trigger is," I say. "I think that's why Family First want the police to evacuate the girls and get them outside. They want to hit them with the ADS."

28

FOR A MOMENT, EVERYONE JUST stares at me as if they all think I've lost my mind. Riya is the first to agree with me.

"That has to be it," she says. "After that night at the warehouse, we never recovered the ADS."

"And, at the lab, Raj mentioned microwaves as a possible trigger," I tell her. "He was just spitballing, and I never made the connection because the ADS doesn't really produce microwaves, but it *does* act on water molecules in the skin, sort of like a microwave would, except it can be directed and targeted. . . ."

I feel my mouth running at a hundred miles an hour. Luca puts up his hands, lost.

"Someone wanna fill me in?" he begs. "ADS? You mean an active denial system? Those things are huge, they sit on top of tanks last time I looked."

"When *did* you last look?" Caitlin asks.

"Six, seven years ago."

"Well, tech has moved on," I say. "We were hit with one last week that's still pretty big but more or less handheld."

"From what distance?" Luca asks.

From her sniper post upstairs, Hala, following the conversation, answers into our comms: "Ours was around a hundred meters away," she says.

Meanwhile Riya's frantically looking through the documents on her phone. She finds something and looks up at us.

"These are my notes from when I interviewed the head of the military base. He told me they can range up to *three* hundred meters," she says.

That dampens the mood.

"That means some guy carrying the ADS could be in any of those apartment blocks, at least two streets back," Caitlin says. "We're literally surrounded."

My glance goes to Riya, wishing she didn't have to be part of this panic, watching what could be the last minutes of her life tick down, slip past, while we try to figure out what to do. While we seem so powerless. I look at Luca and Caitlin.

"We need two more people up in the attic," I say. "Covering the areas facing east and west."

I glance at Caitlin. Technically I'm the best sniper. But I want to stay with Riya. In case.

"Police are opening the front gate," Ethan advises over the comms. "They're coming in."

"Luca, let's do this," Caitlin says. They run for the stairs, heading to the attic to cover the extra sniper posts.

That leaves just Riya and me at the door as the police start hammering on it. Riya turns to me.

"Put your hands up," she says. "In case they're trigger-happy."

She shouts through the door in Hindi, identifying herself, calming down the situation, while also playing for time. But she takes too long; they start ramming at the door, trying to break it down. Riya shouts again and the battering stops. She opens the front door, slowly, telling them what she's doing the whole time, keeping them feeling like they are in control. I keep my hands raised.

The police team push inside, covering me with an automatic rifle. Riya holds out her detective badge and ID, tries to establish a connection with the men. Four of the policemen are inside, each of them armed. There's a ton of urgent chatter back and forth between Riya and the first cop on the scene. He's a young guy, in a blue uniform and cap and a bulletproof vest. He keeps his rifle trained on me and Riya switches their conversation from Hindi to English so I can follow.

"This young woman works for the owner of the school," she says. "She can be trusted."

Hesitant, the cop lowers his gun.

"I'm Riya. What's your name?" she tries.

"Dev," he answers. "Who else is here?"

"Just the girls and the headmistress," Riya says, not missing a beat.

"Where are the girls?" Dev asks.

Riya dodges the question. "Look, I have very good reason to

think the girls are safer inside. . . ."

Dev ignores her. He jerks his head and snaps at his three colleagues to go find the girls. They disappear into the building.

"They are on the ground floor, at the back," I call after them. The last thing I want is police crawling all over the building, or anywhere near the attic, where our four snipers are lying in wait.

Now Sunil comes onto Riya's phone.

"It's my boss. Detective Sunil Patel," she tells Dev, flicking on the speaker.

"I'm literally door-to-door with Maneesh at the apartment blocks around the school, with the picture of the ADS," Sunil says. "Someone saw a man pull it out of a van not long ago. But they don't know where he went and we haven't found him yet."

"Dev," Riya says. "Detective Patel and I have been working this case from the start, and I believe Family First *wants* you to take the girls outside, so they can kill them. Please, try to understand . . ."

It sounds outlandish, and in any event, Dev is clearly not in charge here—he is a highly trained order-taker. Worse, all this information is making him nervous. He tunes us out, and listens to a crackling voice on his radio, paying no more attention to Riya. She looks at me, desperate, then her eyes move over my shoulder to where a column of wide-eyed girls is marching through the corridor, approaching the foyer. The other three armed policemen walk behind them, ensuring they all stay together and keep moving. Some of them start to cry, others to ask questions, but Jaya encourages them to stay quiet.

Dev turns to us.

"This school will be attacked at noon—in three minutes," Dev says. "My orders are clear. Get everyone evacuated now."

What an *idiot* this guy is, saying that right in front of the girls. A ripple of fearful gasps rises up into the tense atmosphere, and the girls all surge forward, *wanting* to get out. Dev opens the front door and, instinctively, I run over and shut it. The sudden slam echoes in the foyer, sending a shiver through all of us.

"Stay back," I yell at the students.

Immediately, Dev's weapon is thrust upward into my face. Riya cries out, but I step back and raise my hands again. The last of the girls are here now, pooling into the back of the hallway.

"Turn around and face the wall," Dev barks at me. "Hands on your head."

I throw Riya an agonized look as I obey. Behind me, Jaya comes forward.

"Officer, is this really necessary?" she demands.

With my hands still on my head I can't see my watch, but I know the deadline is right on top of us.

"Anything, anyone?" I mutter under my breath, willing our attic team to give us some good news.

"Nothing," Ethan replies. "We're scanning but they're likely waiting for the girls to exit before they show themselves. I don't know how we'll see them in time. . . ."

Riya hears that and exchanges a look with me. She tries talking to Dev again, tries appealing to the other cops, but they keep back behind the girls and generally behave as if she doesn't exist. I watch

the policeman hold open the door once again. The girls are shep-
herded out toward the threshold. Toward their deaths.

I turn, braving Dev's wrath.

"I have to stop this," I say to Riya.

Riya shakes her head at me. "And get killed?" she says. "It's not
your time. If anything, it's mine."

But there's no space for this conversation now, and the strange
thing is, I don't feel afraid of dying at all. The world starts to move
in slow motion, and for this moment at least I feel that I have the
capacity to take control of everything around me. I sense Dev's gun
turn toward me again. I see in my mind how I can dodge low and
bring him down.

But there are three more armed men behind me.

Riya is right, I realize. I *will* get killed. And the girls will be sent
outside anyway. And yet—I don't have it in me to just stand here and
watch them all troop out and be obliterated.

I duck low, stepping toward Dev. From the corner of my eye, I
see Riya slam the door shut yet again and shout at the girls to stay
back. Dev swipes at me with his rifle, catching me under the chin,
sending a juddering vibration through my skull and knocking me
off-balance. I stumble, but I grasp hold of Dev's gun as I fall, unbal-
ancing him too. We both hit the ground, hard.

I lie there, stunned, trying to get up before Dev does. In my line
of vision, behind Dev, I see Riya turn and grab one of the school
blazers off a peg. She shrugs it on. It makes no sense to me, but I
can't fathom it out now. My head is thick from the blow I just took.

I fight to stay alert. Riya's voice floats into my brain. She's yelling, but not at me—at Jaya.

"Keep the girls inside. . . ."

Grappling with Dev on the floor, I look up as Jaya brushes past me, to the front of the foyer, pushing the girls back inside. The other cops are shouting, directionless. Now the front door opens again, and Riya, in her school blazer, touches the comms unit in her ear.

"I'm going out. Watch for the direction of the ADS," she says to the sniper team. Then she looks back at me, her gaze intense.

"Keep doing what you do, Jessie. The world needs it." She turns away.

I scramble up, yelling at her to stop, trying to get my footing, as Dev strikes me again. I don't even feel the blow, I move straight past it, but I can't reach Riya before she's through the door. I make it outside, but only in time to see her standing in the center of the playground. She suffers for a second under the burn of the ADS and lifts her hand to point to the east. Then she drops where she stands.

29

There's a burst of staccato chatter from our sniper team, words that just scatter through my head as I run toward Riya.

"We got him. We got him," Caitlin says.

"Confirmed, ADS shooter is down." Ethan's voice comes in.

Behind me comes the beat of running footsteps. I glance behind. The girls are being rushed out across the school grounds by the police. Nothing happens to them. I skid down to my knees beside Riya. A low noise of pain, an inhuman sound, comes from her. She convulses, then stops—but still, her chest rises, like she's gasping for breath. Fluid bubbles into her mouth.

"Somebody help her," I scream. But in the front playground and driveway, everyone I see is moving away from me and from Riya, the police and girls rushing to evacuate. Sirens whine in the far distance, but no help comes.

"You saved the girls," I whisper, but I can't tell if she hears me. There's no response. I can't even see her properly through the tears that fill my eyes, but I take hold of her hand, which lies motionless across her body.

"Please, Riya, don't . . . Please . . ." My words drown in a sobbing gulp that I can't control. I lean forward to kiss Riya's forehead, and as I do, I feel her fingers entwine with mine, and her grip tightens. Then her hand drops. And I know she is gone.

In my ear, the sounds of the mission continue, a dull, background soundtrack between here and London. I hear it, but none of it means anything to me. It's like the world has been dropped into thick, clear liquid, absorbing away any real sound, any true meaning. I reach into my ear and slide out the slim gold comms unit. Then I shift downward, next to Riya, so my head is on her chest. It's so silent. No breath, no heartbeat, but she's still warm, her scent is still there, under the layers of fear and sweat. My eyes close and for a precious few moments, the reality around me fades.

It's only the insistent ringing of Riya's own phone that rouses me. On autopilot, I reach into her pocket to find it. It's Sunil.

"Riya?" he says. "Riya? We found him, the bastard . . . he's dead and the ADS is right here."

He pauses, waiting for her to reply. My mouth opens to speak but nothing comes out.

"Hey," says Caitlin, running up from behind me. "I've got this. Come on."

Her arm is around my shoulders as she gently takes the phone out of my hand. I hear Caitlin talk to Sunil. Dazed, I get up, my legs shaky. Hala is right there, her arm grasping hold of me firmly, and then pulling me into a hug that I can't even feel. I just stand there, cold, chilled right through to my marrow, even though the sun beats down on us, harsh, relentless. As if it's any ordinary day.

"The girls . . . ?" I say, eventually.

"They're fine. They're all okay," Hala tells me. "We'll keep them safe till the antiviral is ready."

I turn away from her to look back at Riya, sprawled on the ground, lifeless. No one else approaches us until a tired Honda groans up the driveway. Sunil's car coughs to a halt. He is outside in a flash and runs toward her body, shaking his head, not wanting to believe what he can see right there in front of him.

He kneels and checks her vital signs, then he stands up and just looks down at Riya, like a regular detective taking in a new crime scene, piecing together the story. After a long minute, he flicks tears off his cheeks before he turns his gaze on me.

"Why is she wearing a school blazer?" he asks, his voice gruff.

"She wanted to look like one of the girls," I say.

And I stop there. I can see he already figured that out when he started to ask the question. And he knows why. That she sacrificed herself to draw out the ADS shooter; to help our snipers take him out before the police forced the girls outside.

Sunil reaches into his jacket pocket, pulls out his detective badge, and throws it onto the ground with such frustration that it bounces twice before settling into the dust. Then he turns around and looks at the special forces police team standing by, surrounding the girls, uncertain of the next move.

He groans, tiredly, and goes over to pick up his badge, smearing the dust away. Then he lifts the badge above his head and trudges toward the girls and the police.

"I am Detective Patel," he says. "I am issuing a warrant for the arrest of the police commissioner. These girls will remain under my guard now."

30

THE FAMILIAR TAP OF KIT'S nails on my bedroom door is followed by her immediate entrance. She's stopped waiting for me to invite her in, possibly because recently, I haven't.

"Hey, Jess," she says to me. In her hand is a steaming cup. Twig-like bits of tea leaves float aimlessly on the surface. She places the tea gingerly on my bedside table, sits down on my bed, and strokes my hair back off my face.

"Drink this. It's good for your nerves."

"Do you really think so?" I mutter. My tone is cynical, harsh, but I can't help it.

"How are you feeling today?" Kit tries.

I take a breath and force myself to say what she wants to hear. "Better."

There, that wasn't so hard, and Kit's face lights up. She gets up and pulls open the shutters, bathing me in gray light from a cloudy London sky.

"More rain today," she comments conversationally. Like that's somehow news when you live in Britain.

Kit responds to my silence by flipping on the TV in my room. Then she pushes at me to move over in the bed and lies down next to me. It's the news channel. In silence, we watch a political piece that isn't of much interest to either of us.

"Do you want this?" Kit says, pointing at the tea. When I shake my head, she picks it up and sips at the hot liquid herself. Feeling stifled suddenly, I lever myself up, walk through to the bathroom, and brush my teeth.

"Glad you're getting ready," Kit calls. "We need you back at Athena today."

I come back into the bedroom and wave my toothbrush at her.

"I'm on leave," I point out.

Kit consults her watch for the date.

"I think you'll find it's been three weeks," she says. "Shower and dress. I'll drive you to the tube. There's an update meeting in the situation room at ten."

People complain about public transport, but when it works, which is a decent part of the time, it's so much faster than fighting through the morning traffic edging its way into the City of London. Kit and I cannot be seen traveling together to Li's building. So while Kit drives down to the parking lot deep under the building, I take public transport to Athena's headquarters, then follow the rear entrance.

Inside the elevator, I hesitate. To move upward, I just need to look at the floor I want and blink twice to choose it. There's half an hour to spare till our meeting time. Usually, I might spend that time going up to the tech cave and hanging out with Amber. But I don't know how to face her after what happened. They all know I became close to Riya in Mumbai. I decide I can't deal with it now—the concern and pity. So, I choose the main Athena floor, where the situation room is located. I can wait there quietly until the meeting starts.

But as the doors open to let me out, Amber is right there, waiting for a ride back to the tech cave.

"Jessie!" she says. She hesitates. "Good to have you back."

"Thanks," I reply, not really meeting her gaze.

Amber waits politely for me to exit. But I don't. I'm not sure why. So, she steps into the lift and waits as the doors close. This would usually be my cue to make a joke or tease her about something, but my chest feels heavy and I can't trust my voice. Glancing up, I find Amber's eyes are on me, unflinching, kind, caring. For this moment, it's like she gets everything that's going on with me, and then some. Before I know it, she steps across the elevator and grasps me in a hug. She holds me, without a word, until the elevator doors open at the tech cave, and only then does she let me go, with a final, gentle kiss on the cheek.

Suddenly brisk, as if she's shaking off that unprecedented display of emotion, she walks out into the tech cave, and I follow. She puts on some music, calling over her shoulder, her voice unnaturally bright:

"I can't tell you how much I've enjoyed the past few weeks, without you driving me insane every five minutes."

I give a half smile, my first in ages.

"You missed me," I offer.

Amber spins to look at me. Her eyes hold their usual gleam.

"Don't flatter yourself," she says. "Missing you would be like missing a toothache."

I smile an acknowledgment, but she looks disappointed.

"What, no witty comeback? Your banter needs sharpening, I see," she says. "And I imagine you've let your physical fitness go downhill too while you've been off."

"I'm in decent shape," I say.

"Why don't you let me be the judge of that?" she says with a small smile. "Now, if you can bear to stop distracting me, I need to get ready for the meeting."

I leave Amber to her preparations and head over to the situation room. I figure I can wait around there with a coffee and a muffin until the meeting begins. But Peggy's already in there too. We hug and she pours us both something hot to drink.

"How are you feeling, Jessie?" she asks.

"Oh, you know," I reply, brushing off her concern. "I'm used to this."

"Meaning?" she asks.

"Meaning, I've done it so many times that I've become accustomed to it."

"Ah," Peggy shoots back. "Thank you for clarifying the literal meaning of 'I'm used to this.'"

She throws me a look and I glance away from her, ashamed of my sarcasm.

"What I meant was, this is what we do, as Athena agents," I say, figuring that it won't kill me to make an effort to talk to Peggy. Day after day, she makes herself available to us, whether for wise counsel or just a kind hug.

"We fight, we go through stuff," I continue. "We win some, we lose some." My voice falters a bit right at the end. Sensitively, Peggy looks down, giving me space to say more, but I'm done.

"Do you think the time off helped you?" she asks.

I shrug and clear my throat. "Maybe it would have been better to stay busy."

"Why?"

Peggy's eyes are compassionate but evaluating. I guess this is where I'm supposed to break down and admit that thinking about Riya causes me pain. That I hate that she's dead, cheated out of the rest of her life.

"Do you feel guilty about what happened in Mumbai?" Peggy persists, in the face of my silence. "That it was in any way your fault?"

I feel my leg moving up and down, nervously. It's not a difficult question, and I've certainly thought about little else recently. But forming it into spoken words requires a different kind of courage that I'm not sure I have right now. Peggy waits, though, not really letting me off the hook.

"Some days—most days—I know it was Riya's choice," I say, my voice barely louder than a whisper. "But a lot of the time I blame myself."

Peggy reaches out a hand to cover my own. "That's normal," she assures me. "It will take time. Give yourself that time."

I look away and take a sip of coffee. Time heals all wounds. This too shall pass. Nothing lasts forever. How desperately I want to believe these platitudes. But I'm spared from any more emotional excavation by Thomas arriving. Close on his heels is Hala. Thomas leaps up to hold open the door for her, and she actually parks her habitual scowl long enough to smile at him. Then, even more incredibly, she hands him the takeout cup that she's carrying in one hand.

"Cappuccino, extra dry," she says. Exactly the way Thomas likes to enjoy his excuse for a coffee.

It's like she's offered him a winning lottery ticket. Thomas is surprised, happy, and ridiculously grateful in quick succession.

"I made sure they only put in half a shot of espresso," Hala tells him.

"That's just . . . perfect," Thomas says, gazing at her.

"You mean the cappuccino, right?" I comment.

Hala scowls at me but I'm sure I see Peggy stifle a smile.

"What?" asks Hala, picking up our little interaction.

"Nothing," Peggy says. "Perhaps we'll talk later."

Now Kit arrives, followed by Li and Caitlin. More chatter and talk bubbles up, rising and falling through the room, bringing it fully to life. I look around the table, at my mother and the cofounders of Athena. At my teammates, who always have my back. And at Amber, who is last to arrive, but first to get herself set up, laptops open, notebook at the ready. These people are more than colleagues and friends. They are my family. My mind suddenly goes to Jake Graham, the reporter, for the first time in many days. We're a family who have chosen to work outside the law. When I think about what could happen to us if we are discovered, it makes me feel sick.

Li brings the meeting to order.

"Amber, bring us up to speed on the situation in Mumbai, please," she instructs.

"Well," Amber begins, "you know the girls have received the antiviral. They continue to be monitored but it is clear that the virus has been neutralized entirely. They are safe from harm on that front."

"And Family First?" I ask.

Amber pauses and looks at Li.

"We thought we'd play you a video. It'll give you a thorough update on them," Li tells us enigmatically. She flicks on the wide screen that takes up the wall at the end of the room.

"This is a preview of a special report coming out on Global News tonight," she says.

The video plays. Establishing footage of Mumbai, then of

Pakistan—then shots of women and girls. Jake Graham's voice talks over it, outlining the program to come.

"In the next sixty minutes," Jake intones, "I'll be uncovering government complicity; deep corruption that leads all the way to the top of the police forces of two countries; and a far right movement called Family First, who used terror, violence, and election tampering to further their mission. And the main purpose of that mission? To subjugate women."

Opening credits roll, and when they end, Jake is walking through the school that was bombed, side by side with none other than Sunil Patel, talking about where the story began. We watch as Jake creates the background to the story step-by-step, and then goes on to link in the Cypriot Private Bank, Imran, and Jingo Jain.

"It's a web of unchecked power that leads right to these men," Jake continues. "Pakistani general Mohsin Khan, and Indian billionaire Sunny Mehta."

Well, this is new. We turn to look at Amber and the Athena founders. Li pauses the tape and Amber chips in, practically bouncing out of her seat.

"We got to the heads of Family First," she says, excited.

"How?"

"Remember when Sunil tapped Jingo's home phone? The call he taped, that you uploaded to me, was between Jingo and an unknown man. But coming right before the attack, with the precise instructions it held, it felt like this man was a key player in Family First. It took a few days to clean up the recording, but we discovered that he made that call from a private jet."

Amber looks at us with barely suppressed triumph.

"What? How?" I ask.

"We could just about hear the pilot talking to traffic control in the background," she continues. "The details he mentioned led us to one particular private airport. From there, we chased down all the leads and narrowed it to Sunny Mehta."

"Good old Sunil, tapping Jingo's phone." I smile.

"Yes, well, Thomas and I may have had *something* to do with breaking this lead too," huffs Amber. I smile at her.

"Well done, guys," Caitlin says. "But—I don't get it. How did *Jake* cover this story?"

"We gave it to him," Kit says.

"You leaked it?"

"In a way," Peggy responds. "I hit Jake with a harassment suit two weeks ago."

"And I applied for a restraining order to keep him away from my house," Kit adds with a laugh.

"Would those even hold up in court?" I ask.

"It's fifty-fifty, but even if they don't, the lawsuits would tie Jake's hands for months and maybe years," Kit says. "No news outlet will publish anything he cares to write about us, for fear of being sued."

"Then, when we felt he might be more amenable," Peggy continues, "I met with him. I suggested that he was chasing rainbows trying to find something on me and Kit. But that I did want to do more to help women and children and that he and I could make a good team. I would feed him a story bigger than anything he'd had before, and he'd get it exclusively, way ahead of every other news station. In exchange, he agreed to stop pursuing us."

"With his report on Global News," Kit says, "the pressure on law enforcement, banks, and governments will ratchet up. Sunny Mehta has already been arrested. By a new police commissioner in Mumbai."

I feel lighter than I have in weeks. Riya sacrificed her life to save those girls. She shouldn't have had to. She was pushed into that choice by Family First. Seeing them decimated and brought down gives just a tiny bit of meaning to her loss.

"I'm assuming you are all well rested," Li says, drawing the meeting to a close. "Prep for our next mission starts next week, but training starts today. As usual, Amber will oversee your routines and report back to me."

"I hope she goes easy on us," I say.

Li fixes me with a placid stare. "Of course she won't," she says. "I taught her everything she knows."

During only my second hour of gym work, I'm struggling. After an hour of cardio on the treadmill, Amber has me boxing against Caitlin. She's great at this, Caitlin. An inch taller than me, with a little more muscle mass and fast feet. I want to stop, want to slow down, want to crawl back into bed and think about Riya, but I'm trapped by this training ring and by Caitlin, right there, in my face, relentless, unflinching.

My muscles begin to burn, creating the tiny tears that will heal up and make them tougher, stronger. Oxygen floods my brain as I gasp for more breath, as I push for my lungs to expand wider, longer, deeper. Caitlin lands a hook on the side of my head, catching my helmet, but hard enough that I stagger back and fall.

I hit the floor. I'm not hurt—not even winded—but for a moment I just lie there. I feel terrible inside. Like weeping. Like nothing is worth it anymore. Grief over Riya fills me up, flooding me, rising through my stomach, up through my chest, forcing its way through my throat, choking me. Hot, rough tears escape the edges of my eyes. They run down my face.

"Hey, champ, you okay?" Caitlin stands over me, loosening her helmet.

I turn my head toward the canvas floor of the ring, so that she can't see my face. I blink hard. The tears will suffocate me if I let them. I blink again. Then I grit my teeth, get to my knees, and ignore the hand that Caitlin holds out. I force myself to stand up by myself, and as I do, frustration takes over: a white-hot glow of anger that surges into me.

I'm up, running at her, hard, fast. Surprised, she dodges and punches out at me again. A glancing blow that I shake off as I turn, weave, and advance on her. I increase the pace, move my feet faster, throw the punches harder, punches that hit her twice, with the force of anger behind them. I see shock in her eyes, but I don't let up, even for a split second. I'm on her, pushing her back against the ropes. She staggers and I land another punch. Sweat drips into my eyes; my top is so wet it feels like it's become part of my skin. With a final dodge and a cuff to the side of her head, I have Caitlin on the floor. Before I know it, I'm on top of her, my knee pressing down hard on her chest, my face up to hers, grimacing, raging, my glove up, threatening a punch down onto her nose. Her gloves come up to shield her face and, dimly, I'm aware of Amber calling my name again and again, her hand grasping for my arm.

"Jessie," Caitlin pants.

Like a swamp draining, my head clears of all the darkness. I sit back, fast. A long moment passes. Then I pull off my helmet and glove and reach out a hand to haul Caitlin up. She hesitates, then takes my hand and eases herself up, but she moves back far away from me, going over to the ropes to catch her breath. I'm just standing there, gloves off, head down. The sound of our breathing fills the room. Even Amber has nothing to say.

I feel terrible. I look up at Caitlin. There's uncertainty on her face, and distrust; things I've never seen there before when she looks at me.

"I'm sorry. So sorry." My voice is tiny in the large space. There's another long silence.

"I've never seen you get to that place before," Caitlin says, finally.

My mouth opens again to explain something I have no words for. But I don't want to admit that I fell so far out of myself that I lost sight of her being my teammate, my friend. If I tell her that, how would she be able to trust me ever again?

"I guess I got wrapped up in it," I say, trying to salvage things. "You had me cornered and I had to push hard to get back in the fight. . . ."

I keep talking about the training, calmly, like I'm the same old

Jessie she knows. It's awkward and strange, but by the time we make it to the showers, things are mostly back to normal between us. We don't mention it again. That "place." That rage. That brute instinct. But now I know I have all of those. Now I know I can use them. I'm not the same. What happened in Mumbai changed me. After I came back from India, Kit told me that I have to remember who I am and stay true to those values. But I don't care what she thinks. All I know now is that I have to make it up to Riya. I have to do better by the women and girls we've pledged to help. And I'm not playing by the same rules anymore.

ACKNOWLEDGMENTS

The antics of Jessie and the Athena team left me needing to find out a lot of detail about things I had no experience in.

A heartfelt thank-you to my friend Dr. Sarah Caddick, who put me in touch with a couple of experts to think through my virus theories and triggers. Anirvan Ghosh put in so much time in thinking through my ideas and reading drafts of the relevant sections. Thanks also to Massimo Scanziani, who helped our brainstorming early on.

Thanks to Edward Cadogan, who introduced me to Colonel Laurence Williams for help with bomb disposal notes, though I probably still took a bit too much license with them.

Peter Hui gave me feedback on cardiac triggers that never made it into the final version of this book, but for which I am grateful.

And Susan Coll introduced me to seasoned pilot T. J. Johnson to look over my stealth copter and missile sections.

Finally, such gratitude and appreciation to my wife, Hanan. For giving me a writing cabin in the garden (and plenty of time to use it) and for reading every page of every draft, even if the shifting of her red pen over the pages makes me want to weep at the time.